The Flight of the Wretched
A Journey to the New World

Canadä

*Borealis Press gratefully acknowledges the support
of the Government of Canada through the Canada Book Fund (CBF).*

Library and Archives Canada Cataloguing in Publication

McCarthy, Michael, 1950-
    Flight of the wretched : a journey to the New World / Michael
McCarthy.

ISBN 978-0-88887-427-6

    I. Title.

PS3613.C36F55 2011   813'.6   C2011-904950-3

*Cover design: David Ross Tierney
Illustrations: Katelyn McCarthy*

Printed and bound in Canada on acid free paper.

The Flight of the Wretched
Wretched
A Journey to the New World

Michael McCarthy

Borealis Press
Ottawa, Canada
2011

Preface

In 1607, the chieftains of Ireland were forced to leave their homeland as a result of the continued onslaught of Elizabethan forces. This exodus was known as the Flight of the Earls, and the result was the new Protestant ascendancy whereby English lords replaced the old Gaelic culture. Even though the chieftains were defeated and gone, the common Irish people remained, principally as farmers. Throughout the next two centuries, their labors were now in the service of the new absentee landlords and the sitting royalty—a hard truth to accept.

All of Ireland was expected to swear allegiance to the queen and king as well as the Church of England; otherwise they lacked power and position in the new political structure. The traditional Irish people refused.

Therefore Irish Catholics were left at the bottom of the social structure; they had no voice, no land, nor were they able to practice their religion openly. Their ownership of the land was gone, even though they continued to work it, and the taxes owed to the new property owners began to climb. In addition, the poverty-stricken Irish Catholics were required to pay a tithing to the Church of Ireland.

Over the next two centuries, the land became divided and subdivided for these tenant and sub-tenant farmers. By 1837, the land was crowded and dependent on a single source of nourishment—the potato. At this point in history, the stage is nearly set for one of the greatest social, political, and humanitarian disasters of all time—the Great Hunger.

This story focuses on two people situated in the middle of these troubled times. With no viable future in Ireland and with their backs against the wall, they set out on a journey full of fear, separation, and uncertainty. Their faith, courage, and moral code guided them on a course to a new life: the flight of the wretched.

Michael E. McCarthy

"The work of Queen Elizabeth and James the First, it was said, would now be perfected. The Irish would now be rooted out by a new and overwhelming plantation of English: another England would speedily be found in Ireland . . ."

John Prendergast, Esq.
The Cromwellian Settlement of Ireland

Chapter 1

O'Malley's Pub

The future is rarely planned in great detail, and it can change in moments. Such was the case for Conor Meighan, a twenty-year-old Irish lad struggling to survive amidst the crowded lands across Ireland. In the 1830s, the nation was headed towards another Irish famine known as the Great Hunger. Crop failures, starvation, and human deterioration had already begun. Families with multiple children meant multiple mouths to feed, and as the children grew to maturity the family lands grew smaller and smaller.

The spread of families increased but the spread of land dwindled. Ireland was bulging with poor people and it was increasingly difficult to feed them. The landlords were not present and therefore unable to see the crisis, and if they did, shrugged off the warning and continued the status quo, hoping some divine intervention would rectify the problem.

The problem was more intense than not enough food for the current population; the social structure was one of division—upper class versus lower class. Any attempt at a solution meant disagreement, distrust, and disruption. The third leg of this issue was religion—Protestants against Catholics, where deep hatred of each other rolled over into every facet of Irish life. The Meighan family sat at the intersection of these political, social, and economic crossroads along with thousands of other poor Irish.

At the western edge of Ireland, the people of County Clare were a rough breed toughened by the elements of rocky soil, frequent rain, and an ever-present wind. Today, the wind seemed to blow non-stop; it blew across the fields in one steady gust against Conor's face. Now the rain came with it, and strong pellets of water struck his face, trying to penetrate his youthful but hardened skin. It was a horizontal rain, typical of the rain that came off the ocean where it traveled on the wind's current until gravity overcame its trajectory, lowering it to any earthly object in its path.

Conor and his family were familiar with these assaults of rain pellets, wave after wave as they walked about the farm, but today Conor hardly noticed the weather until the damp cold air chilled his muscles. This condition once again caused involuntary shivering as his body, weakened by lack of food, could not maintain its core temperature and caused his muscles to twitch and his thinking to be slowed, his mood low. Conor continued his journey home wearing his tattered, saturated woolen shirt and soiled pants.

The Meighan farm in the rolling hills of Kilmaly, County Clare, raised dairy cows, potatoes, corn, wheat, and children for years. The landowners in Ireland were being encouraged by the British government to move away from crops and instead use the land for grazing. The government's reasoning was, in part, to avoid frequent crop failures, as the Irish were heavily dependent on potatoes. Change is difficult, especially when generations have used the potato as their main staple. Conor's father resisted British government recommendations.

Tonight, an unexpected incident would change one offshoot of the Meighan clan forever. The flow of events started with dinner, when the family gathered as they had for generations; in spite of the lack of food and a sparse dinner, it was a time for all the Meighans to draw together.

Da sat at the head of the table as the children lined each side and Ma took her place at the other end. It did not matter if the children were fully grown adults or tiny tots—their place was at the side of the table until they established their own home. Tonight was no different, and the family progression at the table started with the three eldest sons: Frank with his wife Emily, then Conor and Andrew, sat on one side; Elizabeth, Joseph, Claire, and Leo, who were the four youngest children, lined the opposite side.

The meal was always the same during these hard times. Ma selected potatoes from the storage bin where last year's crop was showing signs of decay. But it was the staple of each evening meal and the supplies were bleak from last year's blight and overly damp storage. Even though most of the potatoes were unfit for normal consumption, these were tough times and she carefully selected a mixture of well-preserved spuds and soft, barely usable potatoes and boiled them in water.

The result was a dinner for the Meighan family that must feed five adults and five growing children. When it was ready, rather than place the pot of potatoes on the table for the family to help themselves, Ma dished out everyone's portion. From the limited amount, she plopped down two small potatoes on Father's plate, as he received the healthiest-looking potatoes, followed by the two youngest getting the next healthy serving.

The eldest, Frank, and his wife, who was with child, received the next portion. Conor was last to be served before Ma took her share. He knew his serving was too soft, discolored, half-rotten potatoes and as he picked apart the soggy skin to expose the interior flesh of the crop, he saw a black core surrounded by an edible white layer. He looked at the potato and sighed aloud.

Frank looked up and said, "Maybe next year will be a better crop."

"Let's pray for it," Conor replied.

"Take one of mine," Da said, moving his plate towards his son.

"No, Da, you need your strength." Both men knew Ma would not allow it anyway. If Conor had accepted the healthy potato, she would have intervened in gentle but firm words that Da needed his strength for the welfare of the family. Da slid the plate back, embarrassed at his privileged stature.

Conor picked around the black blight trying to find a nutritious bite and after two attempts on each spud, pushed the plate away. He sat in silence as the rest of the family pecked at their portions for healthy bites to keep the hunger pains away.

"I'd rather eat the dirt in the field than these," said Andrew.

Ma's reply was sharp. "Andrew, don't whine. Be grateful you have something in front of you." Complaining was not allowed, so Andrew went back to dissecting his meal.

Ma suffered the most but said the least; her portion was the remainder in the pot after the family was served. Even though her good health was vital to the family, her meals were barely sustainable food. They drank tea from a collection of leaves in the bottom of the kettle, and the leaves were re-used at each meal until devoid of all flavor and effect before a fresh batch of leaves was added. However, the fresh leaves were not that fresh, mostly leftover tea leaves from better days. Their diet was simple, sparse, bland, and lacked nutrition—as it was through most of West Ireland with little hope of improvement.

Claire rose and collected the dishes, piling the remaining inedible potatoes onto one plate. Even the animals would not eat these leftovers, so she took the scraps to the "rot pile" at the edge of the field, which had limited value as compost. Even though food was scarce no sickness had invaded this house thus far.

After dinner, Conor broke the quiet. "I'm going down to Michael O'Malley's tonight and have a pint with the boys." Da looked up but did not say a word. Ma scowled. Conor continued, "I heard the English may send food for the starving and struggling people in the countryside. I don't know if it's true but I'd like to find out." The news, however timely, came through the pub before any other source. Newspapers published the stories for those who did not go to the pubs.

Da looked disappointed but Ma spoke up. "How will you pay for a pint? We can't afford food and you want to drink in the pub. Are you going to ask Michael for credit?"

Conor knew both his parents disapproved of the pub life. Other than reports of politics and gossip, the pub was nothing but a source of trouble. However, the news of food distribution was important for all of Ireland, including County Clare. Da was a skeptic; he did not believe the English would give an Irishman a slice of bread until he bit into it and even then he would say it came from a Scot.

Conor answered his mother. "I helped Brian McPherson fix his wagon today. He couldn't pay me but he said he would buy me a pint tonight."

Ma persisted, "If he couldn't pay you, how is he going buy you a drink?"

"Ma," came Conor's only reply.

Silence fell on the dinner table again. The Meighans were thinkers, not talkers. Their communication skills were acute, but only when needed.

It was a busy night in O'Malley's Pub for a cold Monday in February and the usual drinkers were present for their nightly taste and talk. The banter was more intense this evening. The anxiety of the critically low food stashes worried the families of West Ireland; as everyone knew, the fall crops of 1836 were far less than expected. Little did the Irish people know that the potato blight and massive famine was coming within ten years and the intensity and devastation of human lives lost would be far-reaching. Currently, farmers had less trade at the markets; families had less meat in the sheds, and fewer root crops in cellars, and the seedlings for next year did not hold promise for a better season. Crops of maize and wheat were strong but the English lords took the greater share, leaving short supplies for the poor Irish families that had worked this soil for generations.

Tonight in O'Malley's, the talk was sharp; it was desperate talk of survival for today, tomorrow, or a year from now. The chatter was laced with the hatred for the English that dominated every aspect of Irish life. Shawn Clark was on a verbal roll about the forces that abused the Irish and, as if cued, the fierce enforcers of the British throne entered the bar.

Four British soldiers walked into O'Malley's Pub. The soldiers stopped about three steps inside the door. The bar went silent. The sergeant, a lad from the east end of London named Peter Clark, was no relation to the Irish Shawn Clark who was in the middle of spurring anti-English hatred before being rudely interrupted by the English.

Clark entered with his usual arrogant posture, hoping some hot-tempered Irish lad would let his tongue get ahead of his ability to filter his good sense. Any reaction by the bar patrons would cause a brutal response from the British soldiers that would demonstrate their cruel control of the population. The Irish had their police force, the Royal Irish Constabulary (RIC) who were also English or loyalists, but the soldiers were an auxiliary presence in the country, who ruled with fear and intimidation. A visitor need only speak to an Irishman to see how strong was the loathing of the British enjoyment of their superior status and call to duty.

At the end of the bar, Conor Meighan watched the familiar scenario play out. Conor was a quiet man, not quick to enter political arguments. His purpose for being in the bar tonight was to hear the latest news on the government response to impending hunger, not to enter a political fight. The winter had been hard on the limited harvest and the potato staple was dwindling, so Conor was hoping the British government would take care of its Irish subjects, but there was no news of that happening. Conor watched the two Clarks glare at one another, each sending a non-verbal message of hatred.

The English sergeant gave a smug smile and moved on down the bar. He locked eyes with Meighan, who was standing next to

Brian McPherson. Clark knew Meighan was not the usual Irish rebel but tonight the two men gazed suspiciously at each other. A tense moment ensued; Clark wanted to find an example for tonight's harassment but Meighan was not a person easily rattled. Clark's look said, "I want a reaction." Meighan returned a hard but non-threatening look. Clark knew Meighan wasn't going to challenge him physically but he also knew that Conor Meighan could articulate a sharp response that could embarrass and disrupt his control.

Conor came from a large family of devout Catholics who lived their faith and who had a long history in County Clare. Most of the Meighan family history included farming, but the English had taken control of their remaining land through forced tithing, and each generation lost more land, little by little. But this interruption by Sergeant Clark was not about taxes, it was about domination.

The long family lineage did not produce extraordinary muscled arms as it did with many others, yet Conor Meighan was strong for his slight build, and he was known for his easy-going, friendly manner. However, when crossed, he had a temper Peter Clark did not want to confront. Clark moved through the room.

There was no love lost to the English controllers. The Meighans like all Irish families were waiting for the opportunity to rebel against the English and drive them back across the Irish Sea, but tonight was not the night; food and survival were much more pressing. O'Malley's Pub was not going to be the trigger point, at least not for Conor.

Sergeant Clark walked to a table where Seamus Burke, Tony Fitzgerald, and two of the McNeil boys, Jack and Tom, were sitting. Peter Clark had been assigned to County Clare over two years ago; by now he should have known better than to start trouble when those four twenty-year-old kids were together. Individually they were good kids growing up during hard times. But when Seamus, Tony, Jack, and Tom got together and started drinking, anything could get broken, including bar stools, windows, arms, or legs. Sergeant Peter Clark miscalculated. The four boys had grown considerably in the last two years, and in the process they had gotten stronger, and more sophisticated about when and how to fight. Clark stopped at their table and looked directly at Burke.

"Did your mother steal any potatoes today?"

It was an attempt to ridicule Burke and all the Irish; everyone knew it. Everyone also knew the stage was now set. Burke looked at Clark but Tony, Jack, and Tom each directed their looks to the other three soldiers and sized them up.

Michael O'Malley, who was behind the bar, tried to defuse the situation. "Now, we are not going to have any trouble in here tonight. You boys, mind your temper," he said with half authority and half wishful thinking. "And Mr. Clark, if you don't mind, we have done nothing wrong, everyone is behaving." Clark gave a slight turn to smile at O'Malley's feeble attempt to bring order. That slight distraction was all Burke needed.

Burke was on the move, out of his chair, dragging his hand behind him to hook the back of the chair into his grasp. Once hooked, the chair rotated like a wheel, spinning towards the unsuspecting sergeant. Tony, Jack, and Tom moved horizontally, heading straight for the three soldiers.

Ordinarily, three soldiers would be quick enough to react to the charge. They did not see Shawn Clark lead the assault from their left flank, a tactical mistake that would cost each of the soldiers more than a few teeth and several days of recovery. The surprise attack happened with speed and precision: the soldiers' long guns were quickly batted away, turning the fight into hand-to-hand combat. The four youths had speed, strength, surprise, and most effectively, emotion on their side.

Meighan stood ready at the bar, prepared to join in if needed, but a bar-room fight with British soldiers was not his style and he was not sure how eager he was to become involved in this attack. Everyone including Meighan was already implicated in any accusation merely by his presence, and the outcome would be severe. He waited.

Seamus Burke was a brawler and the years of his personal and family oppression had accumulated deep within his soul. The pent-up emotions from his father's death at the hand of the English enforcers, the forced loss of family land that led to reduced crops and frequent hunger, the stripping of his native language, and prohibition against practicing his Catholic faith all accumulated in this moment. Today's abuse, like the harassment his family had received in their daily comings and goings, was now focusing in one central point. This aggressive, arrogant sergeant in front of him represented all that personal history, and the fire of frustration and humiliation felt deep within his chest at that second exploded into fury.

Seamus lost control. He had knocked the sergeant back with the force of the revolving chair. As soon as the chair struck, Seamus let go of his grip and the chair fell, covered with the fresh blood from the sergeant's head. He then planted his feet in a strong fighting stance as his left fist came with blazing speed to the sergeant's jaw, causing bone and teeth to break and splitting his lower lip, sending more blood splattering across the floor.

Clark stumbled to gain his footing but Burke sent a flurry of punches to the face and head. Peter Clark went down and Burke's assault continued. Clark never regained his footing or his composure. Within four minutes the fight was over and the sergeant lay on the floor motionless; he was dead. Peter Clark's brain could not withstand the powerful forces coming from the left and right side repeatedly and had finally shut down. The other three soldiers had been beaten and stripped of their weapons. Michael O'Malley let out the only words: "Holy Jesus and Mary, Mother of God."

Seamus Burke was in a rage but there were no more English victims left to beat. Tony Fitzgerald grabbed Seamus around the chest and dragged him outside, followed by the McNeil brothers, who ran off in the darkness.

Conor Meighan, Mike O'Malley, Shawn Clark, and the other Irishmen looked at each other wondering what to do, as each man knew the trouble that would follow with the British forces.

"I'll go for Dr. Zimmerman," said Shawn and headed towards the door for the six-mile journey to Ennis. Two other men said, "I will go with you."

Conor and Mike helped the soldiers off the floor and into chairs. The soldiers pushed them away, resisting the kindness and covering their shame and damaged pride.

Frightened at being in the middle of a scene of a British defeat with the blood-splattered floor and walls, Conor saw the vivid forewarning of trouble ahead; he knew life had just changed and his future was now uncertain.

Up to this point in his life, Conor had worked the family farm of three acres of wheat, corn, and potatoes. The wheat and corn went to the landlord. He also worked in their local town when any job was available. Most of the employment had dried up and with no work, Conor was mostly idle. As a result, Conor became another mouth for the Meighan family to feed without contributing to the welfare of the household.

He did not want to leave his family and move to a foreign country like America or Australia as so many others had done, but Conor had no future in Ireland. His older brother Frank was in line to inherit the three acres of land. Conor was more of a burden to the family than help. Now the incident in O'Malley's Pub had solved his dilemma about whether or not to leave Ireland.

Conor immediately left the pub, long before Dr. Zimmerman arrived and before additional soldiers from Ennis responded. He ran home as fast as his legs could move, pushed by adrenaline that fuelled his energy until he was so winded that his lungs gasped for air. He panted in short, sharp bursts as if no amount of air would satisfy his need for oxygen. He moved onward. His pace was now a rapid walk stimulated by nervous energy and conflicting thoughts along with the confusion about the night's events and whether to stay and report his observations to the British authorities or remove himself as if he had never been present. He continued directly to his brother's cottage because he couldn't face his parents with such upsetting news—a decision he would regret for the rest of his life. He pounded on Frank's door until he woke him up.

"Frank, there was a terrible event at O'Malley's place tonight. I have to leave."

"What happened?"

"The less you know the better; however, one soldier was killed and three others were badly beaten. Tell Da and Ma I had nothing to do with the fight or the killing, but because I was there, I have to leave. Frankie, I am going to catch the next boat out."

"Where will you go?" Frank was still groggy from sleep.

"I don't know. I will take the first boat I can. I just hope it's not a boat for London."

Frank's wife Emily came into the kitchen to ask what was going on.

Conor walked back over and gave her a hug. He said, "Goodbye, Emily." She did not realize it was a final goodbye. Conor turned and walked to his older brother, whom he had loved and respected for many years. He patted Frank on the shoulder. "Goodbye" was his last word as he headed out the door. Conor hustled down the lane in the darkness, never to see his home again.

Chapter 2

Meighan's Pub

Conor knew the British would be looking for him and every man in O'Malley's Pub. He had a good idea his fate was dire if caught: a penal colony in Australia if mercy was shown or a firing squad if they did not believe in his innocence. Such thoughts about the outcome did not take into account the ordeal he would endure if captured, the torture of interrogation, the beatings, and the humiliation of putting his family through a trial. His decision was to put distance between himself and the incident.

The busy port city of Limerick had boats leaving for America, Canada, and Australia every day and he quickly formulated a plan to catch an outgoing boat. But Conor was worried about leaving from Limerick, which was too close to home and too close to the British stronghold, which, like a disturbed and swarming beehive, would have its members searching everywhere in great numbers with a passionate hatred.

Instead, he reasoned as dawn approached, he would take the ferry across the Shannon River to Tarbert and head through County Kerry. He had a cousin in Listowel and from there, he would cut across to County Cork and down to Cork City to leave his country from there. If he hustled, the trip through back fields and cautious travel on the open road would take him three days as he bartered and negotiated his way to Cork. This morning, at the edge of the Shannon River, he mixed in with some Tinkers who were boarding the ferryboat with their wagons and families. No one noticed.

Conor crossed the river on the early morning ferry to the southern terminal at Tarbert. His plan was to work his way to the small market town of Listowel in northern County Kerry. The tradesmen and market vendors used the pre-dawn ferry to move their wares to the marketplace. The boat had a group of "Travelers" referred to colloquially as Tinkers, gypsy-like nomads who spoke their own unique dialect known as the Cant, and sold and fixed tinware with a reputation for untrustworthiness in their business practices. Their roaming of the countryside was an old tradition, thought to originate with Cromwell's invasion of Ireland in 1649, when many landowners were evicted by the conquest. The Tinkers' home was now the road.

Conor avoided the group as he feared, if given the opportunity, they would turn him in to the authorities quickly in order to gain favor with the local law enforcers. Co-operation such as this helped the group to survive without being harassed. Yet at the same time, local townspeople were potential customers. This relationship was a delicate balance for survival, which also kept the Travelers on the move.

Conor went to the port side of the ferry to avoid contact with the Tinkers—the term he knew. He approached a wagon being led by an elderly herder, whom Conor could identify by his woolen vest. If Conor had the inclination, he could have studied the knitted vest with its decorative cable lines and patterns to determine the man's region and family history. He was not so inclined because his mind was active with worry and suspicion.

The old man could read Conor's story from his appearance as well. Conor was average height, which was not unique to his region, but the rest of his appearance told the story. His fair skin was weathered by daily exposure to the elements. A mixture of Irish sod and sea salt was as much imbedded in his skin as his freckles. One might think that Conor had missed a few Saturday night baths but soap was scarce, so he had frequent water splashes rather than soap scrubbings.

A hand-made knit cap with straight stitching, which covered his fiery red hair, indicated a practical knitter was in the home rather than an artisan. His woolen pants were loom-made but well worn, with numerous patches to cover the hard abuse in the fields. His woolen shirt likewise was tattered, showing age and wear as large Irish families engaged in hand-me-downs to get the most use from available clothes. They lacked the opportunity and resources for outfitting each offspring. Even if the old man observed Conor sitting in the back row of the English House of Parliament, he would immediately recognize him as a poor farmer from the West of Ireland.

The old man was trying to soothe his mare. The horse became skittish when a wave would hit the boat, and in the twilight the horse got scared. Conor was familiar with horses; his father had two when he was younger. Now Da was down to one horse; he could not afford to buy a new workhorse after Pokey had died. Conor moved slowly and quietly around the front of the horse, so the horse could see him. He gently stroked the mare. He had a soothing way, which was easily recognizable by man and beast. The horse responded immediately. Even the herder relaxed, as Conor's presence calmed both.

"You know animals."

"Indeed, since I was a kid."

"This one," the herder stroked the long neck and mane, "is a good puller but doesn't like crossing the river."

"Doesn't like crossing, is it? So who gets the anxiety first, you or the horse?"

The statement surprised the herder. Conor had quickly assessed the herder's issue—when boarding the ferry, the horse became skittish. At the same time, the herder became worried about the horse's behavior on the boat, so each caused the other anxiety. Conor continued to stroke the mare and whisper soft statements, reassuring the horse.

The herder said, "I make this trip twice a year to Tralee. I always dread the crossing. Two years ago this mare bucked and kicked and I lost my load. At least two bales ended up floating down the Shannon and out to sea. Some bloke in Nova Scotia is probably wearing the wool as we speak. Where are you headed?"

Conor hesitated. He did not want to announce his plan carelessly; stating that he was going to Cork was not a good idea. Even revealing his immediate destination of Listowel was risky. Conor also knew that the herder was going through Listowel, which was on his route to Tralee. After some thought, Conor said, "I am going to visit my cousin on the way to Tralee." The statement was true but Conor could be evasive if needed. His plan was to visit his cousin Joe Meighan, a pub owner in Listowel, for a rest stop and layover.

The two men, along with the horse and wagon, disembarked at Tarbert and headed south towards Tralee, while the Tinkers turned westbound at the road for Ballylongford. "My name is Breandan," Conor's traveling companion finally said, and he looked at Conor, waiting for the reciprocal introduction, which was slow in coming.

"I'm Conor," he said timidly.

The winds off the west coast of Ireland were chilly and damp. In his haste to leave home, all Conor had taken to wear to fight off the cold was the coat on his back and his knit cap. The two men walked at the side of the horse that was pulling the wool-loaded wagon. Breandan did not pry into Conor's personal business or the reason for his journey and Conor was not about to volunteer information to this stranger.

As they walked, they talked of the potato blight "We are in the second year of bad potatoes," Conor said. "My mother and father cannot feed all of us. They fear the children will get sick and not have the nourishment to fight off the disease. The young ones sit in the field and eat dirt to fill their stomachs."

"That's terrible," said Breandan sadly. "Many families are suffering the same way."

"Indeed, they are," Conor replied and the two walked along.

Conor was fatigued because of his long travels through the night to catch the ferry but he did not complain. Breandan could see that Conor was tired and he offered Conor a ride in the wagon. "You ride in the back and get some rest."

Conor at first refused. "No thanks, I'm fine." But after Breandan's second offer, he said, "Maybe I will take a few minutes to rest." He climbed into the wagon and nestled between two bales, partly to keep warm and more importantly, to hide from passersby. After about an hour of deep sleep Conor awoke abruptly. The wagon had stopped moving. He heard voices.

Breandan was speaking to a man but Conor could not make out the topic of the talk. The tone sounded casual and lacked official commands. Even so, he was afraid of being discovered and not knowing the conversation made him nervous. Finally the wagon started to move. He remained still and waited. Breandon and the wagon must have traveled a half-mile before Conor raised his head to look. No one was around. He climbed down and rejoined Breandan on his walk.

Late in the afternoon they arrived at a fork in the road. To the left was the path to Listowel and to the right the route continued to Tralee. Conor bid farewell to his traveling companion: "Thank you for your company; I wish you well." He headed down the left road into town.

Once on the main street of the little market town, he found his cousin's bar, aptly named Meighan's Pub. It was squeezed between a bakery on one side and a general goods store on the other, with a small river flowing behind the buildings. Inside the pub was a typical afternoon gathering of drinkers—early starters, all-day drinkers, and casual visitors. Joe was behind the bar and when he saw Conor, each greeted the other simultaneously and warmly.

"Hey Joe."

"Hello Conor."

The two cousins had not seen each other since the funeral of their grandmother two years before but it was as if time had never moved. Both cousins were equally excited to see each other. Joe introduced Conor around the bar as a proud family member and Conor was quickly accepted into the Meighan's Pub family, a different level of family from Conor's experience. Joe took Conor into the back room, which had a stairway to the living area upstairs. Joe called up to Bridget, his wife, to come down.

"What do ya need now?" was the sharp reply.

"Just come down and bring Liam." Conor could hear the moan from above. Bridget was not ready for this interruption but Joe knew she would feel better once she learned a family member had arrived to visit.

Bridget was about half-way down the stairs when Joe announced that Conor from County Clare was there. By now Bridget was in view carrying a small baby. "Conor, so happy to see you," she said.

"Bridget, good to see you too, and who is this little one?"

"This is Liam; he is thirteen months now."

"He has the sparkle of his mother in him," Conor noted.

"You are so kind," Bridget said, then she asked, "What brings you to Listowel?"

"I am just passing through," Conor said. The silence just hung after the statement. Bridget and Joe were waiting for further explanation but Conor was not going to supply it. Bridget was Irish enough not to pursue it; Conor and Joe would talk in private and Bridget would get the details later. Nevertheless Conor wanted to protect his story and the pub was no place to disclose secrets, especially when he was on the run from the authorities.

Joe and Bridget prepared a special dinner for their unannounced guest—a boiled ham bone with a potato and some white beans added to the pot. Joe, like his father who ran the pub before him, usually had food available but since the current hard times had started, food was scarce; Joe was only able to get food for his family. He no longer had food on hand for his customers, but beer, whiskey, and the chatter were always available at the pub.

"Can I get you a pint of the black stuff?" offered Joe.

"Thanks," replied Conor, who could not turn down a glass of the foamy Guinness.

After dinner, the purpose of Conor's visit came up again. Conor started, "Joe, I need your word that nothing will be repeated."

Joe realized a good story was about to be shared and an excitement overcame him. Conor also realized Joe's long history of story-telling as part of his lifestyle in the pub. "I will not breathe a word of it," Joe promised.

"I am on the run from the Crown." Conor knew Joe would comprehend the need for discretion with this news; after all, a fugitive was in his house and place of business.

"Sweet Jesus of Nazareth. Of all the people, Conor, I would not think you would have this trouble."

"Joe, I was in O'Malley's Pub when a British sergeant was killed and three others were badly hurt. All of us are on the run."

"Sweet Jesus," Joe said again. "Why did you come here?"

"I am just passing through and I need a place to sleep tonight."

"Why did you walk through the front door?" Joe was starting to get mad. "Everyone knows you are here."

"I'm sorry. I understand your concern, I wasn't thinking. I will leave."

"No, you can stay. You will be gone in the morning? Where are you going?"

"Joe, I am not going to put you in the position of knowing my plan. I will leave before sun-up." Conor did not want Joe or

Bridget to suffer any harassment from the British, so he added, "If you have to tell them anything, tell them I am going down into the 'Ring' and I plan on hiding in the hills." In southern County Kerry the mountains form a ring with a circular valley in the middle. This "Ring" is a tough place to find someone who wants to hide.

Joe fixed a cot in the back room. After the bar closed, Joe locked up. "When you get up, just head out the back," he said, pointing to the back door. "Godspeed."

"Thank you, Joe. I hope I have not caused you any harm."

"The Brits can . . . , well, you know."

Conor was exhausted and fell asleep quickly; but sleep did not last long as he dreamt about his journey. He was leaving Ireland on a boat to go anywhere—Africa, America, Australia, Canada, India, or China. His mind was racing; his future was so uncertain. And even though his decision to leave was made in seconds, the results would affect generations.

He lay on the cot thinking. Sleep eluded him now, as he tossed and turned. He reviewed all the events that led up to his flight:

- I should have listened to my mother and not gone to O'Malley's.
- I should return home for I had no reason to run, I did nothing wrong.
- Surely the soldiers would say that Seamus Burke, Tony Fitzgerald, and the McNeil brothers were the cause of the deadly attack.
- But Shawn Clark and others were also involved; I would get lumped into that group of assailants.
- And then I ran: innocent people do not run, they stay and tell the truth.
- Certainly, they would understand how scared I was.
- If I continue to run, I will never see my family again.
- If I go back and end up arrested, I will be beaten, and sent to Van Diemen's Land or face a firing squad.

Conor's discomfort did not stop with thoughts of O'Malley's or where he might end up living or dying. He thought about the lack of land, food, and future in County Clare for the second son of a poor Irish farmer. The cot became uncomfortable. He was in distress. His breathing was loud and his words were forming on his lips as if to speak but there was no one to talk to in the pitch black of this lonely night. His thoughts made him feel completely alone, completely isolated from any trustworthy support.

He could not find solace in a definite plan. Joe had been no help nor did he expect Joe to counsel him in his dilemma. His thoughts revolved backward and forward. He decided to return home in the morning and then quickly changed his mind again. For hours, the night played havoc with his anguish. Conor was a proud Meighan, he would do what was right; he just needed to figure out what that was.

Intertwined in his debate over these legal principles and personal scruples, and adding to his restlessness, was his faith. Conor's religious upbringing involved achieving goodness through Christ-like behavior combined with the Golden Rule, where one treats others as he hopes to be treated. This pathway to achieving his personal happiness and satisfaction in his earthly life was also the same pathway to eternal salvation. So, what would Father Carroll say about the events in the bar? Would he have a different consideration? Conor's breathing slowed as he settled into a calmness elicited by confidence in his faith.

"My son," he thought of Father Carroll's words, "you are now part of a long history of hatred. Your presence in the bar was by chance, unplanned as to the events that took place, but you were there. Seamus Burke, as rough a boy as he is, did not intend to commit a murder that night. He lost control in a fury of passion and contempt. He will hang for his crime, along with the McNeil boys and Tony Fitzgerald for their accompanying assault resulting in murder. The magistrates have an obligation to control the population and they do that through example and intimidation. Your dilemma is not about the salvation of your soul; it is about surviving the justice system in western Ireland." Conor lay on the cot, eyes wide open in the dark, staring into the darkness as if it were the loneliness of hell.

Still taunted by the morality issue, he reasoned that Christ returned to Jerusalem to face his accusers and take his punishment even though it meant going to his death, but Conor's bravery could not match Christ's moral example of courage in confronting evil. If he returned to face death, history would not remember Conor's moral bravado; he would be an additional line in the story of treachery of British rule in Ireland. As he rolled onto his side and took in a full breath of air, his mind relaxed.

Conor was half sleeping and still half debating his future when he decided it was time to go. Just before dawn, he was up and gone before Joe or Bridget started to stir, as barkeepers tend to sleep later than farmers. Conor found the road heading southeast towards Cork. His decision was really quite simple, regardless of the outcome. There was no future in County Clare.

Chapter 3

Cork City

I n the cool morning, as a hazy sun rose in the eastern sky, Conor
continued his journey to Cork using the side roads that connected small towns and farmlands, rather than the main roads
used by patrolling soldiers. The route was difficult through the
hills and winding pathways, and was complicated by Conor's
unfamiliarity with the terrain.

When he arrived at a town, people asked the purpose of his
visit, for rarely did a stranger pass through these out-of-the way
places for no reason. His response was polite but curt, even though
Conor knew the Irish way of friendly greeting while passing through
a town; to do otherwise brought suspicion. Even so, he did not
engage beyond a local resident's "Hello"; rather than a friendly conversation, it was followed by silence. The empty moment violated
the unwritten custom of a reply, and led to uneasy feelings towards

this unexpected stranger. Conor kept walking with purpose while the eyes of the town watched until he left their area. Suspicion of him sometimes lifted when he pointed ahead and asked, "Cork?"

"Ah yes, young man, follow the road straight ahead," came the relieved reply.

In the small market town of Kanturk, Conor felt safe as he passed openly through the narrow streets using the market activity as a cover to cross the Dalua River and head south towards the rural farming area that is mixed with forest. He passed Kanturk Castle, built by the Gaelic chieftain MacDonagh MacCarthy.

The solid, handsome structure was never finished because MacCarthy was ordered by the English Privy Council to cease construction at the final phases of the roof. The English feared this native Hibernian was building a fortress and the council felt the castle was much too large for an Irish subject. The castle had not been inhabited in the past two centuries as it stood, five stories high, nestled in the scenic countryside.

Once again the weather blew a heavy rain to the interior, but the damp moisture did not slow Conor down as he cautiously hustled towards Cork.

The docks of Cork were active with the shipping of food and Irish-made materials like clothing, wool, and linen. Conor was amazed at the movement of food through this port. While thousands of people were near starvation in the west of Ireland, food was still in plentiful supply here. The English had placed heavy security along the docks to make sure the supplies were not hijacked and distributed to the needy in the interior of the country.

Conor was cautious with the passing of each soldier, fearful that he would be recognized as a wanted person from County Clare. He felt as if he had a brand on this head for all the soldiers to take notice, so he walked with his head down, only looking up to maintain his direction.

Conor did not have money to buy a ticket on a passenger boat. He joined the hundreds of others begging and pleading with the captains to let them on their boats for free passage to more promising lands. He checked each ship.

The captains were on constant alert for stowaways and immediately threw them off the ships. The English soldiers would then beat the lads and drag them away. The captains followed up by throwing crew members off for letting the stowaways on in the first place. After that, the captain hired a new chap who was waiting on the dock, for a lower wage. It was Irish economics at its worst as many Irishmen, like Conor, were desperate for work, especially if elder sons took control of the family land. Younger sons were left in want of work. British policies of increased taxes and tithing were also forcing foreclosure after which the land was given as a reward to English nobility and retired military command personnel. Hunger, famine, and death were just by-products.

Now on the dock, Conor watched a young lad hiding behind a crate of cargo waiting to be loaded. As he watched from a distance he could see the lad sticking his head out now and again waiting for the opportunity to jump aboard unnoticed. Conor knew the lad's doom—he would make it aboard, get discovered, and be dragged off by the crew at the captain's orders.

Conor did not want to risk getting caught, but this ship offered the best negotiating location, because it was the farthest ship down the line of boats along the parallel dock and the soldiers did not walk that far unless summoned. As Conor approached the ship *Carolina* he still watched the potential stowaway waiting for his opportunity. As luck would have it, another stowaway had just been found on board, and as he and two crew members were being disembarked by the First Mate, Conor decided to take advantage of the circumstances by using a direct approach.

As Conor passed the crates waiting to be loaded, he saw the lad who had been hiding. It was Seamus Burke. "Seamus," Conor said quickly.

"Shhhh," came the muffled reply.

Conor kept walking. The ship's captain, known officially as a "Master" rather than "Captain," was directing the loading of the ship and as Conor approached, he found the captain was different from the picture he had formed based on what he had heard about sea-going men. Conor expected an older, stout man with grey hair and beard, a gruff voice, and little tolerance. This captain was younger—middle-aged, tall, thin, clean-shaven, and articulate.

"I see you could use a couple hands with strong backs," said Conor.

"Oh, another Irish kid looking for a free ride to America."

"Is that where you are going?" Conor asked.

"As if you didn't know," was the captain's short reply.

"My friend and I . . ." motioning back towards the cargo although no one was in sight, "would like to help you sail your ship."

"Have you ever been on a ship at sea before?"

"Yes, twice," Conor said, which was a little white lie. Two trips out in a fishing boat did not equal sailing experience across the ocean. But Conor left that part out. The captain knew it was a lie. The proper sailing protocol for Conor would have been to identify the ship and its captain as a measure of his experience. Conor did neither.

"Listen, son," began the captain, "there are a hundred lads like you every day looking to help me sail my ship. I am looking for a crew member who is going to stay with the ship. What am I going to do in New York when you and your friend, wherever he is, get off and I have to sail back with a short crew? There are no lines of sailors waiting on the docks of New York City to sail back to Ireland. I need men who are going to stay with the ship."

"I understand. But you are nearly ready to leave. The only available experienced sailors are the ones proven unworthy by sneaking castaways on board. You will be faced with this decision whether you hire us or not. If you hire us now, we will prove our worth by loading the remaining cargo, and if you don't like us after that you can dismiss us right then and there."

The captain hesitated. He liked this young man and the way he approached the situation; besides, he was watching the tide and sailing time was near. "Okay, I will hire you on a tentative basis until the cargo is loaded and then I will determine if you will sail with the ship. But first," the captain interjected, "who is this other person?"

"It's Seamus. He is right here." Conor walked around the crate and grabbed Seamus. "I got us a ride," he whispered, then, "Captain, this is Seamus. We have been friends since we were kids in the west of Ireland." Conor knew that the reputation of Western Irish was one of a strong work ethic. However Conor's reference to their friendship was another white lie, an unsettling statement. He and Seamus had known each other for their entire life but they were not friends. Seamus was a fighter. Conor was quiet and more reserved. Their lives had followed different paths but a dreadful circumstance in a pub had brought them together here.

The Captain smiled. Both he and Conor knew the blarney that was being passed between them but the Captain went along with it anyway. "Welcome, Seamus. We have hard work ahead of us. I would like to catch the tide at noon today. So time is important. If you can't work hard and fast, you will stay here on the dock when we sail. Now, go see Mr. Bailey for your duties."

Captain Albert Ryan was an experienced sailor and leader of men. He had good judgment about people and his crew had confidence in him. His instincts told him Conor and Seamus were trustworthy and hard workers. The captain also had a different reason to use caution. He had a special passenger on this trip, and Conor and Seamus might help mitigate any trouble with the regular crew.

His ship was generally a cargo ship; however, his long-time friend and business associate Paddy O'Grady had needed a favor. His daughter, Kathleen, was pregnant out of wedlock and Paddy needed to get her out of town or his business would be ruined because of his daughter's loose moral behavior. He asked Captain Ryan to take Kathleen to New York. Within a few years, Kathleen could return with the baby and a husband, if she found one, according to Paddy's contrived plan, and all would be fine. Kathleen was already on board in a special berth that the First Mate had made ready. Captain Ryan didn't like Paddy's philosophy on family matters but his compassion went out to Kathleen and he would try to make her journey safe and comfortable.

Conor and Seamus were assigned to carry bales of wool off the dock, up the plank to the ship's cargo hold. Two other sailors, Ray and Mutt, were in the hold stacking the bales. Conor and Seamus thought they ended up with the better job on the outside rather than being stuck down in the hold. Conversely, Ray and Mutt laughed at the new lads who had to carry the load a farther distance up the plank. Little did they know that Conor and Seamus were well suited for carrying and stacking bales of anything—they were farmers.

Captain Ryan was pleased with his prospective sailing mates and asked them to join the venture across the sea. "All right, lads, do you want to work hard like this on the open water?"

Conor and Seamus were thrilled at the chance. "You will not regret this, Captain," said Seamus. Conor nodded.

Seamus slapped Conor on the back as a "thank you" gesture. Conor said to himself, "Please don't hit me like that."

At noon, the ship sailed out of the port of Cork to catch a west wind that blew down the river from Cork City and pushed the boat eastward towards the Irish Sea. Once in open waters, they navigated south around the lower peninsulas of Ireland.

Chapter 4

The *Carolina*

The sea was calm on this crisp February midday; gentle swells raised and lowered the ship as it headed west towards America. A light wind caught the angle of the sails and pushed the wooden vessel away from the coast of Ireland for the long journey across the North Atlantic. Conor was kept busy managing the sails, as he was ordered from the Captain's deck. He was quickly learning the names of the sails as he hesitated for a moment waiting to see which sail the others grabbed. Soon he knew the main gallant sails, the mizzen, and the jib sails.

Late in the afternoon, Captain Ryan called Seamus and Conor to his berth at the stern of the ship. The first mate, Mr. Bailey, was sitting at the captain's table as they entered the berth. The quiet atmosphere and lack of quick greeting made the pair suspicious. The Captain was making notations in his log. He motioned the two boys to sit down.

"Lads," he started, "I allowed you on this ship to have passage to the New World. What I want to know is, why you are leaving the Old World?"

Conor said, "What do you mean?"

"Don't be coy with me, son." The Captain's tone reflected serious concern. "You didn't pick this boat at the end of the dock haphazardly. You didn't hide among cargo because you wanted to make a deal. You fellows are on the run from something. What is it?"

Seamus tried to deflect the question again. "Captain, I was going to jump on board because I didn't have money to buy a ticket. Conor convinced me that asking for a job and working our way to New York was a better way to operate."

The Captain was straightforward. "If I threw you overboard, would you be able to swim back to Ireland?"

"Captain," Conor said, "we all have secrets that we try to protect. If I assured you that it meant nothing to you or your ship, could this be the end of it?"

The Captain pondered the words; he liked Conor's style. Still, he was uncomfortable not knowing their purpose for being sneaky and evasive. He stated, "When we left Cork, I became king. I rule everything that happens on this ship. I am the judge, the jury, and the executioner. You will follow every word I say without question. If I hear, see, or suspect that you undermine my authority in any way, I will turn you over to Mr. Bailey here for as many lashings as I care to watch. After that you become shark bait. Any questions?"

"No sir," said Conor.

Seamus was a little slower to react. His arrogance and fighting nature bounced around in his head. He was not used to obeying authority figures or bullies. He decided to meet the Captain half-way. "Okay," he said in a low defiant way.

"Mr. Burke, you can go. Mr. Meighan, stay."

Seamus waited momentarily to see Conor's reaction, and when Conor made no signal, he slowly opened the door, looked around, and left the berth. The Captain motioned to Mr. Bailey to leave also.

Conor had a good sense of people too. He knew that he had a rapport with the Captain and he felt he could be frank with his statements. As soon as he and the Captain were alone, Conor spoke up immediately. "There was a fight in a pub. People got hurt. We had to leave Ireland or we would have felt the wrath of the Crown."

Captain Ryan pondered the thought of a fight in a bar with injuries—routine, he thought, dismissing his concern. "Thank you." The Captain nodded and sat down at the table. "I have another matter to discuss with you. I have a special passenger on board and I need someone to watch her. I was hoping you could keep an eye on her."

Conor thought this was a strange request, especially after the speech about him being the king and all. "Who is this person and why is she so special?"

"You are pretty direct, Mr. Meighan. In one way I like that. In another way, I caution you."

"Captain, you have been good to me. I respect you. My directness is not a disregard of your authority."

The Captain paused for a moment, then decided to proceed. "There is a young lady on board. She is the daughter of a friend of mine and she is with child." The Captain hesitated as if he wasn't sure what information should be disclosed. Soon enough all would know anyway. "She comes from a wealthy family and I don't want any of my crew bothering her. Or anyone, for that matter."

"I will keep an eye on her."

"And that means Mr. Burke, too. Can you control him?"

"I believe so."

"Ump," the Captain sighed. "You can report any transgressions to my First Mate Mr. Bailey. We will have dinner tonight in my berth and I will introduce you." Captain Ryan was done and said, "Off," as he waved his hand.

Conor left the berth but was surprised that Mr. Bailey was standing outside the door. Conor nodded as he slid past.

The Captain's assignment to Conor was a test of allegiance, truthfulness, and trustworthiness. Unbeknown to others, Conor was placed under the close watch of the First Mate. The Captain ran a tight ship and new crew had to earn his respect. He instinctively trusted Conor. However, if Conor failed, he would face the Captain's wrath.

Conor went below deck and found Seamus in the crew's quarters, an open area in the bow of the ship with hammocks stacked three high and five in a row, all hanging from the floor above. Fifteen crew members were squeezed into the narrow room on the starboard side. If the ship were to take passengers, they would be lined along the port side at the bow with not much more comfort; however, the only passenger on this trip was the Captain's special guest. In the aft was the galley. The cargo and supplies were in the bottom hull of the boat.

For meals, the passenger ate first and the crew ate according to their shift and the pressing needs of sailing. The food was adequate and edible, but limited.

"What did the Captain want?" asked Seamus. "What did you tell him?"

Conor did not want to talk with three other crew members lying in the hammocks. "He gave me extra duties," Conor replied faintly.

"Why, what for?"

"I don't know, he just did." Conor motioned for Seamus to follow him on deck. Conor climbed to the upper deck and walked to the bow of the boat. He turned to talk to Seamus. Conor gazed straight to the back of the ship and the pilot at the helm was looking directly at him. He looked straight up. Mutt was sitting in the crow's nest and watching the two lads.

"Great," thought Conor. "No privacy." Conor said faintly,

"The Captain wants me to keep an eye on a lady—a special passenger."

"Why you?" asked Seamus.

"I don't know. I just have to make sure no one bothers her."

"That's it?"

"He is a friend of the lady's father."

Seamus was quiet and Conor thought he was thinking about the mysterious lady, but Seamus had something else on his mind. "Hey," he said, "I want to change my name. I want you to call me 'Mike.'"

"Why?"

"Because I don't want people to remember that Seamus Burke was on board. I need a different name. I can say my first name is Mike but my parents always called me 'Seamus' after my grandfather."

"And now all of a sudden I am going to call you Mike?"

"Yeah."

Conor let out a long exhausting breath. "Okay."

"And Conor, thanks for helping me. You have been great in getting me on board and handling the Captain. I would not have been able to do this without you."

"No worry."

"I mean it. I am going to name my first son after you, to honor your friendship."

"Thanks Seamus, I mean, Mike."

They both laughed.

Conor went below to clean up for his special dinner and introduction. In the sailors' quarters was a box of old clothes and uniforms left behind by sailors who had died, were tossed overboard, or just left their clothes behind. The clothes were second-hand but clean. Conor scrubbed and got dressed. He looked and felt better than he had in a long while.

Shortly afterwards, Conor went to the Captain's berth and was greeted at the door by Mr. Bailey. "We have been waiting for you," he said. Conor followed his escort into the berth.

Chapter 5

The O'Grady Family

The O'Grady family had lived in Ennis, County Clare, for centuries, working the land, but currently Patrick O'Grady was working the people. O'Grady was a merchant who imported tobacco. He was a linguistics expert with a quick tongue who could sell the shirt off the owner's back and throw in his or her own pants as an extra bargain. He was well known throughout County Clare as "Paddy O."

His oldest daughter Kathleen had her father's command of the language but she chose not to be a verbal hawker in the image of her father. She was more like her mother Emma than her father, reserved and respectful of people's time and personal thoughts. Her presence sparked life through her large smiles and lovely face. Her striking good looks naturally drew people in for an engaging conversation.

Kathleen was tall for a Western Irish girl but her dark eyes along with her dark complexion were her most notable features. Those who paid attention to the Irish folklore would consider Kathleen a 'darkie.' A darkie, or Selkie, has a connection to the sea and the seals that live off the coast of Ireland and Scotland.

In the folklore, the seals are transformed into human form by shedding their skins but they never lose their connection with the sea, and water is never far away. Selkies possess great beauty and are noted for their romantic nature. Kathleen's lineage did not have an explanation for her dark features; therefore she was considered to be connected to the Selkie folklore and was referred to as "The Darkie." She found the reference amusing. Kathleen was comfortable with herself and the world around her.

Kathleen had completed six years of education and knew how to read and write in English, but she also knew many of the old Gaelic sayings. Of course, the Irish language was outlawed in Ireland, so any conversations had to be held in the home usually with her mother and her two sisters, Anna and Grace. Kathleen also played the violin and fiddle. In the evening, she would play the soft music of Turlough O'Carolan.

Kathleen worked as an aide at the county Fever Hospital in Ennis. She assisted with the daily chores of cleaning and changing bedpans, and giving sponge baths to patients; she also ran errands and delivered messages. She wanted to study in the health field but women doctors were nearly unheard of, so her best option was to consider joining a convent that cared for the sick. Her eighteenth birthday was soon approaching and a final decision had not been made regarding her life's vocation.

She was well liked by the hospital staff as well as the patients, which made the decision easier, but leaving home for the convent would not be easy. Most patients at the hospital were short-term because the fever would overtake them quickly, or they were sent to Dublin for longer-term care, and many were sent home with no hope for survival. Kathleen gave them as much comfort as she could and tried to provide an environment in which they could die with dignity.

On a cool, cloudy, and dark October evening in 1836, Kathleen left the hospital for her usual walk home through the streets of Ennis. This night, she was about two hours later than usual as she had sat with Edward O'Donnell during the last hours of his earthly existence. After he passed and she reported the event to the charge doctor, Kathleen left for home. She was sad for the loss of Edward, an older man who possessed a vigorous spirit throughout his sickness. She felt as if she had lost a friend, which left her in a melancholy mood that made her keep her head down, lost in thoughts of Edward's final struggle.

As was her custom, she walked past Callaghan's Pub. The typical crowd could be heard from the street, bantering and sharing the talk of the night.

Kathleen walked past, ignoring the bar's activity. Shortly thereafter she heard footsteps behind her. The footsteps kept pace with Kathleen even as she quickened her step. The click of her follower's heels was easily heard against the stone walkway, and fear grew within her. Kathleen thought the heavy footsteps were that of a fully grown man, so she decided to turn abruptly on a side street to see if she could get a look at her follower. She only made out a large shadow and thus could not identify the person.

Now, she was on a small street with a couple of shops that had closed for the day. The footsteps now became a run. Kathleen had only a few short seconds to decide what to do, but it was too late when an arm wrapped around her neck and a hand was pressed over her mouth. She had just reached the intersection of an alley and was dragged down the alleyway, meant for horses, and pushed to the ground, still unable to see her assailant. There, in this alley of Ennis, County Clare, Kathleen was tragically dese-crated in body and spirit in one of the greatest crimes against humanity imaginable.

She was left alone. Disheveled. Abused. Torn. She gathered her tattered underclothing as she sat up and tried to regain her compo-sure. Her coat was soiled but her aide uniform was still intact. Tears rolled down her cheeks from the physical pain and the emotional trauma that overwhelmed her. She slowly stood up and waited. She listened with frozen fear for others who might come at the call of her assailant and take advantage of the powerless girl in the isolation of the alley. She looked down the alley, and knew she did not want to return that way. She looked in the other direction, which was a longer distance back to a main street, but she was in shock and not sure of her location. She stumbled in the longer, unknown direction.

Her senses sharpened, Kathleen took a deep breath and now she could hear sounds clearly. The smell that stuck in her nose reeked of alcohol and sweat, and her mouth was dry. She felt dirty, soiled by the crime that stuck to her skin and invaded her soul. By the time she limped and staggered up the alley and reached the main street, she was able to stand fully upright. She brushed her clothes, gained control of her tears, and started her trip home.

Kathleen stood in front of her house. Having to tell what hap-pened would be difficult indeed, and her father would react with great anger and shouting, questioning how this could happen. He would want to organize a posse to roust anyone with alcohol on his breath—not to mention the commotion he would create in Callaghan's Pub. Kathleen's mother would be devastated as well as her sisters. In the end, Kathleen decided to say nothing. She entered the row house and walked the stairs to her second-floor residence. Upon entering the apartment, Emma was the first to greet her. "Kathleen, you are late, is everything all right?"

"Yes, everything is all right, Mother. Edward, an older man whom I liked, died today. I stayed with him until the Good Lord took him home."

Emma smiled, proud of her daughter. Kathleen went to her room to change and clean up. When she returned to the living room, where the family was gathered, again Kathleen's mother sensed something wrong. "Something's bothering you." It was a statement more than a question.

Kathleen explained again, "It's just the loss of Edward; he was such a good man and no family was there for him." Her mother's concern was calmed at least for the time being.

As the days passed, Kathleen continued her daily routine of going to work and walking home. She was careful not to stay late and she took the longer route home, away from Callaghan's Pub. She was a strong woman but she had pride and she hurt. The walk home on that fateful night past Callaghan's Pub could have destroyed Kathleen's spirit, but such was not her nature. Kathleen had an internal strength that did not let a horrendous crime defeat her true self. She suffered internally but she endured externally. She never wanted to see or hear of Callaghan's Pub again.

As Christmas 1836 approached, Kathleen's worst fears became reality. She feared she was pregnant. How would she explain this circumstance to her family? As a good Catholic, being pregnant out of wedlock would overshadow any explanation of the crime that had happened to her. Her father would not understand and the scandalmonger talk of the townsfolk and the parishioners of the Cathedral Church of St Peter and Paul could not be endured. She waited as long as she could, but by the end of January, she was certain of her condition.

Kathleen waited until after church on the last Sunday in January to tell her parents. Her two younger sisters were out of the house visiting their friends when she determined it was time for a talk. Paddy was sitting in his chair enjoying one of his cigars.

Kathleen decided to say it outright: "I think I am pregnant."

Her mother said, "What?"

Her father said, "Who?"

"Yes, it's true. I think I am pregnant." Answering more of her mother's question than her father's inquiry.

Her father repeated his question: "Who is the father?"

Kathleen took a deep breath and stood her ground. "It does not matter who the father is, I will not marry him. He will have nothing to do with my baby."

"I want to know who he is. He will pay for this baby and his indiscretions upon my daughter."

"Daddy, it does not matter."

"Are you kidding me?" Now his voice was loud and all occupants of the building and many on the street could hear Paddy O starting his verbal confrontation. He was on his feet. "No young man is going to take advantage of my daughter and walk away without anyone saying anything." Kathleen was about to re-affirm how little the identity of the baby's father mattered when her mother interrupted her.

"Paddy, lower your voice and control yourself," ordered her mother as she pointed to the windows and the ceiling.

His face was flushed with red, the veins were bulging across his forehead and along his neck, but he quickly redirected his thoughts. "What are we going to do?"

Kathleen took note of the statement, which included the word "we." "Father, we are not going to do anything. I'm going to have the baby and that's that." Pregnancies out of wedlock and unwed mothers were not unusual in County Clare but harsh stigmas followed both the mother and her family.

"No," was Paddy's reply, followed by, "we can't have you living here, pregnant with a baby out of wedlock, and say nothing. I have a business to uphold. Customers need to respect me." Paddy O's voice was up again for all to hear as he continued, "I have built this business so I wouldn't have to dig dirt for a living. I have given you a house with a roof over your head and food on the table and a respectable place in the church."

"Paddy, calm down," Kathleen's mother interjected again. "We need to talk this through in a civilized manner."

Paddy overcame himself and slapped his hand on the kitchen table. "I can't believe this," he shouted. Kathleen and her mother jumped.

Kathleen's mother turned to her again and said, "As you were saying, you think that you are pregnant." This was Mother's way of saying, you can tell us the whole story if you want to, otherwise Kathleen had the opportunity to state her plan.

"I will have the baby by myself."

Silence fell across the room. All three minds were churning; each O'Grady was searching for answers, for words to be said aloud, for a strategy to be stated that brought solace, comfort, or a positive outcome.

After a long silence, Paddy O said, "I have a plan." Kathleen did not like the plan and she had not even heard it yet. It wasn't Paddy's plan to make. "We will send you away to stay with the Magdalene Sisters during this period. They will take care of you and help you with your baby."

Kathleen shouted back, "No Dad. I will do no such thing."

Paddy's eyes narrowed, his face reddened again, his body filled with intensity. He was ready to explode. Kathleen saw it coming. He rarely lost his composure but when he did, it was volatile.

Paddy could feel the rage inside him. He had built his business and he had a reputation to think about. All of Ireland was suffering from disease, hunger, fever, land stripping, and abuses from the English. Amid all this misery, he had used his savvy business skills and established a viable trade through shipping and importing goods, an unusual success—for a Catholic to deal effectively with Protestant customers. In Irish terms, he was successful. A scandal like this would destroy all that he had worked to create. He had no intention of letting this happen. Now he was face to face with his daughter whom he loved greatly, and he tried to constrain his anger, but the intensity still made him shout louder than he should have.

"You must go away." He heard his own words and understood in an instant what they meant. He was removing her from her home; he was abandoning her. He sat back in his chair. His own conflicts tore him up on the inside. The discussion was over. Each retreated to their private thoughts. The air hung heavy in the small apartment on the second floor of the O'Grady household.

Kathleen withdrew to the room she shared with her sisters. She needed time to be alone. Tears welled up in her eyes but she refused to cry out loud. She felt alone and deserted by her family. Her father's priority to focus on his business confused her. How could he consider sending his daughter to those terrible slave masters, the Magdalene Sisters, to save his business rather than find the right answer to take care of his daughter and her baby? She had never felt so alone, so isolated from the comfort of her world. She lay on the floor staring at the white-washed ceiling and walls with its cracks spidering across the room and watched the aged plaster dividing away from itself into separate islands, losing its anchor with the wooden lath behind it. "Time," she thought, "separates everything. Now, it's my time."

The next evening Kathleen left the hospital and walked to the Cathedral Church of St Peter and Paul, to see Father McKenna, a Franciscan at the cathedral. She walked past the new church being built on Chapel Lane, observing the vast cathedral. As she moved by the construction area, she said hello to the up-and-coming architect James Joseph McCarthy, whom she had seen around the church before. "JJ" McCarthy was a student at the Figure and Ornament Schools of the Royal Dublin Society and he seemed to be having a serious discussion with Dean O'Shaughnessy, who was overseeing construction. For a moment she saw how handsome JJ was, but Kathleen kept on walking. Tonight was not a night to be flirting with promising architects, nor was she inclined to make romantic gestures towards any man. Foremost in her mind was the serious dilemma she had to resolve.

Fr McKenna was a young priest whom Kathleen respected for his spiritual guidance. He was easy to talk to and able to narrow any issue to a simple and pious closure. This problem, however, was not simple, and Kathleen did not see an easy solution to her predicament. When Kathleen reached the door of the rectory, she hesitated. Her biggest fear was trusting Fr McKenna not to say anything about their conversation. Even though she had no reason to doubt Fr. McKenna's trust, the doubt lingered in her mind.

If, in a year's time, the truth came out, what would the result be for her father, and for her baby? Both thoughts had grave, lifelong ramifications. The thought of the truth being exposed was disturbing. And besides, the church had made its position known about unwed mothers: having a child out of wedlock was unacceptable. Although she trusted Fr. McKenna, his reaction could be either comforting to her situation, or rage and accusations of sin-filled behavior.

She turned to leave. After a step, she stopped. She needed insight into her problem. How would she deal with her situation and her uncompromising father?

She looked down the street and saw JJ McCarthy talking with the Dean. She saw confidence in JJ's movements and stature. He too was making enormous decisions, although these were decisions about the future of the church's structure which needed to endure weather and destructive forces for centuries to come. Kathleen needed to be bold like the McCarthy that she saw. Inspired by her own reasoning, she left the rectory and went home.

The next day, Kathleen announced her plan to leave. She would find a way to survive in the new and exciting America. "I have a plan to travel to America and have my baby there," she said to her parents, not having any more details worked out in her head.

Paddy simply said, "I have a friend who can get you there safely."

Chapter 6

County Cork

Unbeknownst to Kathleen, Paddy sent a dispatch to his associate in Cork City, who handled his shipping business, asking for a special favor. "I have a dire emergency for which I need your help," he wrote. "My daughter needs to travel to America quickly and safely; please ask Captain Ryan to grant this special request."

Paddy received his reply within the week: "Captain Ryan wants assurance that there is no legal trouble, otherwise he is leaving three days hence." Paddy said aloud, "Oh my, three days!"

He threw down the letter and called to Kathleen. Both Kathleen and her mother ran to his small office in the back of the apartment. "You must pack quickly and go to Cork for your transport," he announced. "They are waiting to sail."

Kathleen's mother was not ready for such a quick decision and departure of her first-born child. "She cannot go this soon; can't she wait for us to prepare a little better?"

"No, the ship is going to sail. I will accompany her to Cork and see her off."

Kathleen steeled her emotion against his dismissal of her so readily and dispassionately. "I am prepared to pack my bag right now." Her possessions consisted of a couple of dresses, some underthings, and her violin. She was finished with her preparation to travel to the New World within moments.

But her mother could not handle the speed of events between the announcement of the pregnancy and Kathleen's departure, with the likelihood that she would never see her daughter again. Emma could understand the rashness of a seventeen-year-old but the dispassionate speed of Paddy to discharge his daughter was confusing.

"I need to knit a blanket for the baby before you go." She wanted some delay tactic, but she knew that Paddy's mind was made up. Neither reason nor emotion would change his course of action. She thought to herself, "Maybe the frequent voyages in his shipping business are keeping him from seeing the magnitude of her departure."

Tears welled in Emma's eyes but she fought them back, a trait of internal strength that Kathleen had learned from her mother. Knowing they were about to leave, Emma opened her arms to hug her daughter and the embrace lasted several minutes with the whisper, "I love you. Godspeed on your journey."

Kathleen pulled away. "I love you too, Mother."

Within twenty minutes of receiving the reply from Cork, Kathleen and her father were off to Cork in a carriage arranged by Paddy.

It was odd that Paddy, in trying to protect his reputation, turned to his business associates for help. Surely they would learn the nature of the dire emergency and the secret of his daughter's condition. In his fury to control events and make the decisions he felt necessary, he lost his business savvy and a true sense of the proper alternatives for his daughter. Kathleen, too, with her streak of stubbornness, had made snap decisions about leaving as a hasty reaction to her father's wrath.

Even though the O'Grady household experienced the devastating effects of an unwed mother, which tore the family apart, County Clare was experiencing numerous other children born out of wedlock. In a study conducted the year before, a sampling of ten parishes showed 646 "bastardly" children within the county and these numbers did not include the children of 741 widowed mothers.

Kathleen may not have known the extent of fatherless children in the area but she did have a keen sense of the treatment. One parish report echoed the Church's stance with the affirmation, "Bastards are never supported by the parish." The report further stated that men looking for marriage shun women with children. The child's future was devoid of hope too. "If a bastard behaved himself well and became an industrious member of society, the circumstance of his unfortunate birth would be forgotten." At the same time several farmers stated that they would "move heaven and earth to prevent their daughters marrying bastards . . ."

The report also noted that men sometimes marry to get rid of charges of rape—a thought Kathleen would never consider. Even if she had the support of her father, life and social interactions in Ennis would ruin any happy existence for this intelligent, talented young woman who at one time had considered a vocation to a religious order. Surely the Church would shun her under current conditions.

As Kathleen entered the carriage for the two-day trip to Cork, she contemplated these circumstances to solidify her decision. Paddy O'Grady too was lost in his own thoughts of financial ruin and isolation because of a bastard grandchild. As the carriage rolled slowly towards Cork on the east coast of County Cork, Paddy had plenty of opportunity to watch his eldest daughter across from him.

He realized the talents of his daughter, now banished by her self-imposed exile, and he would miss her. He could not find the right words or the healing words to express his consternation with his daughter and even his own explosive reaction. Paddy glanced up at Kathleen and the sight of her forlorn expression melted his self-loathing. "I am sad you are leaving us," was all he could say.

"Daddy, I'm scared." An unusual statement from Kathleen, who rarely showed her vulnerabilities, but the realization of dangerous and distant travel suddenly came to the forefront.

"Now Katie"—a term he rarely used since she had grown—"you will be fine. It is time anyway for you to be thinking of your freedom and leaving your parents' home."

"Ah, you're right," she said, but not because she believed his words about maturing into adult life. He still was not taking the future welfare of his grandchild into consideration—but to argue would mean leaving Ireland with distressing memories. Nevertheless, she was disheartened by his lack of regard for her and the child as she slid lower into the hard bench of the coach, trying to find some comfort and ease the bumps of a rutty and pot-holed roadway. The remainder of the trip was either in silence or with guarded niceties about inconsequential views seen out of the carriage windows.

The trip over the well-traveled rutted dirt highway took them through the small town of Mallow on the Blackwater River, where they made an unexpected stop at St. Mary's Church off the main road. The driver called for the horses to halt: "Whoa."

"I have a package to deliver," he announced to Paddy and Kathleen. He hopped down out of the carriage landing in the small lane in front of the large stone and brick church. "I'll be back in a moment," he said.

Paddy looked at his daughter. "They say America is beautiful in the spring."

"Yes, I'm sure it is. I'll find a nice apartment in the city overlooking the harbor. It will make me think of home and the times you took me to Limerick to watch the boats being unloaded with your tobacco and other goods."

Paddy did not like the recollection of happier days as he was about to send his daughter off, and wanted to change the subject. "Yes, I hope it doesn't rain as often." They both smiled at the thought and the conversation drifted into an awkward silence.

The driver returned to the carriage and announced, "We're off." As soon as the coachman hit the driver's bench, the stagecoach jumped forward as if to make up for lost time.

Upon arrival at the docks along the River Lee in Cork, Paddy had one more piece of business to tend to with Kathleen. "The O'Grady's have a long history in County Clare, which I am very proud of, but I think you should drop the 'O' in 'O'Grady' so people in the New World will not automatically think you are Irish."

Kathleen stared at her father for a moment. "Are you that ashamed of me?"

"No, that's not what I meant. I think people will accept you faster and might think you are English or something."

"And they might not think we are related?" said Kathleen. "And you are hoping that I will represent myself as English. Daddy, how could you?"

"Just drop the 'O' for your own good."

"Sure Daddy, I'll drop the 'O.'" She turned and looked out the window. "Another piece of the abandonment," she thought.

The driver pulled up alongside the massive cargo ship, the *Carolina*. As he opened the carriage door, Paddy yelled in a gregarious voice, "Good morning, sir," to the captain standing on board the ship.

"Ah, Paddy, I see that you made it in time," replied the captain. "We are going to sail today as soon as we are loaded." The captain left the gunwale and walked down the short gangplank to the dock. Paddy met him with hand outstretched. "Captain Ryan, I would like you to meet my daughter, Kathleen."

"Oh my," said the Captain aloud but inside he said, "How am I going to protect this young beautiful girl from the sailors?" He found his voice again. "'Tis nice to meet you, madam," and took her hand and kissed the back of it.

Kathleen blushed and said, "Yes sir, nice to meet you, too."

Paddy took the Captain's shoulder and drew him away from Kathleen "I need you to get her safely to New York. She is with child." Then he added in a lower voice, "The father is not known."

"I see," said the Captain.

"And please, give her this envelope when you arrive." Paddy handed the Captain a sealed envelope. "And for your troubles, this is for you." He placed a gold piece in the Captain's hand.

"She'll be safe with me."

Paddy returned to his daughter standing alone in silent agony on the dock. "How did it come to this?" she asked herself. "My father is handing me off to this stranger."

She looked at her father and saw a man who thought he was making the right decision for his daughter and family. Even though he had made his commitment to see her off, he stood there confused as to the next step and felt awkward in his movement towards Kathleen. "I wish you Godspeed on your journey," he said as he loosely hugged her.

"Many blessings to you, Mother, Anna, and Grace," Kathleen replied in a low sad voice.

"I wish this could be different," Paddy said, unconvinced that he could ease this departure with a few words. He backed away with a step, turned, and climbed into the carriage. When the door slammed shut, the driver yelled "Go," and the horses led the coach away. Kathleen stood motionless on the dock staring at the departing coach with an urge to yell out, "Come back," but another emotion told her to hold her silence.

Tears welled in her eyes. All that she had known, loved, and become familiar with in life was now gone. She felt overwhelmingly abandoned. Her knees were weak and she felt as if she would collapse at any moment. The air in her lungs felt shallow and vacant. In her moment of panic, tears rolled down her cheek and she swallowed hard to suppress an outward sob.

The Captain took her elbow and said, "Let's get aboard."

Chapter 7

Atlantic Ocean

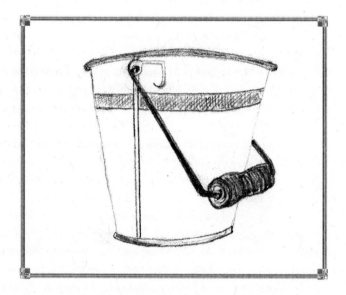

Captain Ryan led Kathleen up the gangplank to the main deck. "This will be your home for the next thirty to forty-five days. I have a berth set for you below for your privacy and living quarters." He turned to his First mate. "Mr. Bailey, take Miss O'Grady below."

Kathleen turned to the Captain. "It's Grady; I'm dropping the 'O.'"

"Very well," said the Captain.

Mr. Bailey picked up Kathleen's bag and escorted her to the hatch and ladder that led to the lower deck. When below, he led her into her berth, a small cubicle protected by a cloth hanging on three sides to give her privacy. Within the enclosure was a narrow bed made from fresh stuffed hay, a straight-backed chair, and a small oval window with a hatch that let some light in.

"I hope you are comfortable," said Mr. Bailey as he set down her bag and left. The cabin was clean but the lower deck smelled musty and the damp air blowing in from the porthole gave no promise of relief. Again a wave of melancholy hit Kathleen. Perhaps she, too, could end this voyage by insisting on going ashore. But stubbornness and determination overcame fear and prevented her from making a quick exit off the boat.

She sat on the chair for over an hour and looked about the tiny quarters, realizing this small area was her only refuge of isolation from a ship full of men. A different fear overcame her, not the emotional fear of separation, but fear for her physical safety. She asked herself, "Can the Captain really protect me?" She stood because some subconscious voice told her to run, but as she did, the boat jerked. She heard voices above yelling, "Now, drop the mizzen sail." The boat was moving away from the dock and there was nowhere to run to. She was headed to America.

The ship set sail and Kathleen sat back down on the chair and stared out the porthole. The river gave way to the ocean and soon the high waves of the open sea rocked the boat. Kathleen was oblivious to the changes until a sudden sway nearly knocked her to the floor. She could hear footsteps coming below and walking towards her. A deep voice spoke. "Miss Grady? Miss Grady?"

"Yes," she answered. Silence sat in the air for moment.

"Miss Grady? Are you all right?" She recognized the voice of the First Mate, Mr. Bailey.

"Why, yes," she said as she pulled back the cloth opening.

"Ah, just checking. The Captain would like you to join him for dinner tonight. Will that be all right with you?"

"That will be fine," she said.

"He will expect you at six o'clock."

"Six o'clock. How will I know when it is six o'clock?"

"The ship's bell will ring five times at five o'clock. The crew will change at that time and it will ring again six times at six o'clock. The captain will be waiting."

"Thank you, Mr. Bailey."

"Umm, yes, okay," said Mr. Bailey. Kathleen realized the awkwardness of the First Mate; she took his discomfort as the result of having a woman on board.

At the tone of 6 o'clock, she left her berth and started towards the ladder to go above. She was surprised to find Mr. Bailey waiting for her by the ladder. "I will take you up," he said.

Kathleen did not say anything but thought it was odd that he was there.

When she arrived at the Captain's quarters under the escort of Mr. Bailey, the Captain motioned her to sit at his dining table. "I have asked a young lad to join us for dinner," he told her. But before she could respond, there was a tap on the door.

"Mr. Bailey, let him in," said the Captain. "And then you can leave us."

"Aye, Captain," said the First Mate and he went to the door.

Conor entered the Captain's quarters. Most sailors never see the inside of their captain's private quarters except in dire circumstances. As it turned out, the ship had not been a full day at sea and Conor was making his second trip to the Captain's berth.

The Captain said, "Welcome, Mr. Meighan. I see that you have cleaned up after a hard day's work preparing for the sail." The Captain was trying to make his two guests feel welcome and comfortable.

"Yes, I feel much better. Thank you."

"I would like to introduce you to Miss Grady. She will be traveling with us to America." Conor wondered what reason he had given Miss Grady for this dinner.

"I am pleased to meet you, Mr. Meighan," said Kathleen Grady with a smile. Saying Grady rather than O'Grady felt odd.

Conor first noticed her dark features because most Irish were fair-skinned with light or red hair, but not this woman. Her black hair and brown eyes had mystery behind them, but her smile had charm. Conor was taken aback by Miss Grady's beauty. He was disarmed immediately. His first word was "Ump," followed by, "yes, 'tis a pleasure to met you."

Miss Grady leaned forward and said softly, "You can call me Kathleen."

"Well then, you can call me Conor," he said with a smile. The two had connected.

Dinner on a freight ship at sea in the 1800s was hearty fare, especially as a guest of the Captain. Tonight, the evening meal was a bowl of salt pork and root crops—carrots and potatoes in a watery sauce. The Captain's mood had led him to include the usual ship's fare of biscuits, known as hardtack, and goblets of beer. Dinner on this first night was exceptionally good. The company of other diners, or the fact that Conor had not eaten well for a while, may have helped the mood. The Captain opened a bottle of wine for his guests, another unusual provision for sea travelers.

Kathleen was delightful in conversation as she spoke of her upbringing in Ennis. "I enjoyed the closeness of the neighbors and the many small shops." She blocked out the thoughts of alleyways and bars.

"Yes, I have been to Ennis a couple of times with my family," Conor said. "It's a lovely town. I come from Kilmaly, west of Ennis. We work the land." Conor's reference to working the land told Kathleen that they were tenant farmers; most likely they had lost ownership of the land when the English took over Ireland in the 17th century and they now worked for an absentee landlord, probably a wealthy baron or earl in London. Even though they had a close connection, both being from County Clare, the six miles from Conor's family farm was a long way from Kathleen's apartment in both status and lifestyle.

Conor continued, "We had another crop failure this year, the potato turned black as it did before, and the government won't let us plant anything else for our own use. The only other choice is to convert it into grazing pastureland. It's a tough life right now for my parents and family."

"Is that why you left?" asked Kathleen.

"No, not exactly, but there is no future for me in Ireland. Even if the crops were good—there are too many people working the land, too many mouths to feed. Soon enough there will be widespread starvation unless the landlord allows other crops."

"I believe it is the same all over the countryside."

"Indeed it is," said Conor. "My cousins farther up the Shannon are struggling with the same issues."

The Captain found the conversation entertaining and he spontaneously laughed out loud.

"What's so funny?" asked Kathleen.

The Captain looked at Conor. "I knew you were never a sailor. You have been a farmer all your life."

Conor knew the Captain had figured out he was never a sailor; this was just an official declaration. "I can't lie very well," he admitted.

The Captain laughed again, but he had business on his mind. He turned the discussion. "I have asked Conor to keep an eye on you," he told Kathleen.

"Why? Should I be concerned?"

"No. I mean that ships are dangerous places. They rock and heave. A storm can be very treacherous and I will not have the time to watch over you."

Kathleen chuckled. "I can take of myself."

"Kathleen, you are a woman on a ship full of men." The Captain's voice was serious.

Kathleen was well aware of the danger that lay in the hearts of men. "I understand," she said, equally serious.

Conor added, "If you need me, just say so."

Kathleen nodded. Fear rose in her throat and she felt a wave of anxiety overcome her. She took a deep breath and waited. Conor watched the moment, sensing that something was wrong with

Kathleen, but he was not sure of its meaning. Then Kathleen smiled and raised her wine glass. "To my protectors."

"To us," replied Conor. After dinner, Conor and Kathleen left the Captain's berth together. Their special dinner had celebrated the introduction of the two passengers, and subsequent meals on the voyage would not be as extravagant as this first night. Hardtack, heavily salted beef, and warm beer would become the usual fare.

Conor said, "I will walk you down to your quarters, but then I have duties in the crow's nest."

"Very kind of you," Kathleen said.

After leaving Kathleen in her makeshift room below deck, Conor returned to the main deck. The rumors among the men were well decided before Conor left dinner and had a chance to give his explanation and even then, clarifying the truth was difficult. He decided to wait for the rumors and then explain.

He looked up at Mutt still keeping watch from above. Conor yelled up, "I will relieve you now."

"You're a bit early, by a half an hour, but I will be right down."

Conor grabbed the ropes to start his climb to the crow's nest. He had one foot secured in the rope net when Mutt was down and standing on deck. Mutt could see that Conor was new to sailing. "You will get used to it. Just remember, never let go." Conor managed another rung on the rope. "By the way, the wind is blowing cold out of the north; keep bundled. Watch for ice and report it immediately to the coxswain. We will be in trouble if we hit an iceberg."

"Thanks," said Conor as he inched his way up the ropes. He settled into the crow's nest, which was much smaller than it appeared from below. He barely had room for his feet, and wrapped them around the centre mast. The mast went through the middle of the nest, which allowed a handle for the swaying to and fro. A half-moon gave the ocean a dark, eerie appearance and the light occasionally caught the cap of a wave, causing illusory figures to jump up and dance on the water. Because of these illusions, he could not see small icebergs in the distance—only large ones that clearly reflected the moonlight.

Ice was a sailor's Achilles heel which could destroy or capsize a vessel at a moment's notice. The wind was frigid, as Mutt had warned him. It chilled his body and the waves were kicking up, causing the ship and thus the centre mast to rock from side to side. The rocking was tolerable on deck but now the additional thirty feet in the air exaggerated it. The wine from dinner and the rocking was making Conor sick. A wave hit the side of the boat, causing it to move suddenly three feet to the starboard side. Conor nearly fell out of the nest. As a result, he spewed his dinner downward over the mainsail. A second wave hit, causing more sickness, and Conor gripped the mast.

The sails were made of flax cloth, a plant material used for centuries in making the large canvas fabric designed to catch the wind. Captain Ryan's well-seasoned ship used this heavy-grade cloth as it was stronger than cotton, though not as pliable—but in the application of sails, it was the perfect material.

The coxswain called up, using his seamen's jargon, "Did you get sick? Did you cast up accounts on the mainsail?"

"Yes," Conor acknowledged, as he figured the reference was to his vomiting. The coxswain rang the bell, alerting the crew members to come to the deck.

Mr. Bailey was the first to arrive. "What happened?"

"Meighan threw up his dinner on the mainsail." Two more crew members appeared.

"Lower the sail," the First Mate bellowed. The crew hustled to bring the sail down.

Mr. Bailey looked upward. "Are you all right?"

Conor did not comprehend the distress of the crew. Surely he wasn't the first to get sick in the crow's nest. "Yeah, I am all right." Meanwhile the ship rocked side-to-side from the waves, and rose and lowered from the swells.

"Come down," the First Mate commanded.

Conor climbed out and started down, clutching each rung.
A wave sent its spray skyward coating the deck, ropes, and Conor
with water that quickly turned to ice. Conor was not accustomed
to such treacherous conditions. He looked down; one moment he
was hanging over the ocean on the starboard side and the next
moment the ship had swayed and he was hanging over the port
side. The skin on his hands was sticking and freezing to the ropes
as he gripped each line coming down. It was tearing off a layer of
skin as he released his grip, even though his hands were calloused
from years of farming. When he reached the bottom, his hands
were bleeding. Conor was quickly learning that a sailor's life was
not easy.

Conor approached the First Mate. "I'm sorry, but I can stay
the watch."

"Yes, you will, but not from up above. Too dangerous."

"Why did you bring down the sail?"

"Vomit has strong stomach acid in it. It weakens the cloth."

Conor looked at the crew members, who were washing the
sail. "I'll help."

"Take your post at the bow and watch for ice."

Conor realized the urgency of obeying orders immediately
and without hesitation. The survival of the ship and its crew
depended on quick reactions.

Kathleen did not sleep well during her first night, with the swaying and heaving of the ship on the high seas. She too felt the effects
of the wine and this seventeen-year-old was not used to alcohol;
she became light-headed quickly and the feeling of disorientation
overpowered her sense of control, a sense that frightened her. She
decided that alcohol was not going to control her and dull her ability to remain aware of her surroundings.

So when she heard the commotion on the deck of the ship,
she decided to go up to investigate and get some fresh air. When
she arrived, the sail had been cleaned and the sailors were returning to their quarters. She spotted Conor standing at the bow

looking out over the vast, dark ocean. She walked up and said, "What was all the shouting about?"

"I got sick in the crow's nest. They put me down here at the bow for my watch."

"That was nice of them."

"No, they do that in rough seas because of the danger of getting tossed around up there, and I couldn't withstand the sway. Are you cold?"

"No, I'm fine," said Kathleen. She pulled her woolen coat tightly around her as the wind blew across the bow. "Can I visit you while you are on watch?"

"I think so."

"So, you didn't say why are you going to America?" she asked.

"There was no future for me in Ireland; I had to leave." Kathleen understood that Conor was referring to the political and economic conditions.

"And you are leaving because . . .?" Conor asked, knowing a little of Kathleen's reason.

"The same reason; there was no future for me in Ireland."

"The Captain did mention that you were with child."

"He did, did he?"

"Yes, when he asked me to keep an eye on you."

"Well, there it is, I am with child and alone," Kathleen said straightforwardly.

"You are not alone," countered Conor. They smiled suddenly at each other.

Kathleen visited with Conor for a short time longer and then went below for the night. Conor continued his watch until the next sailor, Bill Tracey, relieved him. Conor filled him in on the night's watch. Tracey, a seasoned and muscular sailor, who lacked the skill of developing and maintaining a positive interpersonal relationship, just grumbled an acknowledgment. To Conor, Tracey seemed angry, more so than necessary, maybe because he was one of the sailors who had to clean the sail; still, Conor knew that even though Tracey was socially inept, hard work and physical exertion brought him satisfaction. Conor apologized for causing his extra duty: "I'm sorry that you had to clean my mess."

But the effort was not acknowledged; Tracey grumbled an inaudible but irritated remark that contained some reference to "your kind" and "you don't belong here."

Conor decided to let the remarks go unchallenged and went below. Once in his bunk, the weight of O'Malley's Pub returned and his subconscious tried to change the events and make a positive outcome for himself. But he could not fix the event, for the stubbornness of Sergeant Clark and the rage of Seamus with the hatred between them could not be intercepted. If only Conor had approached Seamus before the soldiers came in or before Seamus entered the bar, he could have headed off the impending disaster and life would have remained easy to understand. He could have walked to Ennis and met Kathleen on his own terms. But Kathleen's circumstances had already started her on her pathway to the ship in Cork. His mind remained unsettled and his sleep was not restful.

Shortly after sun-up, the Captain left his quarters and walked out onto the bridge. "Aye, Captain," greeted the boatswain. The Captain nodded in response to the greeting and looked out across the boat. His pensive mood was distracted by a passing seagull, which squawked as it flew by. The Captain was surprised to see a gull this far from the coast.

"Are you lost," he asked aloud, "or are you flying away in fear from danger?"

"Ahh, he was following a mermaid, Captain," said the sailor and then laughed aloud.

Captain Ryan's thoughts were far distant from the sailor's seafaring fantasies. He watched the gull land on the crosstree beam and considered the bird's dilemma of searching for land. His mind shifted to his boat and crew. "Yes, these men are like you," he thought, "some are lost to the call of the sea, some are lost to the call of life, and some are even running in fear from some scar of tragedy. Ah yes, society's misfits, sinners, and criminals sail my ship."

A large wave hit the ship, causing a shock against the forward movement. The jolt made the gull jump and fly off. "Go, you wanderer, and find your way, find your treasure," the Captain said, smiling to himself.

He reflected on his three special passengers, each one running, motivated by life's cruel injustices, trying to find their inner peace, their perch on which to rest. America was that place of refuge to many. "I hope they find it," he said in a half-whisper.

"What's that, Captain?" asked the boatswain.

"Nothing, I was watching the winds, looking for change."

"No change, sir," he replied.

"Yes, I see," answered Captain Ryan softly. "No change."

He returned to his quarters to write in his daily journal.

Later in the morning, Conor had to endure the chiding of his fellow sailors about getting sick in the crow's nest on his first night. It was all taken in good fun by the crew members—except for one. Bill Tracey had a chip on his shoulder about life. He was a longtime sailor, strong and hardened by the sea, weathered by the sun, and shunned by the world. "He shouldn't have been up there," started Tracey.

Conor let the comment go by, again. It was not his decision to be in the nest.

"He shouldn't be on this ship, it's not a passenger ship."

None of the sailors wanted to engage Tracey because of his aggressive temper.

"You should be back growing daisies and potatoes, where you belong."

"I'm doing my best and I will work hard," Conor finally replied.

"You probably can't even swim. I have half a mind to throw you overboard just to watch you splash about and attract the sharks," Tracey said, laughing. "Maybe I will do just that."

"That's not necessary," Conor stated.

Tracey didn't hear or pay attention to Meighan's attempt to calm the situation. Tracey threw down the rope he had in his hand and took a menacing step towards Meighan. Laughing and exposing the rotted teeth in his mouth, he reached out to grab Conor. Lightning struck. From somewhere in the back of the crowd, Seamus bolted forward and caught Tracey with a left hook to the side of head.

Seamus knew the knock-out sequence instinctively—stun with the left hook, break the nose with a quick right jab, knock the air out of the lungs with a left shot to the chest, and the fourth punch was an upper-cut to the base of the jaw. Tracey hit the deck with a thud. Seamus turned and looked at the crowd. His look challenged anyone else who wanted to harm his friend. No one moved; no one said a word. The message was clear: "Don't threaten us."

It took two splashes of seawater to bring Tracey around. Seamus stood by, in case Bill did not realize the lesson just meted out to him. Tracey shook his head to wash away the water and clear the shock of the lightning attack. Once stabilized, he picked up his rope and walked away.

The word quickly traveled around the ship not to bully Burke or Meighan, and this included Kathleen. The Captain was pleased with the lesson taught, learned, and remembered by the sailors. His tactic of assigning Conor was working out better than he had anticipated.

Life on the ocean in early March was a mixture of sunny warm days and treacherous storms, added to the threat of floating icebergs. The crew and its three novices could never relax against the sudden forces of nature surprising them from the air or in the water. In the evening Kathleen brought her violin to the deck and played the charming concertos of O'Carolan. Conor was enthralled by Kathleen's gentle violin; it added to her charm.

"Where did you learn to play such beautiful music?" asked Conor. "All I ever heard were the rowdy jigs and reels."

"From my grandmother; she studied O'Carolan's music and taught me the soft planxties—music written for the harp."

"Who is O'Carolan?"

"Turlough O'Carolan was a seventeenth-century Irish composer," she began. "He was struck with smallpox when he was eighteen years old, which left him blind. He learned to play the harp and made his living by traveling to the homes of the wealthy, where he would write and play for the landowner. He dedicated a planxty to his host in return for his room and board. His music was never written down, just handed down."

"You sure have a touch for his music."

"Thank you. Do you play an instrument?"

"No, the only music we had were the hymns we sang at Mass at church."

"Oh, I don't know, I have you pictured as quite the hooligan in the pub twirling the céilí dance. I imagine you created a stir." The origin of the céilí dance was a social gathering for music, storytelling, and poems, but also choosing a companion, thus a spouse. Maybe Kathleen was hinting at learning Conor's past.

"No, I am not the pub kind."

"Surely you have spent time in the pubs?"

Conor had built a trust with Kathleen and he found it easy to speak to her. "I stay out of pubs, especially now."

"Why now?"

"Seamus and I had trouble in a pub; that's why we're here. Well, Seamus had trouble." He thought for a moment. "No, I guess I had trouble too."

"I can see Seamus having trouble, but you . . .?"

"I was there and that made me part of it."

"Part of what?" Kathleen could see that he was distressed by the thought of a pub, and hesitant to explain.

Conor said, "We were in O'Malley's Pub one night. There was this fight and a British sergeant was killed. It wasn't planned; it just happened. And now I am fleeing County Clare."

"I don't see you as picking a fight with a British soldier or spending time with Seamus," said Kathleen.

"We weren't together; Seamus was with his friends. I just happened to be there on this particular night," said Conor. "I didn't know whether to go back and tell my side of the story and hope they understood I really did not have anything to do with it. Or whether I should just leave Ireland and be done with it."

"You were wise to distrust how the British would react to your innocent presence." Then she added, "I am glad you left."

"I felt bad leaving my family without saying goodbye."

"That is sad. Family is important."

"At least you had time to say goodbye," reminded Conor.

"It was hard saying goodbye and leaving, but I did what needed to be done."

"Didn't your father send you here?"

"No, I chose to go to America. He wanted to send me to the Magdalene Sisters."

"What did the baby's father have to say about all this?"

"What do you mean?"

"About leaving with the baby?"

"There is no father," Kathleen reported matter-of-factly.

"Oh?" Conor showed genuine concern.

Kathleen thought for a moment whether to tell her story. It was a deep secret she wanted to bury away and never bring to the surface. She had vowed to herself never to speak of her history, but this young lad from the hills of her own beloved County Clare had captured her trust and she could feel her very essence being warmed in his company. Her determination eased with the compassion and concern Conor had shown and now she was considering opening up.

"I was attacked in a dark alley by a man I could not see," she finally said. "I don't know who he was but he is the father. I could not tell my parents what happened—they do not know. I can never tell them."

He took her hand. "You have been keeping this inside?"

"I am okay as long as I don't think about it. It's hard. I try to be strong. I don't want anyone to know."

Conor gave her a minute and then said, "I will not repeat this to anyone." Kathleen half-smiled with the reassurance but her thoughts were lost in the drastic change in her life. "Are you scared?" asked Conor.

The question loosened her pain. "I am so scared. I am scared that in the next moment I will get surprised, shocked by some force that will overtake me. Footsteps in the dark scare me, alcohol breath makes me sick, and not knowing where I am is so frightening. All these things scare me."

"All that and an overbearing father—you must hate men."

"No, not really. I love my father and at times, I really miss him. But he is stuck with one way of thinking. He can be very difficult sometimes."

"Kathleen, I am glad we are traveling together." Conor reached out to hug her. She stepped back. The moment was awkward. Conor wanted to comfort her but she wanted distance.

"I am sorry. I can't be affectionate, at least not right away."

"Just know I am here." The moment hung so Conor continued, "Oh, that's a dreadful story."

"My father is so unpredictable, he would have traveled the streets of Ennis accusing and assaulting every drunk he found, so I refused to say how I became pregnant."

"You couldn't talk to your mother?"

"It would be the same as telling my father, only with the added accusation of not telling him first—the man of the house— the one who reacts to the troubles of a daughter."

Conor reeled back in his own thoughts as he recalled his father about ten years earlier grabbing Timmy Regan by the back of his collar and dragging him down the lane to Timmy's parents' house. Timmy's feet hardly touched the ground as his father pulled and lifted the offending boy for hitting his sister Claire. No injury to Claire but that didn't matter; Dad saw his girl get hit. Timmy was in transit, his feet dangling within seconds. That's what fathers do.

But Kathleen's situation was different; the assailant was unknown yet Conor's fury over the violation was just as strong as if the person were standing there. Conor felt that same anger and immediate emotion that said someone had to pay; someone had to feel the same pain and loss. He wanted to strike out with the same wrath as her father against the unknown man, whose savage attack had desecrated Kathleen's innocence and left her devastated.

"I wish I had been there to save you."

"Oh, Conor . . ."—she didn't know how to say the words—"I wish you were there too." Instead she just sighed.

The ability to speak of her ordeal that October night was a relief; it was a comfort to let it out. At times she wanted to shout words of hatred to rid herself of the suppressed emotion, but now it eased out in a controlled and comfortable release. Finally, the proper ear was listening and reacting to the delicate yet explosive forces of rage, fear, regret, guilt, uncertainty, and a host of other reactions that had gripped her soul. The pressure was released, even if just a little, in the expression of her personal story.

"What does your father do?" said Conor to keep the conversation going.

"He is a tobacco merchant," said Kathleen. "He is a good man with a good business sense but he has a volatile side that is dangerous."

"You come from money," Conor said, as a statement but with a slightly questioning inflection.

"Not really," answered Kathleen. "We live in a flat above a store in town but we rarely went without food on the table."

"Lucky you. We rarely had enough food on the table in the last couple of years."

"Oh my," said Kathleen.

"Our comfort was in each other. My brothers and sisters took care of me when I needed it. And now I have abandoned them."

"Hardly; you took the problem away from them."

"I hope so."

Kathleen and Conor spent as much time together as possible. They were the last to acknowledge this budding romance, but the crew saw nature at work and the Captain was again pleased with developments.

Every time Conor and Kathleen met, the romantic tension was there and Conor played his role as protector with enthusiasm. However, whenever Conor felt an intimate moment was at hand, such as wanting to take her hand, he kept himself in check by backing away. He did not want Kathleen to rebuff him, and that forwardness might make her uncomfortable and reject him as being too pushy.

One night, on watch, it struck him. He would ask Kathleen to marry him so he could father her baby. His admiration for Kathleen had developed into love and he saw the common values and the humor between them. He was anxious to propose the idea to Kathleen. The next morning while they were having breakfast tea, Conor suggested, "Kathleen, I would like to marry you and father your baby."

Kathleen was shocked by the proposal. "You want to marry me out of pity, is that what I just heard?"

"No, I didn't mean it that way. I meant that I want to marry you, and that would mean I would be the father of the baby." Conor wondered if that sounded any better.

"I don't know, sailor boy, if I want to marry you," she said, showing her playful side but her cautious nature. "I'll have to think about it."

Conor didn't anticipate that response. He thought it was a good plan for a dreadful situation and he had seen plenty of unions for convenience sake rather than love, including marriages for the purpose of gaining property, inter-family harmony, or political survival. This relationship already had more subtle affection than existed in many marriages based on circumstance and convenience.

"You are heading into a new rough and dangerous world. You need someone to look after you," he added.

The difference between males and females was crystal clear. He wanted to be practical; she wanted romance. "Conor, I like you, but are you ready to get married?"

"I wasn't until I met you. I have changed because of you. I see that I am ready to settle down with someone and I was hoping that someone would be you." At last, he had found some romance.

"I will think about it," was Kathleen's coy reply.

"Kathleen, the situation aside, I like being with you. I want you by my side all the time. I enjoy our conversations. I want to marry you. I want you with me for the rest of my life."

That was the romance Kathleen was waiting for. "But do you really know me well enough?"

"Do I know you? I can see very well who you are. I see your style, your grace, your wit, you are educated and compassionate; I have a clear understanding of whom I am asking to marry me."

"Okay," she said. In spite of Conor's exposing his romantic side, she remained coy. "I am still thinking about it."

"I also see us clearing a farm . . ."

"I what to live in a city," she interrupted.

"Yes, the farm is on the edge of a small village with shops and people moving about."

"Yes," she said. Conor smiled; she had agreed to the small village.

"Yes," she said again. "Yes, I will marry you."

Conor could not contain himself. "I am so happy!" Conor continued, "You know the captain can perform marriages on a ship."

Kathleen thought for a moment. "Whoa, so quickly?"

"Just a thought," said Conor.

Kathleen considered the necessity of being married when arriving. "Once we get settled in the New World, we have to get married in a church to make sure it is legal in the eyes of God."

"Of course."

Conor and Kathleen presented the idea to the Captain. No need for elaborate preparations on a ship: the Captain called the available crew together and, just past noon, he carried out the solemn ceremony while Seamus served as the official witness. The sea was calm as the Captain started with the words, "I am honored to preside over this union . . ."

Kathleen, usually confident in her quick decisions, suddenly felt unsure whether she was rushing into a marriage for the right reasons. In the short time she had had to think this through—which, truth to tell, had been weighing on her mind even before Conor brought up the idea—she had decided this man was special and she soon found her resolve in the emotional connection with Conor, and that made the difference. She had found love in this strong but gentle man, devout in his beliefs and strong in his character, but most of all she saw his devotion and attention to her. These thoughts reminded her that she need have no doubts, no regrets for this decision.

The Captain asked Conor, "Do you take this woman to be your lawful wedded wife and live with her forever in the eyes and the grace of God?"

"I do."

He then continued with Kathleen: "Do you take this man to be your lawful wedded husband and live forever in the eyes and grace of God?"

"I do," she said.

The captain then read from the New Testament, the Gospel of St. Mark, Chapter 10, verses 6-9:

> But from the beginning of the creation, God made them male and female. For this cause a man shall leave his father and mother; and shall cleave to his wife. And they two shall be in one flesh. Therefore now they are not two, but one flesh. What therefore God hath joined together, let not man put asunder.

As soon as the small ceremony was over, Conor returned to his duties when the Captain called to raise the topgallant sail to catch the northwesterly wind. Two crew members, one of whom was

Conor, were dispatched to the crossbeam to release the heavy, stiff cloth that could catch an angle of the wind and force a push to the port side as well as a forward motion. The captain changed course a few degrees to the north to compensate for the side-push. The rear mizzen sail was also dropped to equal the push along the length of the boat, otherwise the boatswain would constantly fight the bow swinging to the port side and sending the ship off course.

Conor climbed the gangway after a quick review by Mr. Bailey of the sail and duties. Now, after a few weeks at sea, his equilibrium was adjusting to the heaving of the ocean's surface, but he still had the anxiety of climbing the ropes with the exaggerated rolling forward and aft and side-to-side, a constant motion making his stomach churn with each change in direction. But he was determined not to vomit again and he fought this internal reaction both physically and mentally. Each climb upward involved a mental strain to calm his stomach and steady his grip because even the slightest slip at twenty feet above the deck might mean a fall—either a fall to the hard surface of the deck or a splash into the ocean.

Such a fall overboard would most likely prove fatal, as a ship does not stop easily and swimming to catch up to a ship is impossible. The only hope would be to drop a lifeboat and assemble a rescue crew to chase after the fallen member. Conor wanted neither an accident, nor such a dire rescue attempt on his behalf just because he missed a rung on the rope. His caution made him move slower and with less confidence than the seasoned seamen who had worked the rigging since they were young boys. The delay caused yells of exasperation and ridicule by the sailors rather than words of encouragement.

"Quit dreaming about your wedding night and pay attention to your work," one yelled.

Combined with marrying the pretty young girl on board, these sailors had plenty of jealous complaint about the novice sailor who caused more work than help. After planting his feet back on the main deck, Conor grabbed the gunwale to steady himself and regain his composure. Kathleen came up behind him and wrapped her arms around him, a surprise affectionate move and public display—but after all she was now his wife and certain liberties were allowed. After his ordeal on the ropes along with the chiding by the crew members and his unsettled internal organs, Conor was not in a romantic mood and he made a quick involuntary movement away from Kathleen. She was surprised by the rejection so soon after their marriage.

"I'm sorry," said Conor, realizing his demand for recuperating time was adversely affecting his new wife. He stepped in closer and placed his arm around her shoulder, but a wave hit the starboard side and sent a cascade of water over the couple. The force of the wave knocked them off balance and sent them sliding down the deck until Conor grabbed the jackline, a safety rope for these types of surprise occurrences. They scrambled for a foothold so they could stand again. With one hand on the gunwale, Conor reached forward and took a firm grip on Kathleen's shoulder; they stood and steadied themselves on the deck. Kathleen smiled as she moved closer and wrapped her arms around his waist. Rather than speaking, he nodded and smiled back.

The remainder of the afternoon passed fairly smoothly and the first mate allowed some private time for the newly married pair. Immediately the need for new routines and new understandings became apparent, including the level of intimacy afforded to the couple. Kathleen's quarters were tight for one person, and a double-width bed was not possible. Conor continued his sleeping arrangement in his hanging bunk with the rest of the sailors. After a few days of mild harassment, the chatter calmed down, but the two were always together whenever time allowed.

In this new phase of their relationship they learned ease in each other's company. "How are you feeling this morning?" Conor asked when he joined Kathleen for breakfast tea.

"I had a rough night's sleep with the rolling, and that north wind had a chill that kept me adjusting my blanket every few seconds. I didn't sleep well."

"I wish I could be closer to give you warmth," said Conor.

"I look forward to it," she said.

Conor reached over and stroked her hair. She offered no resistance or hesitation but accepted his touch as a sign of affection. "You look lovely this morning," said Conor as he rose to go topside and start his daily chores.

Conor and Kathleen enjoyed their time on the ship even though they had little privacy. Kathleen was sick most days for the early part of the voyage, which they considered to be the result of too much sea sway and the pregnancy. Of course the ship food also contributed to her heaves, and Conor tended to Kathleen whenever he could.

They were now more than half-way across the ocean to New York. As they entered the Gulf Stream flow from the warm Caribbean, turbulent weather awaited. Frequent storms hit but most were short-lived and the Captain's experienced crew managed the crisis with ease. However, one morning a more intense storm came roaring from the northeast, an unusual direction but a sign of powerful weather with high winds and even hail. The ship was tossed about, over, under, and through the waves.

The captain ordered the men to take the sails down, allowing the boat to sit on the water without power and to rock at the mercy of the turbulent sea. This technique was called "laying a hull" and the current conditions were right for this maneuver to work effectively. It prevented the additional rocking of the ship from the pushing of the sail against the resistance of the water; rather, the ship just rose and dropped with the swells.

Even so, the swells turned into violent waves sending water airborne across the top deck in a surge of water—taking ropes, materials, and men with it—only to be repeated within a few seconds as the storm gathered momentum. The waves reached heights of thirty-five feet showing a sea of all white foam, the leftover froth of agitated sea crests. Even when the Captain ordered the ship to lay a hull, the ship tossed fore and aft, crashing into the waves.

A tempest such as this was a bad omen to the sailors, who believed that it contained a message that an undesirable person was on board. These superstitious sailors many times blamed the tempest on the presence of a priest on a ship: no priests were on board for this voyage, but there were strangers.

Now, once again, the sailors climbed the rigging under extremely hazardous conditions to secure and tie off the sails. Men were climbing, yelling orders, and ropes were swirling up while other rigging was being pulled taut by two and three men hanging on tightly, for loss of grip meant disaster in the sequence of securing lines and sails. After the initial flurry of hoisting and securing the rigging, Conor looked to the Captain for a signal and permission to go below to be with Kathleen. The Captain realized Conor's intention, nodded from his perch on the bridge, and yelled, "I may need you; come if you are called."

"I will," replied Conor.

Once below, Kathleen wedged herself in a corner on the lower deck to brace herself in the tossing ship. With her legs pressed hard against the hull, she steadied herself, all the while tightening her leg muscles longer than her muscles could endure. Eventually, she needed to stretch a cramp in her leg, but she had a hard time moving. When Conor arrived, she said, "Thank goodness you're here; I'm stuck and can't move."

"Here, give me your hand," he said.

She was barely half-way to her feet when a wave hit the boat, and water poured in from above—salty seawater from a shattered porthole. Kathleen was knocked to the floor of the lower deck and flung to the far side of the boat where she hit a stack of fresh-water kegs. Conor reached for her as she slid by but he could not get a grip on her.

The boat rocked the other way and Kathleen slid back on the wet surface. Conor reached out to grab her but he had to let go of his grip on the support beam and thus the two of them slid back to the ship's port wall. Conor put out his feet to cushion the blow but could not stop the hard knock against the wooden frame of the hull. Kathleen let out a scream.

"Conor, help me," she yelled, even though he was right next to her.

"I'm right here," he said softly.

She was in pain. Blood showed on her dress and across the floor.

Kathleen screamed out again, "I need the privy."

Conor helped her to a bucket behind the curtain. He saw more blood and now Kathleen was near hysterical in her screams, coupled with pain and having lost control. He held her tightly as she raised her trembling body above the bucket, her face covered in sweat. While her muscles tightened and showed the veins in her neck and down her arms, there was a light thud. Kathleen lost the baby. The tiny fetus of a four-ounce baby boy lay lifeless in the pail.

Emotion, pain, and survival competed for Kathleen's attention. Conor held her tight in his arms. He moved her down the cargo space to create a stable wedge for the two of them during the storm's height to minimize the rolling.

After a long silence, Kathleen said, "I pray everyday . . ."

"I do too," Conor interrupted.

" . . . I have prayed all my life, but in these last few months I didn't know what to pray for. I wasn't sure of my thoughts or what this baby meant to me and why things happened the way they did. I didn't know whether it was a blessing or a punishment. I thought it was cruel to crush my dreams of working in the hospital and then I thought, maybe this is my purpose, to have this baby. And what about not knowing his father and still loving the baby anyway. So I wondered if this was going to be my challenge in life.

"I believe we have a purpose in life and sometimes that purpose is not clear. And if we lose our way, these shocking changes put us back on course.

"But I was with child, a child I did not plan for, and all the changes that occurred because of it and my focus in life have changed again. Now the child is gone—what came and what went away?"

"I don't know. I don't know if we will ever know," said Conor.

"Is it you, Conor?" asked Kathleen.

"Me?" he said.

"Was this a long hard journey to find you?"

Conor took a deep breath. "It could be; for both of us. Maybe God planned to have us leave Ireland and find a new and better home?"

"I don't know if I believe that destiny works in such drastic ways," said Kathleen. "Maybe time will tell."

They rode out the storm together in silence and in each other's arms.

The storm settled by early evening but much rolling continued as the sea still churned. Conor and Kathleen, soaked from the rain, the leaked water from above, and the sweat and tears from their ordeal, moved slowly towards the bucket, a tangible symbol of their sadness. With reverence and grace, yet swiftness, Conor took the bucket and looked at Kathleen for a reaction. She shook her head in a sign that she did not want to see into the pail and her tentative, shaky motion indicated this was an end, a conclusion, but not a forgotten period in her life.

"How do we want to do this?" he asked.

"I don't know," she said quietly, looking at the floor.

"When Frank and Emily, my brother and sister-in-law, lost their baby they took it, I mean the baby, out back and buried him under a tree."

"They lost a baby boy?"

"Yes, they did."

"Did they name him?" she asked.

"Edward, after my grandfather."

"Edward," she said, and pondered the words. "Can we name our baby Edward, too?" Kathleen recalled the gentle old man she comforted in the hospital. The name would be a tribute to him.

"I think so. I don't see why not."

"Should we baptize him?" asked Kathleen.

"I think it is too late for that." He paused and added, "I think he has already seen the Gates of Heaven."

"Indeed," she replied. But with all the realization of a majestic union with God in Heaven, as her faith had taught her, a wave of sadness again overcame Kathleen and she wept openly.

Conor moved the bucket around to his right side out of view of Kathleen and placed his left arm over her shoulders. He pulled her in for an embrace while she let the emotion of loss and grief release its grip from her inner soul. He wanted to say something comforting about this child of unknown paternal origin but thought better of it, and decided on the right words in a reassuring tone: "We will have children of our own."

"Yes, we will," she said, and wondered how this man with strong calloused hands, embedded dirt from the fields across his face and neck, could be so sensitive, so outwardly compassionate for her. She thought about this baby as her responsibility, but the fact that Conor was so accepting of dual parental ownership was overwhelming.

An old shirt was lying to the side and Conor picked it up and used it to cover the top of the bucket. He said, "I'll be right back."

"Wait, I want to come with you," said Kathleen, but as she struggled to her feet she realized the extent of the physical injuries she had sustained during her ordeal.

Once topside, Conor and Kathleen went to the bridge where Captain Ryan was taking navigational readings of the now dusky sky. "How are you doing?" he asked.

Conor said, "Kathleen lost the baby."

The captain lowered the sextant and looked at Kathleen. "I am sorry to hear that."

"Thank you, Captain," she said.

Conor said, "Captain, we are trying to decide the best thing to do with the baby." He raised the bucket.

The captain turned to Mr. Bailey. "Find some cloth."

"Aye, sir."

Within a few moments, Mr. Bailey returned with a white cloth that had been stored as wrappings for deaths at sea, but the cloth was too large for such a small being, so he tore a portion off the larger sheet and handed it to the Captain. Captain Ryan nodded for Conor to place the bucket on the deck. When he did so, the Captain made the cloth ready and wrapped the tiny fetus in the cloth. "We will bury him at sea," he said when he was finished, and walked towards the railing. Kathleen gasped for air and the Captain looked back to check whether she was ready for this final act. Kathleen understood and nodded to proceed.

The Captain said aloud for all present to hear, including the sailors close by, "May the Lord accept this young baby."

Kathleen interrupted, "Edward."

The Captain looked back at her.

"Edward, his name is Edward," she said.

The Captain continued, "May the Lord accept Edward into His loving arms," as he gently tossed the baby off the side of the ship into the dark water. The baby had no weight and therefore no sound of a splash was heard.

Silence.

No one moved; no one said anything. The sailors kept their thoughts to themselves about any evil presence or repercussions from the gods.

After about ten seconds, Kathleen sniffled and held back her tears, and Conor placed his arm around her waist to lead her back to the lower deck. That night Kathleen did not sleep well. She tossed and turned, restless with thoughts of the past several months and the loss of Edward. As soon as the sun was up she went topside and found the Captain alone at the bridge.

"Good morning, Kathleen," he said. "Did you sleep well?"

"No, not at all," she replied.

"I am not surprised, given all that you have been through." He hesitated for a moment and wondered to himself whether he should proceed. He decided to continue. "My wife lost a baby, too."

"Oh," said Kathleen, surprised the Captain would reveal such a personal family secret.

"Yes, he was a boy too. We were going to name him Sean, after my father. But my dear wife never recovered from the loss and I wasn't there to comfort her. It's a lonely life being a sailor's wife." He paused for a moment and continued, "I sometimes think it was better that he died in the womb because I'm sure he would have followed me into sailing the ocean. His mother would have grieved his loss to the sea as she does her husband's. Maybe it saved her some of the pain."

Kathleen answered, "I am sure Sean would have brought her great joy and even if he did go off to sea, she would've been comforted by knowing he was with you."

"I don't know, maybe. You think you will have more children?" the Captain asked.

"I hope we do," said Kathleen. "Is she Catholic?"

"What?" he said.

"Your wife, is she Catholic?" Kathleen asked again.

"No, she's Lutheran. She lives in Prussia where I met her in a small port on the Baltic Sea."

"Do you see her often?"

"A couple of times a year, that's all. Why did you ask if she was Catholic?"

"I wondered if she had faith. Faith to guide her through the sadness."

"Yes, her faith is strong and she has family, too."

"Both are important," said Kathleen.

"The best of the morning to you," said Conor, stepping off the ladder from sleeping in the hole. Kathleen approached Conor and kissed him on the cheek.

"Ahh," he said, "'tis a good morning."

Kathleen turned away from Captain Ryan and walked along the gunwale with Conor, thinking of the poor suffering women of the world who had lost their children before birth. She grasped Conor's arm and appreciated his supportive nature.

Baby Edward, however, was not the only death during the voyage. A sailor by the name of Michael Grady, a young but seasoned shipmate, had lost his life working the bobstay, a rope to secure the bowsprit. After climbing out onto the bowsprit and reaching for the loose bobstay to tighten it, a maneuver he should have been better secured to perform, he overextended his reach, lost his grip, and fell into the water.

Rather than having a safety rope around his waist for such surprises, he had thought a quick shimmy out the bowsprit to tighten and re-tie the rope was an easy task. The sea was generally calm, with high swells, but a sudden drop at the edge of a swell brought the ship down with a hard slap, jarring Michael, and making him lose control.

Michael fell and was swept under the ship while it was under full sail; he drowned. An attempt was made to recover the body but a ship under full sail is difficult to turn quickly and Michael was lost at sea. He was twenty-four years old.

Chapter 8

New York

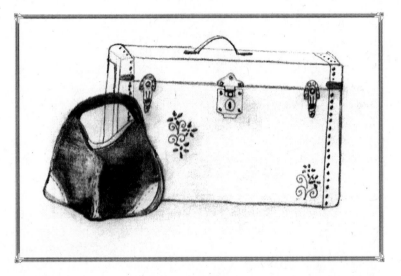

A warming sun on this early April morning combined with a strong wind gave the ship a steady surge across the water. Conor and Kathleen were enjoying their morning tea on the port-side railing, hoping to get another view of a right whale breaching and surfacing for a blow—which they had seen the last few days.

Captain Ryan summoned Conor and Kathleen to his berth. The captain was working with his charts and navigation instruments when they entered his chamber. He looked up and motioned them to sit down at his table.

"According to my calculations, we should be sailing into New York Harbor tomorrow."

"Oh, that is good news," said Conor. He was not sure how to react. This voyage had been an incredible crossing of joyous highs and grueling lows. The arrival in New York was a symbol of an ending of one existence and the beginning of a new and unfamiliar journey. However, Kathleen was looking forward to planting her feet on hard soil again.

"Captain," started Conor, "I want to thank you for making this trip possible for me, Kathleen, and for Seamus, too. I have learned a great deal under your guidance."

"I wish you well with your new life together. Kathleen, your father gave me this, to give to you upon arrival."

The captain handed her an envelope, which she opened. There was a letter and 50 pounds sterling in British currency, a sizable sum for a dowry and a freshly landed immigrant. "That's a lot of money."

"Your father wanted you to have a good start."

She opened the letter and read: 'My dear Kathleen, I am heartbroken that you must leave your mother and me and your two sisters. This is truly a sad day for me." Before reading on, Kathleen stood and turned away from the Captain and Conor, as she took a step. She did not know whether to continue or not as emotion swelled in her heart and tears formed in her eyes. She read on: "Please know that I love you and wish you great health and happiness in America. All my love, your Father."

Kathleen stuck the envelope into the pocket of her woolen sweater and tucked the sweater into her bag as the warm breezes blew off the coast. She looked out at the distant water and drew in a deep breath to clear her feeling of vulnerability, and moved back into the chair. "This is a great comfort to get us started; thank you." Kathleen stood up again and gave Captain Ryan a kiss. "You have been most kind."

Conor reached over and grabbed Kathleen's hand; he could feel her tremble as her muscles twitched under the emotional strain. "What are your plans, Captain?" asked Conor.

"Quite simple. We are going to unload most of the freight in New York. Then we sail to Charleston, South Carolina, for a load of tobacco before heading back to Limerick, Cork, and then London."

"Godspeed, Captain." Conor and Kathleen left the cabin to finish their daily duties and prepare for their arrival in New York.

As the Captain had predicted, the ship sailed into New York the next day. Cheers came from the crew and passers-by as the ship moved around the lower western edge of Manhattan and sailed up close to the docks. Everyone shared the excitement. One by one, the crew lowered the sails and tied them off. When this was completed, Seamus stood with the Meighans and watched the scene.

"Where are you heading?" Conor asked.

"I am going to head up towards Boston. I have cousins living there. They immigrated about ten years ago."

Conor pondered for a moment. "I don't feel bad about Sergeant Clark or that he died. He deserved his fate, and I think everything else worked out for the best."

"Yeah, he got what he deserved." That was the only time that Conor and Seamus discussed the incident in O'Malley's Pub. Seamus added, "You know how I asked you to call me Mike?"

"Yeah."

"I think I am going to take the last name of Grady, too. After you, Kathleen."

"Mike Grady," they both said together.

"I need to be careful. I am sure there are a lot of Loyalist sympathizers here, too." Changing names between the Old World and the New World was not uncommon for immigrants. Some people, like Seamus, wanted to hide, while others wanted to blend in with their new American society and get rid of the link to their ethnic origin. Still other people, through no choice of their own, had undergone a name change while completing immigration papers.

However, Seamus had stolen the sailor Michael Grady's papers after he drowned. Seamus reckoned that after arriving in New York and then traveling to Boston, another port city, no one would discover his deceit and trace him back to Ireland to his true identity. No one realized Seamus had taken the papers; the Captain, in collecting Michael's personal possessions, reasoned that the papers went to the bottom of the sea with him.

Finally Seamus added, "If you are ever in Boston, look me up." Seamus, Conor, and Kathleen bid their farewells but before they were finished, it was Seamus who was most sentimental. "Even though this was a short time together, I learned from the two of you and I saw how you took care of each other. I'm glad that we sailed together."

Conor realized that Seamus had learned a new definition of friendship. His old definition included a basis of fear; the new definition included trust and admiration. "I valued your help in the tough times, too," said Conor.

As the ship drifted slowly forward and approached the dock, three crew members jumped off and quickly tied the lines to the dock. With the tightening of the ropes, the ship came to a stop.

Conor and Kathleen were allowed to disembark after the Harbor Inspectors finished their work. Seamus was required to help unload the cargo before being released.

The New York piers were busy with activity and people hustling from one place to another. Conor and Kathleen walked down the pier with Kathleen's one bag that contained a change of clothing and a violin. Such was their beginning in their new land.

As they walked along, Conor spotted a small elderly lady in front of them struggling with two bags. She dropped a small pouch but did not realize it. Conor picked it up and called to the lady. "You dropped this, madam."

"Oh, thank you, young man. You are very kind to help an old woman."

"No problem, ma'am."

"Where are you heading to?" the lady asked.

"We are not sure. We just arrived."

"Me, too," the lady stated. "I was on the most awful ship, the *Mississippi* that came from Liverpool by way of Cork. Do you know where that is?"

"Yes, ma'am."

She was going to continue regardless of Conor's answer. "Well, the ship was overloaded with too many people and there were not enough places to sleep and the babies crying all the time. I didn't get any rest. Is that your sister traveling with you? Where are your parents?"

"This is my wife." Conor liked the sound of his introduction of Kathleen.

"My, she is so young-looking. Anyway, I have to find my way to the Dunbar Hotel and tomorrow I head up the Hudson River to Albany. I have been writing to these transporters for months and I hope all my plans are set." She stopped talking for a moment, looked at the bewildered couple, and then asked again, "Where are you headed?"

"We are not sure. We just arrived," Conor repeated. The three of them walked down the pier as they chatted.

"Yes, you said that. I meant right now, are you headed anywhere?"

"No place in particular."

"Well, son, you need to be careful in New York, it is full of thieves. I read that they will steal your shirt off your back if you don't pay attention."

"Yes, ma'am." This lady liked to talk and ramble on but Conor and Kathleen were kind people who allowed the elderly lady to talk to her heart's content.

A young sailor not yet twenty years old passed them by in a hurry but turned back. "Goodbye, Mrs. Hurley," he said to the elderly lady. "Cheerio."

Conor stiffened at the British slang.

"Goodbye, Warren," she replied. "You go and visit your grandmother soon."

"Yes, I will," said the sailor as he hurried down the busy dock, dodging in and out between slow-moving passengers trying to get their bearings and steady their feet on solid ground.

The three travelers came down the pier where a carriage man stood waiting next to a single-horse cart with blistered paint and broken leather seats. The carriage man looked old from a distance and his clothes were as tattered as the carriage seats. As they approached, it became apparent that the old man had had a difficult life—his face was aged by years of hard work and hard drinking. The capillaries in his nose, long burst by alcohol abuse, had given him a swelled reddish knob, and the weathered leathery skin surrounding it was covered with a scrubby growth of whiskers.

The hard look cracked with a sudden smile. "Good day, madam," he addressed Kathleen. "Need a carriage?"

"No," Kathleen replied. It was not surprising that the man had mistaken her for a woman of means, what with her clean fresh look, unlike the tattered appearance of other immigrants. Her dress was well-tailored and fitted to her youthful form, and her dark hair had been brushed in long strokes in a smooth straight cut, unlike the high society fashion of curls and ringlets. Adding to her striking appearance, she wore a white bonnet, tied at the side of her chin, which framed her face. Her father, "Paddy O," had instilled a sense of pride in his children. Kathleen had no trouble making a good first impression. People were drawn to her beauty, giving her an advantage that opened doors where others had to resort to their verbal skill or engaging humor.

Kathleen had this advantage but the carriage driver did not. His offers of a ride were often met with skepticism because of his public persona of a wrangler, a shyster, and a drunk. To prove himself otherwise required a reputation of honesty and fairness. Neither Kathleen nor Conor nor Mrs. Hurley had the benefit of knowing this man's true reputation. So they walked on.

The old man stood stoic but his smile sagged into a somber glare as he watched another fare walk away. His disappointment at losing a customer was deep, but he tipped his hat anyway and bid them farewell in the form of a greeting: "Welcome to New York." He turned his attention back to the docks as another weary traveler approached.

The streets of New York were crowded with people from all over the world; some had been settled for generations, while some generations were just starting. With the arrival of another ship, as anywhere, the characters ranged from the kind to the cruel, the charitable to the greedy, translating into the hunters versus the prey, the strong versus the weak. The New World did not mean new humanity. Those fresh off the boat learned quickly that vast new opportunity in the land of freedom did not mean people were different—only their style was different. Kathleen was about to learn this lesson.

Turning off the end of the pier, Mrs. Hurley tripped and fell into the street. Conor and Kathleen dropped their bag and rushed to her aid. They helped her up and brushed her off. "Are you all right?" asked Kathleen, as she noted a scratch on Mrs. Hurley's elbow.

"Yes, dear. I believe I am fine now. That was quite a fright, falling at my age. You will see as you get older and less stable with each step." Then she added, "I am not as young as I used to be."

"Are you sure you are not hurt?" asked Kathleen again.

"I am fine," she repeated. Even though she was aging, Mrs. Hurley was a tough woman and not likely to surrender easily to minor falls and scrapes.

Kathleen turned around and noticed that her bag was gone. Looking down the street, she saw a young boy running off with the bag. "Conor, he stole my bag," she yelled.

Conor dropped the violin and ran after the boy, who had more than a 100-yard lead. The boy went around a corner and disappeared. Conor ran to the corner and looked down the street where numerous people were walking about. No boy was visible.

Conor looked back and saw Kathleen. She was crying hysterically. He thought it better to return to Kathleen than leave her alone with the woman. Conor wondered if this woman was part of a set-up. Yet she seemed too old and frail for such activity.

"I told you they would steal from you," the old lady said when Conor returned. Kathleen was in tears.

"It was just a dress," Conor said.

"Conor, my sweater and the envelope were in the bag," Kathleen was barely audible.

"What? Oh no!" Conor decided to run back to the corner, and he dashed a second time down the street. He turned at the corner and disappeared down the side street.

The old woman said, "This is such a shame; you stopped to help me and look what happened. I feel bad for all this."

Kathleen was also suspicious of this elderly lady's timely arrival as well as the appearance of the young boy whom she never saw trailing them. And now, she was angry. Her new life had just run down the streets of New York, leaving her and her new husband penniless.

Kathleen's nature did not allow her to show the depth of this devastating event, but anger was not buried as deep. She wanted to confront the old woman but thought better of it until she was able to discover more about this woman. All in all, with the confusion of the fall, the stolen bag, and Conor running off, she let out a wail: "Oh no."

A New York policeman walked up. "What's the matter?"

"A young boy grabbed my bag and ran off," Kathleen sobbed.

"Ump, it happens every day," the policeman growled. "What did he look like?"

"I don't know, blue shirt maybe."

"Maybe? Where did you last see him?"

"He ran around that corner"—pointing to where Conor was last seen. "My husband is chasing him."

"Your husband? What does he look like? I'll go and find them."

"There he is, coming back now."

"No bag and no thief," observed the Constable of Police, otherwise known as a "cop."

"I couldn't find him," said Conor as he walked up.

Kathleen looked at the officer and said, "Do you know this lady?"

"No, I don't. Why?"

"Just wondering." The older lady, Mrs. Hurley, was confused by the question as well.

The policeman took some details from Kathleen. The elderly lady reported that she did not see the thief and had nothing to report to help the officer.

"We have these 'snatch and grabs' every day as the ships come in. We have policemen patrolling down here all the time and it still happens, as if they know our patrols." The policeman paused to think. "Where are you staying, in case I get this ruffian?"

"We don't have a place," announced Conor.

"They will be staying with me at the Dunbar Hotel," interjected Mrs. Hurley. Conor and Kathleen looked at each other, puzzled by her statement.

"If I have anything, I'll stop by," the policeman declared.

"Thank you," said Kathleen.

The old lady took over. "Officer, if you could point us in the right direction to the hotel I would appreciate it. As you know, I am new to this town and certainly do not know it as well as you."

"Five blocks straight ahead, turn left for another two blocks. It's at the corner of Trinity Place and Liberty Street; you can't miss it."

"Thank you, you have been very kind to investigate this terrible crime."

"No problem, madam."

The policeman was not done with his work. "You're from Ireland?" he said, looking at Conor.

"Aye," said Conor.

"Catholic, I suppose," he said in a demeaning voice.

"Aye," said Conor again in a defensive tone.

"Are you a Hibernian?"

"Who?"

"You know, the Ancient Order of Hibernians, The Defenders, the Whiteboys . . ."

"Never heard of them," said Conor, peering into the eyes of the policeman to discover the purpose of his questions, even though he knew secret Irish societies existed.

"Yeah, I'm sure you never heard of them," the policemen said with a mixture of sarcasm and contempt, yet not too confrontational.

"We don't want any trouble and you'll have hell to pay if there is."
Then he added, "If you don't know these troublemakers, my
advice is to stay away from them."

Conor was not aware of the hostilities that had been brewing
in New York and Pennsylvania between the Irish and a solid base
of British loyalists who still had old English opinions even though
America had gained its independence. Religion remained the root
of the issue between the Irish Catholics and the Protestant Anglicans and neither side was willing to forgo their beliefs for the sake
of harmony. Catholic churches were burned and, in retaliation,
Protestants were attacked. The animosity spread over all phases
of life, including shop owners who hung signs: "Help wanted, no
Irish need apply."

Soon a secret society was formed within the Irish community, the Ancient Order of Hibernians, who saw as their role to
protect the churches and subsequently their faith in the New York
community.

In Pennsylvania, the Irish were hired to work the coal mines.
The conditions were primitive and dangerous, with routine loss of
life due to the lack of safety standards. The mine owners and the
railroad men, who were enjoying new-found wealth with the
expansion of the rail lines throughout the country, ignored these
conditions. But because of the conditions, regular American citizens wanted no part of this work, with its low pay. The Irish took
the jobs because they were all that was available. The mining company provided the housing as well as the grocery and general
goods stores, and before long these laborers were deeply indebted
to the company and locked into an unbearable and unbreakable
relationship with the company.

As a result, a splinter group of the Ancient Order of Hibernians,
known as the Molly Maguires, responded to the conditions and
the injustices of the coal mines with violence in form of murder,
arson, and general terrorist attacks. As history would show, two
things resolved this turmoil: labor unions and the Civil War. Once

the miners had a voice through the unions, conditions changed. Likewise, the Civil War recruited many resident Irish and those fresh immigrants from off the ships. Their courage and bravery in both Union and Confederate armies gained respect and ultimately acceptance, but when Conor and Kathleen first arrived that was still to come. In 1837, Kathleen and Conor arrived into a hotbed of turmoil, hatred, and distrust that they would see first-hand.

Now they looked at each other with dismay and a deep sense of loss. Within a few minutes of arriving, a fleeing thief had crushed their hopes and dreams. There was nothing more to take from them except a violin, and they had no place to go. Without saying a word aloud, by a shared nod, they agreed to go with the woman to the hotel.

Kathleen said, "We are Conor and Kathleen Meighan, and your name is Mrs. Hurley?"

"Yes, I am Ellen Hurley from Crookhaven, Ireland. Do you know where that is?"

"No, ma'am."

"Crookhaven is nearly the southernmost point of Ireland in County Cork. An odd name given what happened today." The woman talked all the way down the street. "Crookhaven is said to have been a safe hide-out for pirates along the coast to remain undetected, thus its name. Others say the town's name came from the design of the cape where the land hooks out, creating a pro-tective bay. Either way it is a beautiful part of the world."

She talked of her voyage and the young man who helped her. "Warren was a good cabin boy and took care of everything I needed. However, he needs to visit his grandmother in the west of England and I told him to go sooner rather than later, as time moves so quickly. She is in a small town—I can't remember the name of the village at this moment, but she is very ill and could die soon. He will regret it, you know. He is a fine boy and I am sure he will follow my advice to make the visit."

She went into her plans of heading upstate and traveling to Upper Canada to meet up with family, but Conor was lost in his thoughts, trying to decide what to do next, how he and Kathleen were going to survive. Amid the chatter of their new acquaintance, they rounded the fifth corner onto Trinity Place and walked the remaining two blocks to Liberty Street where there was a small park on the corner.

"Oh, such a lovely place," said Mrs. Hurley, looking at a gathering of rose bushes in a cross pattern. "That looks like Christ's cross, and so pretty. The colors are so diverse and passive amid all the bustle of activity. I will always remember this blessed spot amidst the busy New York streets."

Within a couple of steps they arrived at the Dunbar Hotel. Inside the lobby, the hotel was clean, with simple décor and an air of comfort for those of modest means. Mrs. Hurley registered at the front desk and made arrangements for Conor and Kathleen to have a room.

"Young man," she addressed the clerk, "please give me two rooms instead of one. I have companions traveling with me."

"I see," said the young man.

Neither Conor nor Kathleen announced to Mrs. Hurley that this was their honeymoon stay, although the two newlyweds privately shared a moment of excited anticipation. A comfortable bed on stable ground in a private setting would provide the newlyweds with an opportunity to enjoy the intimate exploration of their union. Kathleen felt an unfamiliar fear as she thought about the coming night. Between the rape and the recent trauma of the miscarriage, she was scared of accepting her husband with the scars of her physical and emotional ordeals.

But she also cherished the thought of their amorous bond being forged in a warm, tender, personal convergence away from the rocking of the ship, the closeness of the sailors, and any watchful eyes of a cruel and often judgmental world. They could be together, alone, finally, where they would define the nature and expression of their love. So, in spite of the fear, she was ready for intimacy.

Conor, too, understood Kathleen's uneasiness even though they had not talked of whether they were ready for the closeness of marriage or not. He sensed his own apprehension about the approaching privacy. In his mind, he questioned how he should approach his wife and whether she expected celibacy or a conjugal celebration once alone. He fought over whether to ask the words or simply proceed with the assumption of masculine privilege until she expressed an objection. "No," he thought, "I can't be that callous or even insensitive. Such is not right."

He thought more of the dilemma and decided to offer to sleep on the floor next to the bed and Kathleen could invite him into her bed if she so desired. At that point, the setting could allow the question and the conversation. Kathleen was a beautiful woman, smart and engaging; he longed for the intimacy.

Mrs. Hurley signed the registration book for two rooms. The clerk looked at the book and then at Conor and Kathleen and then he asked, "Is this man your servant? We have special quarters for servants." He hesitated and then added, "We don't allow Irish servants."

The clerk had singled out Conor but then noticed the fashionable traditional dress of Mrs. Hurley and the striking but modestly dressed Kathleen, both of whom had heavy Irish accents. They were not the concern of the clerk. Conor, on the other hand, wore dirty, sweat-soiled, and tattered clothes. His appearance as a manual laborer was considerably more noticeable and offensive to the clerk, and he took exception.

"They are my companions, young man, and I am paying full price for their rooms. So you need not worry about these people."

The emboldened clerk spoke back: "We don't allow Irish Papists here."

The reference was to Irish Catholics and the fact that such Catholics showed allegiance to the Pope, so they never denounced the Holy See in Rome in favor of the ruling monarch of England. A deep-seated controversy between the Irish Catholics and the Anglicans went back to Henry VIII some 300 years earlier, strengthened by Elizabeth I and ultimately overwhelmed through the brutal force of Oliver Cromwell when the Irish people were subjugated to religious domination.

This religious storm manifested itself in deep hatred over the centuries, which included the English Penal Laws banning open expression of the Catholic faith in the British Empire. The Penal Laws did not stop by outlawing non-Anglican religions, but prevented Catholics from owning land and voting—a complete social, spiritual, and economic suffocation.

Now, within a few hours of their arrival in New York, where religious freedom was the promise of America for new immigrants, they met the cruelty and hatred of the old country. It seemed to Conor that people always wanted to create a social hierarchy—to keep some people down and catapult others to lofty heights. In a country designed to even every man's chance, human nature and old prejudices now superseded the intellectual concept that all men were created equal. Another lesson learned in the New World. But Mrs. Hurley was not to be dismissed.

"Young man," she said with ferocity, "these people are traveling with me. You are not going to tell me *who* I can have as companions and who not." Mrs. Hurley was on fire in a controlled yet an effective display of deliberate anger, aggressive demands, and experienced articulation. "You have a lot of growing up to do, if you think you can push this old woman around. Now, get to your duties and get these people a hot bath drawn before dinner." She reached to her bag, feeling for an object.

"Oh no," thought Conor, "she's going to strike the clerk with an object from her purse—not another assault between the English and Irish."

Instead, Mrs. Hurley reached into her purse and pushed a coin across the large mahogany desk. The sheepish clerk, who did not have the courage to challenge this surprised rebuke, took the coin, pocketed it, and turned his back.

Mrs. Hurley drew a deep breath and waited with fury in her eyes. Seeing that the clerk had declared the argument over by withdrawal, she turned to the stunned couple and stated, "You will be joining me for dinner tonight. Go have your bath and meet here in the lobby at 6:00 p.m. I have an important matter to discuss with you." With that statement, she turned and said to the porter, "Please take me to my room."

Conor looked at Kathleen. "What is that about?"

"I don't know."

"Dinner at six and we will find out."

In the meantime, a chambermaid drew a hot bath at the end of the hall, first used by Kathleen, followed by Conor. Thirty-six days of salt air, stress, and fatigue were washed away.

At 6:00 p.m. Conor and Kathleen waited in the lobby for Mrs. Hurley. When the clerk saw them coming, he turned and busied himself with things at the opposite end of the counter. The elderly woman came down the stairs dressed for an evening with the Queen, in a fine yellow linen frock and a matching silk scarf.

"The porter stated there is a fine restaurant across the street. If that's all right with you?"

Conor replied, "Anything is fine with us. Let me give you a hand." He held his arm out for her to grasp.

"You are a true gentleman."

At the restaurant, Mrs. Hurley insisted on a dinner of fine beef and fresh vegetables. The three enjoyed the hearty meal and talked of Ireland.

"I think I will miss the constant breeze of the southern coast," she said.

"I will miss my family," said Kathleen immediately.

"Aye, me too," said Conor.

At last Mrs. Hurley brought up the main subject. "I feel bad that you lost your belongings today. I even feel responsible, for if you had not tended to my fall, your bag would not have been stolen. I can tell something very valuable was taken from you in that bag. I can't bring it back and for that I am truly sorry. I also sense that you have no direction to take here in America. Is that true?"

"True," said Conor.

"I would like to propose a deal. I am traveling to Peterborough, in Upper Canada, to live my final days with my daughter. As you can see, I have a hard time getting around and need help. To tell you the truth, I am afraid. Afraid that what happened to you will happen to me. That someone will knock me down and take all that I own. I would be lost. If you accompany me to Peterborough, I will pay your way."

"That leaves us in . . . Upper Canada, right?"

"I will get you back to America. But I must warn you that I am set in my ways and I do not want you to return to New York City. This city is not for you; it is for hustlers and thieves. Do we have an agreement?"

"I don't know. This is a big decision," said Conor.

"Let me get this right," Kathleen began. "You want us as traveling companions and you will pay all the fares and expenses? You don't know us."

"But I do, I know that you made sure I had my pouch that I unknowingly dropped. You helped me when I fell. You bravely chased a criminal through the streets of New York, but most of all, you put up with my chatter without complaining. You are kind souls. I am afraid, and yet, I trust both of you. I have the means to pay for this trip, if you accept."

"When do you need to know?" asked Kathleen.

"Tomorrow morning at ten o'clock, I leave on a coach for Albany. Be in the lobby at ten, if you accept."

"Understood," said Conor.

Later, Conor and Kathleen returned to their room. There was not much to talk about or decide. Kathleen summed it up. "Either way, after ten o'clock tomorrow morning, we have to check out of the hotel. We have no place to go and no money available. The offer from Mrs. Hurley is our only prospect, our only hope."

Conor countered, "What about entering this untamed and undeveloped interior of New York State and the cold reaches of Upper Canada? And what about Mrs. Hurley?" His suspicion of her being part of the theft had waned somewhat but it still lingered. He asked, "What more could she take from us?"

"She is afraid of being old and traveling alone," Kathleen said. "At least the three of us would be together to protect each other." The two agreed; they would join Mrs. Hurley on her trip north to Albany and into the interior of the New World.

As decided, Conor offered to sleep on the floor. "I will be comfortable," he said, reassuring her of his willingness to place her at ease.

"Oh no," said Kathleen, "you belong right up here next to me." He smiled as she pulled the blankets back to further the invitation. Once they were comfortably next to each other, Conor reached around and placed his arm behind her head, grasped her shoulder and pulled her close. She reached across his chest and snuggled in closer. The night belonged to them.

At sun-up, Conor's eyes sprang open. The sun serves as an alarm clock for a farmer. However, this day the bed was comfortable and he lay there watching Kathleen sleep. He felt lucky and overjoyed with his new wife. Finding her had been the best of his Irish luck. Slowly he drifted back into a deep sleep. He was awoken again with a start; this time, it was a knock at the door.

He jumped out of bed and yelled, "Who's there?"

"Your breakfast," was the reply.

He opened the door and a young porter entered with a rolling cart containing coffee, tea, and fruit. "Compliments of Mrs. Hurley. Anything else I can get you?"

"What time is it?"

"Eight-thirty, sir."

"Oh my, eight-thirty," he repeated. "Thank you, we're fine."

"Oh, one more thing," the porter stated. "Mrs. Hurley sent for these things." He reached for a bag waiting in the hallway. The porter set the bag next to the breakfast cart and left.

Kathleen rolled over and said, "It's morning already?"

"Yes, time to get up and get ready."

"I could sleep here three more days," said Kathleen.

Conor opened the bag and found traveling clothes for Kathleen and himself. Ellen Hurley assumed they would agree to her offer. They prepared for their journey up the Hudson River and met Mrs. Hurley at 10 a.m. in the lobby.

Chapter 9

Hudson Valley

A Concord stagecoach pulled up in front of the Dunbar Hotel promptly at 10 a.m. The Concord was the finest, most durable coach of its day, built in Concord, New Hampshire. The coach was made from the finest woods—oak, ash, and mahogany—and leather, and it was finished with hand-rubbed green paint with yellow, gold-like trim. A team of four horses

pulled the coach, and its driver, Robert, was a tall, tanned, muscular, and pleasant man in his early thirties. He jumped down from
the driver's seat and took Mrs. Hurley's luggage; however, she
kept a small handbag with her. The driver reached for Kathleen's
violin, which was carried in a hard leather case. Kathleen held it
fast. "It's a violin and it's fragile."

"Yes, madam, I'll put it to the side of the luggage and in a
position where it won't bounce around."

"Thank you," she said.

Conor held the door open and with his other hand helped
Kathleen step into the coach. She was surprised to learn two other
passengers were already on board. Mrs. Hurley followed and
uttered the surprised exclamation, "Oh, we have others accompanying us. Well, how do you do?"

The two men nodded their head in reply, indicating a more
cautious approach to a conversational exchange. They were both
dressed in fashionable business suits that radiated their well-to-
do status.

Once they were settled, the stagecoach traveled north along
the east bank of the Hudson River and out of New York City to
make the four-day trip north to Albany. The two unannounced
passengers squeezed together on one side and Mrs. Hurley's trio
on the other, which made the seating tight. This style of horse-
drawn coach allowed for three people on each side of the cabin
with the passengers facing each other, but three people meant one
adult and two smaller people, like children. Mrs. Hurley, as was
her style, struck up an acquaintance with the other passengers and
introduced Conor and Kathleen as her travel companions. She
made sure they knew the three of them were together.

The other two returned the cordial greeting. "Hello, I am Mr.
Caldwell and this is my associate, Mr. Roberts." Mr. Caldwell was
clearly in charge.

As the five became more comfortable in each other's
company, they shared their stories. Mrs. Hurley started the questioning. "And what do you do, Mr. Caldwell?"

"I work for the federal government and the Secretary of State, Mr. John Forsyth. And Mr. Roberts here," pointing to the other man, "is my assistant."

"Oh, you are a very important man," said Mrs. Hurley. "What do you do?"

"Whatever the Secretary asks," he said, being coy. "And what about you, ma'am?" he added, directing the conversation back to Mrs. Hurley.

"I am just an immigrant from Ireland heading to Upper Canada."

Mr. Caldwell knew very well she was being coy too, as she was well dressed for an Irish immigrant and he knew people of wealth and stature in Ireland were more likely to say they were British than Irish. "Upper Canada, you say; why are you going to Upper Canada through New York? Wouldn't it have been easier to travel through Quebec?"

"I have my reasons," she said curtly.

"So you are going to Albany?" he asked.

"Yes, as a matter of fact, I am. I mean, we are," said Mrs. Hurley.

"I am curious—why didn't you take the steamboat to Albany?"

Steamboat service had become the main method of transportation between the two cities since Robert Fulton had made his famous journey aboard the *Clermont* from New York to Albany in August 1807. That first trip was made in thirty-two hours at a rate of five miles per hour and through these intervening years, with improvements to design and function, service had also improved. Hence Mr. Caldwell's question as to why they were taking a four-to-five-day coach journey rather than a little more than a day's voyage.

"I don't trust them," was Mrs. Hurley's only explanation.

Mr. Caldwell narrowed his look at Mrs. Hurley and said, "Well, you know that you will have trouble crossing the border into Canada, don't you?"

"Why?" she asked.

"The United States and British North America are having some disputes that you are apparently unaware of. The Secretary is trying to come to a compromise with them now."

Conor was listening intently. He had agreed to take Mrs. Hurley into Upper Canada, but the news that the British-controlled colony was on unfriendly terms was disconcerting: he feared being detained or sent back to Ireland.

"Well, Mr. Caldwell," Mrs. Hurley stated, "I am a British subject, am I not, coming from Ireland?"

"I don't know; what do your immigration papers say?"

"They say I am from Ireland and that I am going to British North America."

"I see," said Mr. Caldwell, knowing there was more to her story about the route she was taking.

"And you, sir," Mr. Caldwell said, directing his question to Conor, "are you going to British North America too?"

"Yes, I am accompanying Mrs. Hurley to Canada."

At this point, the tone was bordering on an inquisition, as Mr. Caldwell leaned back in his seat, thinking and rubbing his chin. "Where are you crossing into Canada?" he asked Mrs. Hurley.

"For your information, Mr. Caldwell," Mrs. Hurley was taking back some control of this conversation, "I am taking the new Erie Canal to Tonawanda, near Buffalo."

"Yes, I know where Tonawanda is."

"And then viewing the Falls at Niagara before crossing at Lewiston into Canada."

"I see," he said again. "Niagara Falls, quite a sight."

"Yes," she said. "I suppose I may never have the opportunity to see them again. So I am stopping there on my way into Upper Canada."

Mr. Caldwell did not believe her route was determined by a stop at the Falls at Niagara. She could still come in through the St. Lawrence River and cross Lake Ontario to Niagara Falls.

Conor, unaware of the geography of the New York interior, listened intently to the discussion about the crossing point, Lewiston, where he might have trouble with British soldiers. He thought for a quick moment to ask this government agent for sanctuary, but thought better of it given his interrogation about their travels. Then he realized that if the British authorities wanted him, it would be for murder, and no sanctuary would be granted for murder.

Mrs. Hurley decided it was time for a change in the topic. "Where are you going, Mr. Caldwell?"

The government man hesitated and then said straightforwardly, "I am going to the Military Academy."

"Oh. Where's that?"

"Just up the river."

"Why are you going there?"

Mrs. Hurley had reached her limit, and he replied, "As I said, because the Secretary has asked me to."

"Mr. Caldwell," Conor spoke up, "what is the trouble you mentioned at the border?"

Mr. Caldwell looked at Conor and smiled as if he had just figured out what this group of three people was up to. "The Irish in Canada want to overthrow the British and force them to leave Canada, just like what happened here in the United States."

"Really," interjected Mrs. Hurley. "The Irish?"

"You seem surprised. Isn't that why you are here?"

"No," said Mrs. Hurley. "I am moving here to find my daughter."

"I think that question was for me," spoke up Conor. "I know nothing of the border troubles with Canada nor the politics within the two countries. I am here to find a new life with my wife, a quiet life without fighting the British. We are not settling in Canada, we are only accompanying this fine lady in her travels. We plan on returning to the United States after Mrs. Hurley reaches Peterborough."

"Yes, I see," said Mr. Caldwell. "The current trouble with

Canada is in Maine over some boundary disputes. Yet you are not going to Maine?"

Conor did not know where Maine was and he did not want to look at Mrs. Hurley for an answer, as that would look like a contrived reaction.

Mrs. Hurley spoke up. "No, we are not going anywhere near Maine."

"Good."

Mrs. Hurley spoke softly, not addressing anyone as she looked out the window. "Border trouble with Canada and going to the Military Academy, I see." She too thought she had figured out these two men from the government. Mr. Caldwell looked at her and smiled, with a slight shake of the head as if she had guessed it wrong. Conor relaxed back into the coach as the conversation lagged.

Kathleen became lost in her thoughts, too. She was thinking about her little baby boy and the strong name he would have been called, Edward. She wondered whether he would have had the same dark features as she did or whether he would have played the violin with the same grace and dignity that she had learned. Kathleen became saddened by her thoughts and she tried to think of other things, but the feelings did not leave her.

Even so, none of her thoughts about the baby included any possibility of physical traits, personality, or looks of the father. Such thoughts were too painful to consider. Even if the baby had survived, she decided that none of any future discussions would have involved the father, whether for credit or blame. Kathleen stared out the window of the carriage. Whoever the father was, he was a non-entity in Kathleen's mind. The passing scenery along the Hudson River Valley in the early spring was breathtaking. In this moment, Kathleen could not appreciate the setting.

She looked over to Conor, who had his head back and eyes shut. Kathleen loved the respect and comfort he provided her. She thought that if she had met Conor in Ennis, she probably would not have given him much consideration because he was a poor farmer. She realized that was a selfish judgment but now, given the dire circumstances of their meeting, she saw a profound quality within Conor's character which would have been unimaginable without the experience of the tumultuous ship-ride across the ocean. She loved him completely. Conor opened an eye and looked at Kathleen as if in harmony with her thoughts. They smiled at each other.

Mrs. Hurley was not silenced for long. "Mr. Caldwell, you are in international diplomacy; do you think England will ever leave Ireland?"

"That's a very big question, Mrs. Hurley. Why would they want to?"

"They don't like the Irish, most of the people are starving, and they get very little from them except trouble, so why bother?"

"Well, I suppose." He thought for a moment. "They rule many corners of the world. It's just another possession."

"That's about as true an answer as any." Mrs. Hurley turned back to looking out the window at the wide scenic river.

The first night's stop was in Clarkstown, formerly known by its Native American name—Nannawitt, or Nannawitt's Meadows—after a Kakiat Indian. Eventually the town derived its name from an early French settler, Daniel DeClerque, and finally anglicized the name to Clarkstown.

Just twenty-one years before the arrival of the carriage, the townspeople had conspired in a makeshift trial of one of their fellow citizens. Not an official trial in a court of law, but a gathering of town residents where the town physician was named as judge and a selection of farmers served as jurors, in a witch trial.

Jane Kanniff, the widow of a Scottish physician, and known as an eccentric, anti-social, practicing herbalist, was tried as a witch after various town wives suffered a series of failed churnings for butter and a cow found in a wagon one night would no longer produce milk. These events needed an explanation, and the focus turned to the odd widow. Jane further incriminated herself with her wildly colored clothing, unusually styled hair, having a black cat, and possessing a talking parrot.

The trial was bizarre enough, but the evidence was just as strange: the judgment was based on whether she weighed more than a Bible. If she was lighter than the Bible, she was believed to be satanic and therefore guilty. If she was heavier then the Bible, she was to be found innocent. The trial was held at a local mill and a brass-encased Bible was hoisted onto a balance beam. Jane Kanniff sat on the other side. As it turned out, she was heavier, thus innocent of witchcraft. Now, twenty-one years later, an eccentric Mrs. Hurley and an Irish peasant on the run from the British authorities unwittingly entered the town to spend the night.

Robert brought the carriage to the town's only hotel, where the passengers exited the coach, stretched, and checked into the hotel. Mrs. Hurley expected a constant escort except when she retired to her room at night, and Conor and Kathleen were glad to oblige her request because of her generosity to them, given their situation.

Today, Kathleen was less suspicious of Mrs. Hurley than yesterday. She could not find a connection between her being generous and also being a thief, so she considered that maybe her first impression was wrong. Conor was a little less certain.

The three went to dinner together in the hotel. Mrs. Hurley started the conversation with the history of her family. She leaned in and started in a hushed tone: "I want you to know, my great-grandfather was an outlaw, a pirate."

"I knew it," said Kathleen to herself.

She continued, "He operated off the southern coast of Ireland, where he used Crookhaven as a base for his scandalous operations. That is where the town got its name, from the likes of him, and he was very good at what he did. He brought his loot back from the seas around the Mizen peninsula and hid it. Nobody knew where the valuables were hidden except the family.

"As the way of all outlaws goes, he was killed during one of his raids. My family has kept the secret of the loot for years. The soldiers, revenue agents, other pirates have all tried to find my family's loot, but they have never found it. I am not proud of these hooligans but they were my family."

She paused and then began again. "I married an outstanding gentleman, who worked in the harbor as a shipping agent. We have a daughter who immigrated to Canada seven years ago. Since then, my husband has died and I have no one left but my daughter. I tried to convince her to move back to Crookhaven but she would have nothing to do with it. She wants to leave all the history of Ireland behind."

"What happened to the loot?" Conor asked.

"You are traveling with it."

"You are joking with me."

"Mr. Meighan." She paused as if he asked a foolish question. "I was not going to leave it in Ireland and move to Canada."

"And you risked carrying this money by yourself?"

"You see, my daughter wants nothing to do with this illegal money which was gained by fear, terror, and killing. Wherever I go, it goes with me."

Conor was finding this to be an outlandish story. He leaned back in his chair with a slight smirk on his face. "I don't believe it."

"You don't have to believe it; I am just asking you to protect me until we get to Peterborough."

Conor thought that Ellen Hurley was getting old and senile. She must be looking for attention. She is looking for me to risk my life for her protection and find out at the end that she is flat broke.

"Have I not taken care of you handsomely and without flashing money about?"

"You have our loyalty," interjected Kathleen.

Mrs. Hurley continued, "I know we all have secrets. Even you have secrets that you do not want to share. Do you think that I will not believe your story?"

Conor realized that this was her reason for telling the pirate story, so he would divulge his stories. "There is no story, Mrs. Hurley. I am the second son of a tenant farmer. I had no future in Ireland. I had no loot stashed in the hills of County Clare."

"Are you making fun of me?" asked Mrs. Hurley with a bit of anger in her voice.

"No, I am a simple man, who works hard. I treat people fairly and I expect to be treated fairly in return. I will give a hard day's work for a fair price. Those are the values I grew up with. My family did not steal or hide in the hills. That is a life that I do not know."

Mrs. Hurley continued, "I wish my family was as fortunate as yours. I remember as a child, my father would wake us up in the middle of the night when he heard people approaching the house. We would run out the back door and hide. People were always after us. They would ransack the house looking for money and not find any. Once the soldiers burnt the house down. I will be glad the savagery ends with me."

"Mrs. Hurley, how much money am I protecting?"

"It doesn't matter whether it is a shilling or a hundred pounds. Please take care of me."

"We will," said Kathleen.

"I need a good night's sleep," Mrs. Hurley announced, and rose from the table.

"I will walk you upstairs," said Conor.

Mrs. Hurley's room was on the second floor and Conor and Kathleen were helping her on the steps. "Mr. Meighan, you are a good and moral person. I trust you."

"You can, Mrs. Hurley."

Kathleen and Conor returned to their room across the hall from Mrs. Hurley. Kathleen asked, "You don't believe her, do you?"

"I don't know, that's a wild tale, but she has lots of money to spend and she is plenty afraid."

"I think we should take care of her regardless of whether she has the money or not, because she is truly afraid."

"I agree," said Conor. "Even though she may be a little crazy."

The citizens of Clarkstown paid little attention to the three strangers having dinner together discussing piracy and personal history. Otherwise, these God-fearing residents might have run them out of town before their night's rest. But as it turned out, all was well.

The second day started without fanfare as the three visitors to the Nyack region boarded the stage and headed north to the village of Buttermilk Falls. The village was situated next to a series of army posts and the U.S. Military Academy. The river made a sharp bend, an "S" curve that was difficult for ships to negotiate.

The military posts that line the river and sit above the bend have a strategic advantage over any ship going up or down the Hudson River. The high bluff that juts out and causes the bend is known as West Point. A thick chain runs from the west side of the river and is buried deep in the water and anchored on the far eastern shore. The cable is pulled to the surface and stops the boat when any unauthorized ship tries to pass. The boat is then a sitting target for the guarding forts on the bluff above the river. The main fort on the southwest side of the Academy is Fort Putnam. Mrs. Hurley and the Meighans had lunch at Fort Putnam. The two government passengers got off at West Point.

As Mr. Caldwell was leaving, he turned to Mrs. Hurley and said, "I am here about troubles in the Republic of Texas and Mexico, not Canada. Just be careful near the border and don't get involved with any Irish rebels."

"Thank you, Mr. Caldwell. I can handle Irish rebels," said Mrs. Hurley. "Also, I read in the Irish newspaper about the Erie Canal and the wonderful accomplishment of digging this waterway some 363 miles long through the wilderness. When the canal opened, the newspaper quoted a man by the name of Jesse Hawley as saying, 'America can never forget to acknowledge that they have built the longest canal in the world, in the least time, with the least experience, for the least money and the greatest public benefit.' When I read that account I knew I must take the trip up the Erie Canal, which is a little out of my way but worth the experience."

"And many Irish helped dig and build the locks and bridges and clear the land," said Mr. Caldwell.

"I hope they were paid well for their hard work," said Mrs. Hurley. Conor noted that Mrs. Hurley had a natural tendency to protect the downtrodden people of her world.

"Yes, I am sure they were," said Mr. Caldwell.

Mrs. Hurley felt the Irish were not paid well for digging and clearing the canal, and she was right in her assumption. The newly arrived immigrants were paid half the going rate of laborers, much to the dismay of already settled Americans. The Irish were happy to have a job and an income and the employers were happy at the bargain wages.

The two government agents exited the carriage.

The coach now contained only Mrs. Hurley, Kathleen, and Conor, although it was still cramped, with little room to move about or stretch out. Mrs. Hurley moved to the opposite side to face Conor and Kathleen to talk directly.

"They were interesting men," she said.

"They were certainly interested in our plans," said Kathleen.

"I didn't think you were listening," said Conor.

"I heard everything."

The coach continued northward to Cornwall-on-Hudson to ferry across the river on a large flat raft with a pull rope to prevent the barge from drifting downstream.

The next stop was Poughkeepsie, twenty-six miles upriver from the crossing. This thriving village on the east side of the Hudson River was largely a Dutch settlement started 130 years earlier and was a bustling hive of activity. A significant event took place here forty-nine years before Mrs. Hurley's arrival, when in 1788 New York representatives ratified the new constitution, thus making it the eleventh state to enter the new union known as the United States of America.

Many people were on the streets and moving about in this market town, which contained many noted breweries, millineries, and an active lumbering trade from nearby and upstream forest regions. The activity in the streets was loud with discussions of politics and business and the commotion made Mrs. Hurley nervous. At night, music could be heard through the windows of the hotel, and at first this was a welcome sound. However, later, as the night wore on, drunken men walked the streets and sang loudly, with aggressive pushing and shoving to go with the songs. At any moment, trouble in the form of fighting was feared. The men also shouted profanities to each other at a not-so-far-off card game. After dark, this district became a party town. Since their talk with Mrs. Hurley regarding the money, Conor kept a keen ear for trouble at her door. He did not sleep well this night.

When the stagecoach pulled out of Poughkeepsie the next morning, the three travelers were glad to leave this village behind. No one had rested comfortably. By mid-morning, all three had their heads back against the seat and were drifting off to sleep, but the constant jarring from the dirt road made it difficult to find true rest. Mrs. Hurley had her handbag clutched against her chest. The coach traversed a flat stretch of road and Ellen quickly lost consciousness. The bag fell from her grip onto the floor. The noise awoke Conor. He grabbed the purse and laid it back on her lap. Mrs. Hurley opened her eyes and glared at Conor when she saw his hands on her bag.

"You dropped it."

"Did I?" she said cautiously.

"Yes, you fell asleep." She closed her eyes again but he knew she was not sleeping. She might have developed a suspicion of Conor.

By one o'clock in the afternoon, and after another river crossing, the stagecoach arrived at Kingston. The last seven miles had been difficult as heavy rain soaked the roadway, making the path muddy and rut-lined. Robert decided to wait in Kingston until conditions improved. Mrs. Hurley could have taken a steamboat up the river, which would have been a more comfortable ride, but she distrusted these boats and the fact that they used fire as a propulsion method was unfathomable to her. The wait lasted until the next morning, when they left for the final fifty-five miles to Albany.

Chapter 10

The Erie Canal
Albany to Herkimer

Albany was retreating from heavy media attention because Martin Van Buren had been elected and sworn in as the eighth President of the United States just thirty-three days earlier. Van Buren came from a small town, Kinderhook, just south of Albany, and the country was in an economic depression, which was about to get worse. Van Buren would take the blame.

In addition, Albany was a city in transition, in its development as well as in the people traversing its boundaries. The city was full of contrasts: rich and poor; established residents and transient adventurers; tradesmen and the untrained; the law-abiding and outlaws. The trio of Ellen Hurley, Conor, and Kathleen Meighan brought their own contrasts of planned futures and unknown destinies, comfortable means and the penniless, moral strength versus ethical short-sightedness, and these differences were about to become obvious.

The Concord coach pulled up to the Albany Hotel to discharge the three weary passengers from New York City. The carriage was covered in the mud picked up along the road and the Albany streets were filled with fresh muck from the rain, dirt, horse manure, and debris thrown into the street. Robert, the driver, made sure Mrs. Hurley and Kathleen got to the front door of the hotel with as little mud as possible on their shoes.

"You are such a gentleman," Mrs. Hurley told Robert as she handed him a small envelope.

"Thank you," said Robert, who was pleased to take the token of her appreciation.

"Now you be careful on your trip back to New York."

"Yes, madam. And you have a good trip on the canal."

"He is such a polite man," Mrs. Hurley said to Kathleen as they entered the lobby.

The three checked into the hotel as they had done in the previous stops. The arrangements had already been discussed. It was Friday and Mrs. Hurley wanted to confirm their reservations on the packet boat, which was scheduled to leave Monday morning to head up the Erie Canal. Conor accompanied Mrs. Hurley to the Navigation Office for the verification of her ticket and to add Conor and Kathleen to the boarding list.

A man at the counter in the office greeted the pair. "Good afternoon, can I help you?" He had a business demeanor, with a white shirt, bowtie, and brown vest to match his brown trousers. The suit coat was resting on the back of his desk chair.

"My name is Ellen Hurley and I have a reservation for Monday morning on a packet boat."

"Yes, Mrs. Hurley. You are all set," the man replied without looking at any papers or forms. "I checked the reservation this morning and we are ready for your departure."

"Thank you," said Mrs. Hurley, "but I have two additional passengers who are traveling with me."

"I believe the boat is full. Let me check."

As the man was checking his folder, Mrs. Hurley said, "Young man, these people must travel with me."

"Yes, madam. The boat is full. We do not have room for any more passengers."

"Are you sure, young man?"

The clerk was insistent. "Yes, it is full. I can put you on a boat Wednesday at the earliest."

"Maybe this will help you find a space." Mrs. Hurley opened her purse and pulled out a ten-dollar bill. The man eyed the money, which was nearly a week's pay.

"I could take this family of five and put them on the Thursday boat."

Conor spoke up. "No, we can wait. Mrs. Hurley, it is not fair to change someone else's reservation and displace a family another four days."

"Nonsense, son. This is business. Leave it to me." Mrs. Hurley turned back to the agent. "That will be fine, I am sure they won't mind."

Conor turned to the clerk. "What will you tell this family? That you were bought off by another passenger?"

Mrs. Hurley interjected, "Conor, this is none of your affair. We have to leave on Monday and that's it."

"Mrs. Hurley, I am surprised you would do this."

"Well, look here," said the clerk as he reviewed the manifest. "We do have room for two more."

"Good," said Mrs. Hurley, and she started to put the ten dollars back in her purse.

The clerk snatched the money. "For my troubles," he said.

Conor knew something was wrong; he knew at least two people

were getting bounced, if not the family of five. He turned and walked away as Mrs. Hurley finished the transaction. They left the office in silence, then Mrs. Hurley said, "You need to understand that I have to go a long way to get to Peterborough. I am on a schedule."

"Everyone has a long way to go. That family now has to pay an additional three nights at a hotel or find a place to stay for a predicament that we were in, not them." Conor wanted to add but did not, "And you should pay for those extra three nights."

Ellen Hurley finished the conversation with, "You will learn what the world is like."

Conor was displeased but powerless. He did not like being unable to control the decisions that affected him and his wife. He was disappointed at Mrs. Hurley's ethics and sense of fair play and he did not want to be part of a conspiracy to disrupt a family. With little other discourse, he wanted to distance himself from these deeds, and he was so upset by Mrs. Hurley's actions that he wanted to walk away from her right there in Albany. There seemed to be plenty of opportunities in this city.

They walked another block when Mrs. Hurley timidly asked, "What would you like me to do?"

"If we are going to delay that family, you should at least pay for their extra hotel nights."

"You are carefree with my money, Mr. Meighan."

"I see," he said and hesitated to speak further, but he had nothing to lose by speaking his mind. "I can walk away from our agreement right now. I have gotten you to Albany without any trouble. Kathleen and I will put you on the packet boat Monday morning and you can be free of our indentured service. We will survive just fine. I have a strong back and there are plenty of job opportunities here." Conor spoke as if this was the final decision. "Thank you for all that you have done for us."

"Now, Mr. Meighan, don't be in such a hurry. I was thinking that maybe you are right; I should help that family."

"Well then, let's go back and make this right." Conor thought that Mrs. Hurley's style was that money could buy her way to any right decision; however, this course of action did not change the fact that the family would be delayed by three days. They returned to the Navigation Office and were greeted by the clerk.

"I would like to make right the inconvenience to that family," announced Mrs. Hurley.

"What family?" stated the clerk.

Conor did not want to be part of any charade and his anger was starting to show through. "The family that you're going to delay until Thursday, and don't play dumb with us."

"Oh, that is all taken care of."

Conor continued, "What do you mean, taken care of?" Mrs. Hurley was surprised at Conor's direct nature when angered.

"I have sent a messenger to explain the change in plans. It is all taken care of."

"I don't think so." Conor's face was red and his Irish temper igniting.

Just then the door opened and the messenger entered. "This guy is plenty mad," the messenger announced. The words were barely out when the door opened again and a large muscular man entered.

The man interrupted any further conversation. "What do you mean that I can't leave on Monday?"

"I was just discussing this problem with these folks," the clerk began. "It seems that they made a reservation for three and we had written it down for one. I am sorry but we do not have enough room."

"Well then, make enough room."

"I am sorry but I can't." Now the clerk had two fiery customers. Conor watched the clerk squirm. "If you only had been here yesterday, we had a half-filled boat. We had room on that one."

"Well, that was yesterday," answered the angry man.

The four people argued all at the same time. Between the "I can't" statements, the "You must" orders, and the borderline threats, nothing was accomplished. The Navigation Office turned into ugly chaos.

The clerk turned to Mrs. Hurley. "I think I have a solution." The ranting stopped. "Albany now has a railroad train from here to Schenectady. If you like, I can put you on the train to catch up with the half-filled boat. But you'll have to catch the train this afternoon."

"When does it leave?" asked Mrs. Hurley.

"In about an hour and a half."

"I just checked into my room. I can't move that fast."

The angry man spoke up. "I can catch that railroad train." No one was sure whether he appreciated the extra travel time or whether he just wanted some special favor.

"I can issue your ticket from here. That'll be four dollars and eighty cents for the five of you."

"Four dollars and eighty cents is a lot of money," said the man.

"Yes, but you won't have two nights in the hotel."

Conor interjected, "You can take that four dollars and eighty cents out of the ten dollars Mrs. Hurley gave you."

"But . . ." He looked at Conor, whose eyes had narrowed; his forehead had tightened and the blood vessels on his neck were clearly bulging from his intensity. "Oh yes, the ten dollars. It is right here." He reached into his vest pocket and removed the bill.

"It's done. You are leaving this afternoon." He pointed to the angry man.

"And you are leaving on Monday morning," he said, pointing to Mrs. Hurley but looking at Conor.

"Settled," said Conor.

Mrs. Hurley added, "Very good, we will see you Monday morning."

The two left the shop for the second time.

"I don't know about you, Mr. Meighan, but I feel better about this whole thing," said Mrs. Hurley.

"Yes, but it should not have happened."

"But those people got a ride on one of those new railroads and still caught the earlier boat." It was clear that Mrs. Hurley was finished with this controversy. "Do we still have our agreement?" Reluctantly, Conor indicated he would fulfill his agreement to accompany her to Peterborough. "Good. Now I have one thing that is bothering me."

"What's that?"

"Your clothes," said Mrs. Hurley. "You have been wearing those same clothes for nearly a week. You need a change. I saw a shop where we can take care of this."

When Conor and Mrs. Hurley returned to the hotel, Kathleen was relieved. "Where have you been? You've been gone for nearly three hours."

"It's a long story, about the boat tickets, and Mrs. Hurley insisted on new clothes for me."

Conor told her about the disagreement over displacing the other passengers from their reservations and the unethical agent at the office. "I was surprised that Mrs. Hurley tried to bribe our way onto the boat and that she was willing to delay a family's travels."

He told her that Mrs. Hurley wanted to buy him gentlemen's traveling clothes with a tie and leather shoes, but he had insisted on the practical clothes of a working man. "I looked funny in the tweed suit she picked out. I am certainly grateful for her generosity but her sense of style didn't match my simple taste."

He paused, then warned Kathleen, "Mrs. Hurley spotted a dress—a long full dress for a special occasion, so I think a shopping trip may be coming for you too."

"I don't know," said Kathleen. "Should I allow her to buy me clothes?"

"She certainly has the money and she spends it freely."

"Well, that doesn't mean that I should take it freely," said Kathleen.

Later that afternoon, Mrs. Hurley knocked on the door. "Kathleen, I have found a pretty dress that would look beautiful on you. I looked at it and thought of you right away." The two women left to go shopping.

Saturday and Sunday were generally days of scheduled rest; however, if Mrs. Hurley wanted to move about the city, Conor was available to travel with her. For most of Saturday she rested, except in the afternoon when she felt like a stroll in an Albany park, and she summoned Conor to accompany her.

"Come and get some fresh air with me," she said to Conor.

"I could use some air," he agreed. "Kathleen, would you like to come with us?"

"No, I prefer to stay here and rest."

Kathleen decided to write a letter home to report her safe arrival while Conor and Mrs. Hurley went for their walk to find a park. She took a sheet of the hotel stationery supplied in the room and pondered her words. Kathleen knew the next part of their journey was a passage into unknown territory and the two newlyweds were blindly hoping that a good life was waiting somewhere at the other end of this newly dug canal. She felt the fear and the excitement common to all immigrants—what she lacked was the courage the others had. She addressed the letter to her mother:

> April 9, 1837
> Dear Mother,
> I have successfully landed in New York and immediately found my way north to the city of Albany. This country is truly beautiful and the trees are so thick and old and tall. It is very different from Ireland.
> The boat trip was rocky, with many dangerous storms, but Captain Ryan was a superb sailor and he got us here safely.

Kathleen thought about the baby but she could not bring herself to speak of him in the letter or describe the terrible tragedy of that awful storm. Tears filled her eyes as she wrote. She knew the family wanted to hear about the baby's development; for them, this trip was about the baby. But for Kathleen, the trip was more than giving birth to a baby out of the eyesight of family,

friends, and business associates; this trip was her new life. She
continued:

> I miss all of you and wish you were here with
> me to see the New World. I met a wonderful Irish lad
> from County Clare, Conor Meighan. We were married
> on the ship and once we are settled, we will be mar-
> ried in a church. He has taken very good care of me.
> When we find our home, I hope someday you can
> make the trip to visit.
>
> All my love,
> Kathleen
> P.S. Thank you, Father, for the envelope.

A tear dropped from her eyes and blotted the paper. It was like
putting her seal to the letter. She knew they would never make the
trip to America. She knew she would never see her family again.
The feeling of separation—permanent separation from her known
life and childhood to a future with few definite plans and
unknown prospects—was terrifying. Her family could not support
her with words of encouragement and counsel, or provide assistance from across the ocean. She and Conor needed to find their
way on their own.

Kathleen just stared at the letter. Again her thoughts went to
her baby and her feeling of loss. If there had been no storm that
night, she would still be pregnant; her baby would still be growing within her. Kathleen was battling an internal conflict; she felt
like blaming God for the storm but she also thanked God for bringing Conor to her. He was a strong, calming force that had entered
her life. Her mind was a tangle of confusion of becoming pregnant,
leaving Ireland, getting married, and traveling with an unknown
lady to Upper Canada. "How did all this happen?" she thought,
"and so quickly?"

She raised her head just high enough to look out the window. A man was walking across the street with a young girl,

probably his daughter, and he stopped. He was scolding the girl for some unknown transgression. Kathleen thought of her father; he too gave public admonishments. She vowed to be a better parent than her father, and if it was God's will that additional children came from Conor, then God had a more perfect plan than she could recognize.

She took the letter to the lobby and told the clerk, "I would like to send this letter."

"Yes, madam. It will go out with the next mail delivery," he said.

Kathleen returned to her room. "Courage is what I need," she thought, "and I think I found it in my faith, my confidence, and with the good assistance of Conor."

By the time Conor and Mrs. Hurley returned, Kathleen had settled her anxiety enough to take a rest from the ordeal of the past few months, which had exhausted her. She was refreshed upon their return.

"I wrote a letter home to say I had arrived safely and to announce our marriage," she told Conor.

"Did you mention the baby?" he asked.

"No, I wasn't ready to write about Edward."

"In your own good time," he said. "Did you mention me?"

"Yes, I did," said Kathleen. "Was that alright?"

"You shouldn't have mentioned my name for fear of the British intercepting the letter."

The early Sunday morning air was fresh with its warm breeze against the sunny sky. Kathleen woke early as the first light was showing in the city. She quietly got up, careful not to disturb Conor, and decided to step out into the main street and observe Albany as the sun rose over the Berkshire Mountains in eastern Massachusetts. The surroundings were tranquil, as the Sunday morning worshippers had not yet set out for church. Kathleen stopped to take in the moment, as she had not experienced such a serene setting since leaving Ennis.

She walked down Chapel Street to a short stone wall that bordered a large house on the edge of the square. She sat on the wall, her mind floating with random thoughts, but no particular thought. She did not allow the heaviness of their impending journey to ruin this simple moment. Across the square she could hear a man's and a woman's voices. They were arguing, with a slur to their words—leftovers from a long Saturday night, she thought. Even the loud argument could not ruin the mood for Kathleen. For all her uncertainties, she found contentment.

"Good morning" broke the silence as a gentleman in a fine woolen jacket, silk tie, and bowler hat walked past.

Kathleen snapped away from her thoughts. "Good morning," she replied. The man continued walking. She looked towards the square and saw the pigeons pecking away at the sidewalk looking for last night's crumbs. A small black-capped chickadee flew close to her seat and landed in the nearby flowering crabapple, which was in full bloom. Kathleen had not seen a chickadee in Ireland and the little bird looked friendly and fearless. She was impressed by the bird's energy and high-spirited song. Her life was good. She wondered if Conor was awake yet, so she started a slow saunter back to the hotel.

Conor was starting to stir when Kathleen entered. "Have you been out?"

"Yes, it's a beautiful morning."

"Have you seen Mrs. Hurley?"

"No sign of her yet," said Kathleen.

"What time is Mass?" asked Conor as he tried to bring order to his morning.

"Nine o'clock, and don't eat anything before Communion."

"Yes, of course," answered Conor as he climbed to his feet.

At 9:00 a.m. Conor, Kathleen, and Mrs. Hurley went to St. Mary's Church, the first Catholic Church in Albany, to attend Sunday Mass. The historical church was built in 1797 at the corner of Pine and Chapel streets.

In private, all three prayed their thanksgiving for the journey across the ocean and for their continued safe journey through the interior of New York to Peterborough, in Upper Canada. The Mass, which was said in Latin, allowed each of them their private meditation. Father Savage, the pastor of the church, met the three after Mass at the front door. "You are new to Albany?"

"Yes," said Mrs. Hurley. "We are taking a packet boat tomorrow to head west."

"Safe journey and may God be with you," said the priest as he made the sign of the cross in the air above their heads.

"Thank you, Father," said all three travelers.

The weather had shifted for their Monday morning arrival at the Albany docks. The skies were grey and cloudy, with a cool wind blowing in from the north—the Adirondack Mountains. Rain was as likely as sunshine, a typical expectation for much of upstate New York. Sixty-five people boarded the packet boat *Tuscarora*, along with a crew of five led by Captain White along with four horses. Two of the horses pulled the boat while the other two horses rested in the front stall of the boat. Every two hours or ten miles, the horses were changed.

Travel on the canal had just started the previous week after the winter closing of the canal. However, earlier this year, in the bitter cold of January in central New York State and fifty miles north of the canal along the West Canada Creek, the temperature had dipped to 22 degrees below zero. No one was around in this desolate area of the lower Adirondack region, nothing was moving—not even the usual nomad timber wolves or minks scrounging for morsels of food. The biting cold of this harsh northern wilderness area penetrated deep into the frost line at the edge of the rocky creek bed where the ground usually remained insulated from the fluctuations of the surface temperature—but the forces of nature were at work.

Four feet below the surface, droplets of water had slipped along a granite edge that supported the riverbed and collected there. Now the frost reached this small stream of water, freezing it and creating pressure on the narrow anchor of rock. Had anyone been around, they might have heard the snap of the rock breaking loose from its foundation. The rock moved a small fraction of an inch and then rested. The small gap allowed more water to seep in along the deep ridge and after another frigid night, more water froze.

The event had little effect on the topography above and the remainder of the world seemed unaffected. This slight movement in the rock started a chain of events in the spring once the ground-level thawing and re-freezing process started with the warm sunny days and cold frigid nights. The ice created wider and wider gaps, thus allowing ground water to penetrate the gaps of the once stable rock. Suddenly the rock gave way and moved more than eighteen inches from its original spot where it had sat securely for centuries.

Geological movement is not unusual and was of little concern to the passengers on the packet as they loaded their luggage onto Captain White's eighty-by-fourteen-foot boat. The solitary wilderness eighty miles west and fifty miles north had a new eighteen-inch channel to allow the additional rush of spring water to run off. That additional flow moved south towards the canal and picked up momentum, with just enough force to erode a long-standing tamarack at the edge of the river ten miles downstream. The tree fell after four days of continued assault on the solid dirt anchor of this thirty-five-foot tree.

Now the tree lay across West Canada Creek and gathered debris, restricting the flow as if a new dam had been built. Water flowed around the tree with increased velocity and enough force to jar a resting black cherry tree cut by a lumberjack during the winter. The force triggered the massive hardwood to spin and head downstream. The vast trunk, with weight and inertia, rammed a log jam at just the right point to send a reverberating wave of force to the front of a man-made log jam known as a boom, designed to collect the timber for lumber mills along the creek. A weak point in the boom gave way, sending the collected trees downstream in a fury of rushing water.

The lumberjacks scurried to fix the broken boom, but not before numerous trees escaped the holding area. Farther downstream a dam had been built five years earlier to harness the power of the creek, but it was now in jeopardy as the uncontrolled timbers headed with strength and energy. The V-shaped cut at the bottom of a hickory tree became the focal point as the tree crashed into the dam, breaking loose the top layer, sending the logs farther downstream. The seeming insignificant cracking of a rock under the natural pressure of ice miles upstream was now causing a dangerous cascade of hefty logs on an uncontrolled course of destruction.

Meanwhile, in Albany, the dock master was talking to the captain, discussing the ice jams just past Little Falls. In early April the run-off from the Adirondack Mountains caused the West Canada Creek to rise to flood stages.

"Captain," said the dock master, "this year the ice-melt was later than usual and ice floes have been a problem."

"A lot of water?"

"Yes, a heavy flow of water, but the danger is runaway logs."

The captain, on his first trip of the season, said, "Thank you, and how was the bottoming out?" The captain was asking about the winter maintenance of the canal when it was drained and cleaned.

"The fog-gang did a good job of clearing the debris."

"Thank you," the captain said again. The captain knew that he would receive further reports along the way as he moved upstream. Once loaded, the boat left without fanfare, unlike the ocean-going ships leaving the dock of New York or Cork, Ireland, where crowds waved and cheered. However, as they moved through the state, people along the banks waved to the passengers whenever they passed. This new custom of greeting the passing settlers became a cultural phenomenon that lasted for well over a century.

Mrs. Hurley was especially nervous on this journey. She had heard stories of robbers holding up boats and Indian raids on the passengers. "Captain, I read that there are all kinds of dangers along the canal route. Do you think we will see any of the painted Indians?"

The captain tried to quiet her fears. "Mrs. Hurley, the Native people are quite friendly and on many occasions very helpful. Did you notice the name of this boat?"

"I did, and I meant to ask you, what does 'Tuscarora' mean?"

"Tuscarora is one of the six nations of the Haudenosaunee, meaning People of the Long House. They mainly live in the western part of New York State, and this boat is named after the Tuscarora warriors who came to the aid of settlers in Lewiston in 1813, when British and Canadian soldiers charged the town killing civilians, including women and children. The Tuscarora warriors saw the oncoming slaughter from their village above the town on the escarpment and ran to their aid. The British retreated and many lives were saved. They were true heroes to these people."

"Another heart-warming story about the British," said Kathleen.

"Well, truth be told," said the captain, "the Americans had first crossed the Niagara River and attacked the Canadian fort and killed General Brock. The attack on Lewiston was in retaliation for killing their beloved General."

"Oh yes, killing women and children, I see the justification," Mrs. Hurley said sarcastically.

"This was war-time, Mrs. Hurley. The Anglo-American War of 1812 between the United States and British Canada, and a lot can happen during war, but my point was that the Tuscarora tribe was friendly and helpful to the local people of Lewiston."

"Oh, I know about both the good and the savagery of men," said Mrs. Hurley.

"The Seneca, who live along the canal west of Syracuse towards Rochester, have helped me a number of times. I could tell you stories about all of the Six Nations Indians and they would all be good stories."

"Will we see painted Indians?" asked Mrs. Hurley again.

"You may see a painted Indian. Generally they only paint for ceremonies," said the captain.

"Oh, that would be lovely," said Mrs. Hurley, suddenly excited at the prospect of a cultural experience.

"The cavalry patrols frequently along the banks of the canal," said Captain White, bringing the conversation back to the original question. "And the robbers have moved inland to harass the settlers, farmers, and horse-drawn coaches rather than packet boats. Governor Clinton and the subsequent governors do not want bad press about this new canal so a military presence is frequent. However, just a few years ago, between 1830 and 1835, nearly eighty per cent of all major crimes in the United States were committed along the Erie Canal."

"My, that's a lot of crime in one stretch of land," said Mrs. Hurley.

"It is, but some of those crimes were committed at the end of the journey in Buffalo along Canal Street."

"A little too much celebration, I guess."

"Yes, so I warn my passengers getting off the boat to be careful, but you will be getting off in Tonawanda before Buffalo."

"Yes, we will," said Mrs. Hurley.

The captain waited a moment, then continued, "I must warn you of Irish rebels along the New York and Canadian border. Tempers are hot over land between the Niagara River and Detroit, Michigan. The New York Irish wanted to take the land from Canada, which is a territory of the British Crown. Even within the interior of the New World the Irish are fighting the British."

"Oh, we have already heard about the Irish and British fighting," said Mrs. Hurley.

Despite the captain's reassurance, before this journey was over they would get to meet the Native Indians, robbers, and the cavalry: the good, the bad, and the helpful.

Mrs. Hurley turned to the captain again. "I would like to introduce you to my family. This is Kathleen and Conor."

Conor noted that she did not define the "family" relationship and he imagined that would be an interesting explanation. He was never sure what she would say or do.

The captain shook Conor's hand and removed his cap in honor of Kathleen. "Pleased to meet you," he said.

Once under way, Mrs. Hurley and Kathleen were shown a berth for women in the forefront of the boat. In the rear of the boat was the dining area, which was cleared in the evening for men to hang their hammocks for sleeping. Space was limited and the boat used every section wisely.

The boat headed upriver on the Hudson to the mouth of the Mohawk River at Waterford, where they began their westward journey. The intersection of the two rivers was previously known as Half Moon, named after the ship the *Half Moon* used by Henry Hudson when in 1609 he explored the river that now bears his name. A small island sits just south of this intersection called Peebles Island, where the Native Mahicans had a trading post ideally situated to capture the frontiersmen from the north and the west, and forged trade with the well-settled communities to the south.

Recently the name of the town had changed to Waterford, with no connection to the city and county in Ireland but rather to the water passageways throughout the area. Now the canal became a waterway of the actual Mohawk River, with aqueducts around rocks and treacherous streams. As the river rose, a series of locks provided a mechanical means to raise the boat to the new level. The boat would pass through eighty-three locks before arriving at the western terminus in Buffalo.

The engineering of the locks intrigued Conor. The gates would close and create a water-tight seal while valves controlled the flow and underground tanks would equalize it, raising and lowering the boats as much as ten feet. Conor had never seen such a mechanical advantage over nature. The boat would rise 568 feet over the length of the canal between Albany and Buffalo, with a few dips in elevation along the way.

Typically boats westbound from Albany to Buffalo carried more people than cargo, as word of the successful economy, jobs, and wealth there was building. However, materials and goods were the greater cargo for eastbound packets: flour, farm crops, and lumber were delivered to the more populated areas. However, the economy was booming along the canal going both ways.

Shortly after they left, a heavy rain started. The passengers remained in the cabin of the boat waiting for the clouds to clear and the sun to appear. The captain, however, stayed at the helm, and one of the hands walked with the horses on the towpath. Now that they were under way, the captain would keep the boat moving both day and night. The only stops were for the occasional load of supplies or to work their way through the locks.

The first day went slowly, with the rain, mud, canal traffic, and the first series of locks. The trip from Albany to Schenectady was a succession of aqueducts, locks, and large numbers of boats. The booming success of the canal meant that boats were going up and down the canal in an endless succession. The congestion at the terminus of Albany, where the transfers were made to boats going up and down the Hudson River, caused gridlock for the two waterways. However, once they passed Schenectady, as the boats spaced out the packet moved along at an even pace. When it was sunny, the passengers would relax and ride on the top of the boat and watch the beautiful spring scenery of upper New York State.

Today was not sunny, though; it was wet and muddy on the towpath and the horses had trouble maintaining their footing. They fought to drag the packet boat against the swift-moving Mohawk River, whose spring run-off of snow added to the ever-present current.

As the boat approached one of the bridges leading to an aqueduct it was exceptionally slick underfoot and the inside horse bucked and pulled, causing him to slide in the muddy trail. The panicked animal lost control and ended up in the river—an occurrence which was not unusual along this section of the river.

The second horse of the team was dragged over to the bank and fought to maintain his footing. But the mud was too slick and the second horse also slid down the short embankment into the water. Such incidents happened frequently, so a ramp had been built a few yards upstream for the partially submerged horses to walk out of the water. The passengers, however, were shocked and quickly went to the windows of the boat to gasp at the two horses trying to regain footing and coordination between them to walk upstream to the ramp. The four-foot-deep canal presented no danger of drowning for the animals; the only threats were the ropes and entanglements during the horses' panic.

Conor went onto the upper deck as the captain laid out a ramp connecting the boat to the towpath. "I'll give you a hand," he said.

"Mighty kind of you," answered the captain.

He and the captain went to the driver's aid in controlling the horses and directing them out of the water. Once the horses were back on the path, they brushed them and calmed them down.

"That was scary," said Conor.

"Naw, happens all the time," said the driver.

The captain had a good laugh at the situation. Conor was surprised; he thought the incident had been serious. Eventually Conor laughed too and all the passengers watching through the windows were relieved. Conor stayed on the towpath and walked with the team driver in the rain. Working in the rain was not foreign to a farmer from Ireland. "I can tell you are from the south of Ireland," said Conor.

"Yes, indeed, I'm a Kerryman," the man said, indicating he was from County Kerry. "My name is William Quinn; everyone calls me Billy."

"Mine is Conor. How long have you been here?"

"I came to America eight years ago with my parents. They settled in New York City but I did not want the big city life. When I turned fifteen, I moved upstate as a boat hand. Now, during the winter, I go back to New York to see my parents."

"You like working the canal?" asked Conor.

"I do. It's fun seeing the towns and all the people along the way, but the walk is long and sometimes lonely. I am out here on the towpath by myself most of the time and don't have anyone to talk to. Did you know that the canal is 363 miles long?"

"No, that's a long way, but I'll walk with you, I don't mind. I can't sit all day doing nothing on the boat," said Conor. "My wife, Kathleen, can knit and sew or play her fiddle. I don't have such things."

He and Conor discussed the digging and building of the canal and the vast frontier. Billy said, "This ditch, as many people call it, has kept America strong. The United States' economy has struggled but the canal is keeping the goods moving and allowing people to settle farther west. It has saved the country from collapsing."

"That does seem like a big statement for such a small ditch, as you called it," said Conor.

"Oh yes, when the State considered the route of the canal, they saw the link to agriculture and all the support enterprises that went with it. And when the canal was finished, they understood the employment opportunities of the canal laborers. The men and the economy were all intertwined, so when the canal was completed, New York State was not left with a stream of unemployable 'ditchdiggers' floundering along its bank. No, they had hard-working men willing to keep the fruits of their labor alive by settling the areas as farmers, lumberjacks, carpenters, blacksmiths, weavers, shopkeepers, and canalers like us.

"New York State is known as the Empire State. Some say it's because of the gateway from the coast to the interior and from the interior to the shipping ports along the east coast and beyond."

"The Empire State," repeated Conor.

"It's great now, but it is going to be even better as business expands," said Billy.

Conor asked, "What do you know about Peterborough, Canada?"

"Where is that?" he asked.

"I don't know. We are accompanying Mrs. Hurley to Peterborough and then we are going to find a place to live."

"Well, if you ask me," Billy volunteered, "I wouldn't live in Canada."

"Why not?"

"Too cold and it's run by the British."

"The British," Conor thought out loud.

"Yes, they govern Canada," continued Billy.

"I thought I had seen the last of the British," Conor finally said aloud.

"Oh, no. There is a strong presence of British soldiers along the Canadian border. Some of our boys are still fighting. American Irish are trying to take the land from Niagara to Detroit from Canada, which means they still get to fight the British. I don't know if they really want the land or just a reason to fight. Anyway, tensions are high along the border."

Another wave of anxiety came over Conor as he once again realized that he had traveled half-way around the world and he had not escaped the far reaches of John Bull and British dominance. He became worried over the prospect of entering Canada with Mrs. Hurley, that somehow British troops would instantly know that he was a fugitive from Ireland.

"What's wrong?" asked Billy, as he could see that Conor was nervous.

"Oh, it's nothing. I was just thinking about the unknown, our future."

"Well, if you ask me," Billy said again without being asked for advice, "I would pick a place along the canal to settle down. There are boomtowns springing up everywhere. I would invest my money in any of the trade markets along the way. You can make a killing."

"And why aren't you becoming an instant millionaire?"

"I am. As soon as I have enough money to invest, I am going to start making and selling packet boats for the canal operators."

"That's great; how much are you going to need?"

"Well, I have been talking to this guy in Tonawanda at the end of the canal and he wants to partner with me to open this business. He has most of the money but he wants me to run it."

Conor was hesitant about Billy's possible future business plans. Conor had been in America for just over a week and he had already learned about the swindlers, dealers, and double dealers not only in the cities but at the edges of the wilderness as well.

"You can find a job anywhere along the canal," said Billy.

"What kind of job?" asked Conor.

"Anything," Billy repeated himself, "anything at all. Even being a farmer. The land is fertile and there are great markets for the cities."

"I don't have money to buy land," said Conor.

"There are plenty of people looking to hire immigrants who are dependable and hard-working."

"That's a relief. I can give a good day's work." This news relieved some of Conor's anxiety over his lack of a plan.

Billy added, "I don't want to be a hoggie for the rest of my life."

"What's a hoggie?"

"I'm a hoggie, a canal driver. It's a slang term and I don't like it."

"Why not? What does hoggie mean?"

"I don't know where it came from but it means that I get low pay for being out here on the path and taking care of the horses. I work just as hard as the rest of the crew but they don't pay me as much. I earn twelve dollars a month and look at that bowsman being paid twenty dollars a month for sitting down all day—as if that is hard work." Billy pointed to the rear of the boat where the pilot sat.

The pilot waved when he noticed the attention.

"Ahh," mumbled Billy, "that's Danny, he's an egit." The Irish jargon for an idiot was meant for anyone with a different point of view.

"Sounds like you don't like Danny."

"He doesn't do anything except hang onto the rudder to prevent hitting the bank of the canal. A little kid can do that."

"And going through the locks is just as easy?" asked Conor.

"It's a little tricky in the lock chambers but anyone can do it."

Conor let the conversation drop but he continued to walk with Billy until his shift was over. The boat stopped to change the horses. The second driver, or hoggie, was Aaron, and he unloaded the fresh horses while Billy loaded his two tired horses that had been pulling for the past ten miles. Billy went into the stall to feed and care for his horses; Conor went to inform Kathleen of Billy's stories of jobs and opportunities.

"The driver, Billy, told me that jobs are plentiful along the canal," he said to Kathleen.

"We will be fine, I am sure."

Conor was irritated that since he had met and married Kathleen, they had had little privacy except for the few hotel stays. The ship, the coach, and the packet boat all had people in close proximity where conversations could be easily overheard. He wanted to talk quietly to his wife during the day, when plans and decisions could be discussed and decided upon. Conor was a private man who did not openly share his feelings or opinions except with those he trusted. Conversely, Kathleen was comfortable in airing her thoughts and views on different topics, although she understood the need for family business to stay between her and Conor.

Mrs. Hurley wasted no time introducing herself to the rest of the passengers and finding out their origins, destinations, and family histories. Her straightforward and outgoing nature solidified the travelers as a group. She had the Irish wit to tell stories of common events that brought humor to life's hard times and tragedies. The stories, however, never mentioned pirates or lost treasures.

The fourth crew member was the cook, Mrs. Wentworth, a widow who kept to herself but was always in the middle of activity as she prepared the meals at the back of the packet. She would occasionally flash a smile but said little to the passengers who tried to engage her in conversation about a good meal or her morning breakfast of pork, gherkin pickles, potatoes either baked or boiled, eggs, bread with butter, and cheese. She just nodded acknowledgment of the compliment. Conor especially noted the heartiness of the food; having left home with little nutrition, he found the wealth of food miraculous and overpowering.

The next day, the boat progressed up the combined waterway of the Mohawk River interlinked with the Erie towards the village of Little Falls, where the captain stopped to talk with a blacksmith in town just off the towpath. The canal water had been moving swiftly as they approached Little Falls, with numerous tree branches and the occasional tree log floating by. The passengers guessed that the captain was discussing the water conditions with the blacksmith.

Shortly, the captain returned, hopped on board, and gave the order to start up again. Mrs. Hurley was the first to question the circumstances. "Why did we stop, Captain?"

"I was just checking on conditions. We are fine."

Mrs. Hurley wanted to know, "What was it that concerned you?"

"Just debris in the water and its source. Mr. Paine, the blacksmith, said it was the upper part of the West Canada Creek that has a winter log jam breaking up. We will be passing it shortly."

Mrs. Hurley heard the word Canada. "Are we close to Canada?"

"No, we still have a long way to go." The captain continued his explanation: "The West Canada Creek starts in the lower part of the Adirondack Mountains and flows down to the Mohawk River. The loggers cut trees during the winter and haul them out on snow skids. The trees are stripped and placed next to the creek, waiting for the spring thaw to carry them down to the mills where the logs are planked into boards and then transferred to boats in Herkimer.

"This year, they had a significant log jam, which is just breaking up now. The boom broke and some logs managed to continue downstream. We just have to be watchful. There is a small dam upstream to divert the water through a mill but the high water and its rush has logs flowing over the top."

The stray logs were scarce but occasionally one would float by or strike the boat. If a log hit the boat, there was a large thud, which could be both felt and heard. The crew, put on alert by this news, would run to the edge and look for damage. The driver kept watch as well and warned the bowsman to avoid any obvious logs. With the boat going against the current, a considerable force was generated in the collision when a log struck. A ramming log could seriously damage the packet boat if struck at the right vulnerable point.

As the packet approached the West Canada Creek, logs became more frequent and now dusk approached, increasing the concern. The captain asked for help to guard against logs. He hung lanterns on the boat edges and assigned people to watch for approaching logs. The canal had other debris floating as well, which made for difficult observations and false sightings. When a log was spotted, the crew was alerted and they used poles to direct the logs away from the boat.

At first, the passengers watched from inside the boat and looked out the windows, but as darkness approached it became difficult to see. So the assigned passengers went to the top of the boat, to the edges, to get a better view. In the early evening it was time to change the watch duties: Mrs. Hurley was assigned to watch the starboard side while Kathleen was given the port side. Conor was in front with Billy to fend off any approaching logs.

All was going well, when the captain announced that they were approaching the mouth of West Canada Creek. Once past the creek, the watch would be over. The horses were out in front fifty feet or more from the boat and they became skittish as they walked over the bridge at the mouth of the creek. The captain could feel the push of the rushing waters coming out of the creek into the canal bed, causing turbulence and eddies. He cautiously counter-steered the boat from the force; however, as the back of the boat crossed into the path of the opening, a rush of water hit the right side of the boat. The captain turned the rudder away from the force.

Mrs. Hurley, who was diligently watching the debris coming out of the creek, lost her footing in the sudden shift. She fell over the edge of the boat into the water. She screamed as she fell and Kathleen yelled to Conor. The boat kept moving forward as Billy yelled, "Man overboard." The driver halted the horses but the inertia of the boat kept it moving. Mrs. Hurley hit the water and quickly came to the surface. The canal was only four feet deep, so Mrs. Hurley was able to get her head above water. But the quick-moving water made it hard for the elderly woman to maintain her footing. A large hickory log came out of the creek moving directly for Mrs. Hurley.

The captain yelled, "Watch out!"

Mrs. Hurley could not move. The shifting and sway of the boat delayed Conor's arrival to the starboard. The log slammed into Mrs. Hurley's chest, making her the ramming point as the log struck the boat. Conor, Kathleen, and the captain could hear the air being forced from her lungs. Conor immediately jumped in alongside of the log as he swung around to belay it off the boat. Mrs. Hurley went beneath the boat. Conor pushed the log downstream to clear the area and was able to grab Mrs. Hurley's jacket as she slid under the boat with the current. He tightened his grip and held fast.

The captain tossed a rope to Conor. With one hand, he held Mrs. Hurley, and with the other he held the rope as the boat dragged him and Mrs. Hurley against the current. The captain called for the horses to pull the boat away from the creek. With a jerk, the boat moved forward, taking Conor and Mrs. Hurley with it. Conor could feel the dead weight of Mrs. Hurley; he knew she was badly injured.

Once clear of the creek, the boat stopped. Conor and Mrs. Hurley were helped out of the water onto the towpath. Mrs. Hurley was lifeless. The captain tried to clear her lungs but her chest cavity was crushed. Mrs. Hurley was dead.

The Captain, Conor, and Kathleen stared at Mrs. Hurley lying on the path as if she would jump back to life. The remaining passengers from the boat joined them. Everyone was stunned. Billy made an attempt to clear any water from her lungs, but all life signs were gone.

The Captain called for a makeshift stretcher and Mrs. Hurley's body was carried aboard the boat in silence. An area was set up in the dining area to lay Mrs. Hurley out and people gathered around to see if she would regain consciousness. She lay so still that all hope soon vanished, but Conor and Kathleen maintained their vigil next to her. Herkimer was a couple of miles ahead so the boat started forward. Kathleen held onto Conor, who was still wet from the canal. She wrapped him in a blanket, as the passengers approached to offer words of sympathy. Conor wept.

After 9:00 p.m. the boat arrived just south of Herkimer and tied up at the docks. The captain sent Billy into town to find the Sheriff to report the accident and death of Mrs. Hurley. The only place open was a saloon just off the towpath. The bartender sent a runner to get the Sheriff while the townspeople went to the boat to help.

The Sheriff arrived and took the report of the accident from the captain. The Sheriff walked over and examined the body. He stated that the coroner was out of town so he would issue the certificate of death. The captain decided that the boat would stay in Herkimer for the night. The passengers were offered sleeping quarters in the local hotel as well as in the homes of local community folks. Captain White, Billy, Aaron, Conor, and Kathleen stayed on the boat with Mrs. Hurley's body.

The next morning, the captain made coffee while Conor and Kathleen discussed burying Mrs. Hurley. The captain placed Conor in charge of Mrs. Hurley's belongings. "As next of kin, you are rightful owners of her effects."

"But I am not exactly family. We were traveling companions."

"Well, no one else on this boat is family and no one in Herkimer is family. So you are the next in line and as far as I am concerned, you are the next of kin."

Without thinking or discussing, Conor made the right determination. "We will continue to Peterborough, Canada, and turn over Mrs. Hurley's belongings to her daughter." Kathleen nodded in agreement. The captain was pleased that that was settled.

Kathleen opened Mrs. Hurley's luggage to find a proper burial dress. She handed the smaller bag, which contained her money, to Conor. They looked at each other. Conor asked the captain if they could have some private time with Mrs. Hurley. He agreed and stepped out, taking Aaron with him.

"What should we do?" Conor asked Kathleen, referring to the unknown amount of money in the bag.

"We are going to have to count it sooner or later. I am sure there will be expenses to bury her, so we might as well count it now."

Conor opened the bag. Inside were a series of smaller bags, some quite heavy. "I don't like doing this," Conor said quietly but intently.

Kathleen added, "Especially with Mrs. Hurley lying here next to us. It is like we're taking her money with her right here."

"Well, we are not going to take her money. The money is going to Canada. We are just going to watch over it."

"How much is there?" asked Kathleen.

Conor opened the first bag. It was paper money in English pounds. He counted three thousand pounds. The second bag had American currency equaling three hundred and seventy dollars. Two bags had Canadian tokens that had just been issued from the Bank of Montreal, called Papineaus, totaling over two thousand dollars. A fifth bag had various coins, which Conor figured amounted to less than fifty dollars but accounted for the heaviness of the bag. The sixth and final bag felt pliable, with small objects inside. Conor opened it to find various jewels, including diamonds and other gems of various colors and sizes that were unidentifiable to either Conor or Kathleen. Conor was shocked at the amount of money and valuables. Mrs. Hurley's story of pirating started to make sense.

"This is a lot of money," he said.

"No wonder she was worried. Now I am worried."

"We will have to protect it still. I will take twenty dollars for expenses," Conor half asked and half told Kathleen.

"That's a good idea," agreed Kathleen.

"Yeah, it's not a good idea to keep going into the bag for money as we need it. People will notice."

Kathleen noted, "She had money for the British, America, and Canada. She planned well."

An undertaker arrived after being notified by the Sheriff. He offered to assist with the burial. A hole was dug at a local cemetery and by mid-afternoon, the captain and a local pastor performed a short funeral service at the gravesite, attended by all the passengers as well as approximately twenty-five people from the town.

Because there was no Catholic priest in the area, the local Presbyterian pastor attended the service and gave a short prayer. Conor leaned over to Kathleen and said softly, but not softly enough, "Isn't it odd that a Presbyterian minister is here at a Catholic funeral?"

"I think it is best to have someone from the clergy here," Kathleen replied.

The minister looked over at Conor and started the service. "Even though I am not a Catholic priest, I would like to bring God's presence to Mrs. Sarah Hurley, whose soul has joined with our heavenly Father. May we bow our heads and pray the words from the Prophecy of Isaiah, Chapter 9 of the Old Testament, which promised us a light through Jesus Christ:

> Nevertheless the dimness shall not be such as was in her vexation, when at the first he lightly afflicted the. land of Zebulun and the land of Naphtali, and afterward did more grievously afflict her by the way of the sea, beyond Jordan, in Galilee of the nations.
>
> The people that walked in darkness have seen a great light: they that dwell in the land of the shadow of death, upon them hath the light shined.

"Amen," came from the group of townspeople. The passengers caught up after a second with their own reciting of "Amen."

Conor leaned over again and whispered, "Tír na nÓg." Kathleen gently poked her elbow into his side, as if to say, "Stop it." Conor's reference to Tír na nÓg was to an enchanted land far off the west coast of Ireland in old Irish mythology that held the power of eternal youth.

After the service, Kathleen challenged Conor's indiscretion, "What did you mean when you said, 'Tír na nÓg'?"

"I was only saying that Mrs. Hurley was getting a non-Catholic service, with the old false gods and superstitions of the Druids."

"Conor, Tír na nÓg was not a Druid belief, and you were making fun of the minister's words."

"Well, maybe I was and I shouldn't have. Mrs. Hurley deserved better respect. Yes, you're right, I'll say an extra 'Hail Mary' for Mrs. Hurley."

The town residents had organized a dinner for the passengers at the hotel. Conor was impressed by the unity and compassion of the Herkimer community, composed of people of mostly German and Dutch heritage. These hardy people were descendants of residents during the French and Indian War as well as of many brave fighters in the American Revolutionary War, including the town's namesake, General Nicholas Herkimer, so they knew the hardships of wilderness living and graciously helped those who needed assistance. However, they did not accept any payment for the dinner even though Captain White tried to pay them and Conor tried to make a donation.

The local pastor refused the money. "You will need your money for your travels and settlement. Our goal is to have your soul at ease. God bless you on your journey."

"You and your congregation have been most kind, thank you," said Kathleen.

The undertaker charged a minimal fee for the coffin and gravediggers. Conor paid them with as many coins as he could to lighten the load.

As they walked towards the packet, Kathleen said, "Mrs. Hurley was a Catholic, we are Catholic, yet it didn't matter to the Presbyterian minister or the people of his parish. They took care of us anyway."

"I think we have to learn about the frontier way of life and how everyone comes together. People back home can learn a lesson from America," said Conor.

"I'd say the English need to learn this lesson, too."

"Oh yes, most definitely, but all people need to be reminded to take care of those in need."

"Conor, do you think Presbyterians can go to Heaven?"

"Oh, I guess," he answered. "Even though I was a little flippant during the service, Presbyterians are followers of Jesus, just like we are. It would be hard to say that these good people of Herkimer can't get into Heaven because they are not Catholics but behave in all the goodness that Christ taught."

"But the Pope and the Church have said that it is reserved for the faithful of the Catholic Church."

"Yes, they have said that and those people have been taught the very same thing. You know, when people die, what do you say—'May they rest in peace.' I think that dying in peace and resting in peace is the key. Mrs. Hurley died in peace—very tragically, mind you—but I think her heart was at peace with the world."

"Yes, I think she was a good person in her heart."

"That is the key to opening the gates of Heaven. Those who die killing, hurting, stealing cannot be at peace in their heart and they feel the anguish of Hell."

"Do you think it is that easy?"

"Oh, the concept is easy—be a good person in all aspects of your life. The hard part of living is the day-to-day stuff when it is easier to put your fellow man down than to help him up. It is easier to kill your enemy than to deal with him, or live next to him. I saw that every day in Ireland. Kill the Irish because they're a problem, kill the English because they . . ." He took a deep breath. "Well, sometimes you have to fight back."

"I know what you're trying to say and maybe some Irishmen are willing to go to Hell for eternity so that others can live free."

"I wasn't exactly thinking that, but you may be right."

"What about our baby Edward? Did he go to Heaven?" asked Kathleen.

"What do you think I am, a priest—with all these questions?" he said playfully, as they turned the last corner before heading directly to the dock at the edge of the canal.

Meanwhile, Kathleen grabbed his arm and hugged it as they walked together, and she said, "It is important to know where Edward ended up for eternity."

"They say he went to limbo, a half-way point to Heaven."

"Yes, but he had no malice in his heart, God bless his little soul. He should be in Heaven right now."

"Yes, he should, but through baptism that takes away the original sin we are all born with—until then he must go to limbo."

"It wasn't his fault he wasn't baptized."

"Nor our fault," said Conor. "Nor God's fault, for that matter. It was an earthly circumstance that took him away."

"And he will not pay for the sins of his father."

"What did you say?"

"Edward is not banned from Heaven in order to pay for the sins his father committed that night in the alley. The father will have to pay for that on his own."

"My point, the father will not rest in peace."

As they approached the boat, Captain White was accounting for all passengers. "Let's go up top and sit for a while," said Conor.

"I would like that," said Kathleen as she grabbed the railing on the ladder to the top deck. They took a bench near the front where they could sit next to each other. None of the other passengers went topside because of the cool evening air but that did not matter to the young couple; they sat snuggled together and looked at the three-quarter moon on this cloudless night. They did not speak, nor did they have to; their grip on each other was enough communication. They found their peace in each other's company.

Once everyone returned and was accounted for, the journey continued, with Captain White saying, "Okay Billy, get them moving"—referring to the horses. The passengers felt a slight tug as they again headed west.

Chapter 11

The Erie Canal
Herkimer to Tonawanda

The packet left Herkimer with a melancholy atmosphere. Passengers and crew felt they had lost a dear friend. The hardest hit was Conor, partially because of guilt feelings that he had not been able to get to Mrs. Hurley fast enough to save her. The other part was the affection he had developed for the little lady who took two strangers under her protective wing, all the while making believe that it was she who needed protection. Each had a dependence on the other.

Kathleen was consolation for Conor. Kathleen spoke of the bizarre circumstances and the uncontrollable nature of life. The accident was not the fault of one person but the confluence of many factors, including the boat's journey and the events upstream on the West Canada Creek. Conor's actions were one piece of the circumstances. Kathleen was a religious person and placed it in the context of God's plan, but both she and Conor knew it was part of man's trial in civilizing a cruel frontier.

As the boat moved upstream, Conor stayed in the doldrums. The weather did not help, as the rain was constant. Passengers stayed throughout the day in the lower dining area. Kathleen tried to persuade Conor to get some fresh air and walk with Aaron or Billy but Conor did not want to leave the boat. He complained of a constant headache and he had little or no appetite.

At first Kathleen thought he had a lingering sadness over Mrs. Hurley's death; after a time she realized he was sick, especially when he started experiencing diarrhea, vomiting, and leg cramps. The captain recognized it as cholera, the dreaded disease that plagued the Buffalo and Rochester area during the early 1830s. Conor was constantly thirsty and requested water frequently, as the disease dehydrated him rapidly. Captain White quickly became concerned that his water supply was infected, but Kathleen reminded him that only Conor was sick and no one else. As they reviewed the past few days, they agreed that Conor must have contracted the unsanitary disease when he jumped into the canal to save Mrs. Hurley.

To further the concern, Conor frequently placed his hand on his chest, indicating discomfort, so Kathleen put her hand over his and she could feel his rapid heart rate even though he was not doing anything requiring physical exertion. In reality, Conor was not experiencing pain from the rapid heart rate; he was feeling the accelerated beating and he thought by placing his hand over his heart, he could get it under control. This happened twice during the afternoon and, in Conor's sickened state, he was unable to articulate these odd physical abnormalities.

Kathleen was nearing panic when his pulse finally, slowly, calmed down and he fell into a deep sleep. It was a drastic change from the highly agitated state into a sedated rest; Kathleen did not know how to read it but the captain calmed her. "He will be all right. Rest is good for him right now."

Externally, Conor was showing calm in his rest; internally his mind was active with distress. The dream started with the death of Mrs. Hurley and how he should have saved her by intercepting the log before it could strike her. It was easy for him to jump into the water and belay the log to a harmless float down the canal. He played out the dream in his mind of actually performing the heroic act. But as the sleep deepened, the true agony of regret was stealing his focus from heroism to anguish, and it came full force in his weakened state.

Now, again, the thoughts of O'Malley's Pub returned. This time he stayed behind and faced the British inquisition in the beating death of Sergeant Clark. He was arrested and taken to jail, where he was interrogated about Irish rebels and planned uprisings. He tried to speak eloquently about his lack of knowledge and, as dreams go, he convinced them of his lack of guilt or evil intentions but the judge failed to understand his circumstance, and therefore, he was to be executed.

Confusion reigned; he tried to sort out the details and his attempts to explain his innocence to his mother and father, to the English magistrate, but most of all, to himself. He awoke in a flash. Kathleen sat next to him and smiled. Immediately, he returned to the dream and played it out again, with the same result but it was not as intense. The mind was adjusting to his reality. The sickness was subsiding. He was coming back to the present. He lay there half in sleep and half in consciousness of the activity around him.

The captain came by and checked with Kathleen. "How is he doing?"

"He has quieted down. I don't know whether that is good news or bad."

The captain said, "This disease can be deadly but if death occurs, it happens quickly; I think that Conor has passed the deadly stage."

"He has woken a few times, but drifted off to sleep again," she said.

"Rest is good," the captain repeated.

Kathleen stayed by Conor's side. She had set up a small screen with some sheets in the dining area to afford Conor privacy. Her experience at the hospital proved valuable in keeping Conor resting comfortably and provided with plenty of fluids.

As time moved on, occasionally Conor would reach over to Kathleen and squeeze her hand to let her know that he appreciated her attention. Kathleen squeezed back to acknowledge she was taking care of one she loved. Their relationship was coming full circle in the spirit, in the mind, and in the physical. Within a few days, he recovered. Everyone was relieved for Conor.

Shortly after passing through Utica around midnight, one of Billy's horses started to limp. He called to the captain that he was stopping the team. He backed the horses off from pulling but kept them moving with the inertia of the boat so the packet did not float by. When the boat stopped from the resistance of the current, Billy stopped the horses. He grabbed the lantern to examine the horse. Just as he suspected, the horse known as Izzy had thrown a shoe. Horses do not actually "throw" a shoe. They more likely "drop" a shoe because the nails work loose and cause the shoe to fall off. Constantly wet spring conditions are a common cause.

"Captain, Izzy has lost a shoe."

"Bring her in," the captain stated, slightly annoyed by another delay. "Aaron, take your team out," was the next command. They switched teams and Aaron's team would have to take them the seventeen miles to Rome for the farrier to shoe the horse in the morning.

By eleven o'clock the next morning the boat was under way again, heading towards Syracuse. The captain hoped his delays were over. He was already behind schedule but the funeral in Herkimer had been essential. He would just have to make up time.

The boat passed through Syracuse in the early evening after the sun had gone down. Conor was sleeping because he was still exhausted from being ill. The city reminded Kathleen of Pough-keepsie with loud bars, arguments, and drunken singing, all of which could be heard from the boat. She had another memory of unruly bars but she attempted to suppress those horrible thoughts.

"Sounds like a fun town," said Michael O'Shaughnessy, interrupting Kathleen's thoughts. He was a single 28-year-old immigrant looking to start a new life.

"Not to me," replied Kathleen. "Too noisy and rowdy."

"Ah, that's what makes it fun. I wish the captain would stop the boat for a few hours so we could have a taste of the fun and maybe a beer."

"Yeah, a beer or two or three," joked Kathleen, knowing the boat would not stop.

"Yeah, three sounds like a good number. Do you think I have time to jump off and grab a pint?"

"Feel free, but don't expect us to be here when you return."

"Tough decision."

Kathleen thought he was really considering jumping off the boat. After thinking a few moments, O'Shaughnessy announced, "Maybe I will. Captain," shouted Michael, "can you stop the boat? I want to get off."

"Here?" came the reply.

"Yeah, I am ready for some fun."

"I ain't waiting," was the captain's reply.

Typical Irishman, thought Kathleen. The thought of a beer and a few laughs was a stronger pull than buying cheap land in the Ohio Valley where he was originally headed.

The captain stopped the boat and Michael walked the short gangplank to the towpath with his baggage in hand. The boat started up and left Michael standing there in the dark, waving to the passengers.

What a sight, thought Kathleen. He's standing on the wrong side of the canal with no bridge in sight.

With faint light from the moon, Michael stood motionless and before his silhouette disappeared out of sight, the passengers could hear his cry: "Captain?"

"Yes, Michael?" the captain yelled back.

The passengers on the topside watched as Michael raised his arms in bewilderment as to how to cross the canal. "About a half-mile back there's a bridge," yelled the captain.

Michael jumped into the air and clicked his heels at the good news of a crossing, and he was last seen heading back eastward with a spring in his step. That was the last they heard of Michael O'Shaughnessy.

Michael had left a festive mood among the passengers and Kathleen felt the excitement too. For that reason, she went below to retrieve her violin. When she returned and sat next to Conor, she opened the case. The polished wood instrument took the muted light of the moon and reflected it back to Kathleen. More than the reflection of the wood came through; it showed a history of a life lost back in Ennis.

But the violin was a symbol of joy, and she gripped the upper neck of the instrument above the fingerboard, and laid her fingers over the strings as she lifted it out of the case. She felt a shiver start in her shoulders and pass down through her torso into her thighs, a sensation attached to a memory of a second-floor flat where her parents and two sisters gathered, united in music. The tingling subsided as fast as it came, but the memory lingered.

She smiled as she placed the violin to her shoulder; her eyes watered but no one noticed except Conor. Gently, he placed his hand on her thigh and squeezed, feeling her leg muscle twitching under the dress. She looked at him and her smile grew broader. For a moment, the boat was empty; no other person existed except the two of them. It was magical and mesmerizing.

A clap and squeal by a child anticipating the music broke the focused attention between them. Kathleen reached down and stroked the hair of the waiting child, passing the energy and love through her hand to the anxious little girl waiting for the violin to emit its sweet sound. Kathleen took the bow and drew it across the strings; it needed tuning and she adjusted the pegs to bring it back into pitch. Once again, the music of Turlough O'Carolan entertained the group as they headed west towards Rochester.

By morning, the boat had entered the Montezuma swamps of central New York State. The swamps were active with Canada geese returning from the south and provided a spectacle of wildlife as the birds flew in formation, "honked" their arrival, circled around, and landed in the cool ponds to feed and rest. The swamps also held other wildlife which endangered the passing human population. Micro-organisms, ticks, mosquitoes, chiggers, and other disease-causing insects were abundant.

Before long a passenger, Margaret Connell, showed signs of a red rash that started on her arm and spread to her upper chest, and she was running a fever. The illness may have come from the swamps or some other source, but when the abdominal pain started, Captain White recognized it as typhus, also known as ship fever. The captain became worried because rodents or lice commonly transmitted it. An outbreak would mean he had an infected boat, and Captain White prided himself on keeping a clean boat free of mice and rats.

An outbreak would also mean stopping the boat, removing all the contents, and scrubbing it clean. Each passenger would need to be inspected for lice. The captain asked Kathleen to check Margaret for lice but none was found. Margaret's symptoms progressed and her condition became increasingly serious.

Margaret Connell was a fifteen-year-old girl traveling with her family to Buffalo. She was an energetic teenager with a large heart and was friendly with every passenger. She knew and called each passenger by name, whether adult or child, and she remembered their personal stories. Everyone appreciated her selfless attention, uncommon for a person her age. She loved to read books and spoke of the far distant places as if she had made the journey herself. Every person on board shared the concern for her health.

The captain reported that the next stop was Lyons but there was not a doctor in that town. However a local resident, Mrs. Hale, lived just outside of town and she was good with herbal medicines.

In late afternoon the Tuscarora glided into the hamlet of Lyons and the captain sent Aaron to find Mrs. Hale. Aaron knew where she lived because he had searched her out on previous trips through this area. He headed south towards her home about three miles from the canal.

Captain White, still concerned about the cleanliness of the boat, waited for Mrs. Hale and ordered all belongings to the top deck while everyone pitched in to scrub the dining area. After that each passenger went above and opened their cases and checked for lice, mites, or rodents. The top of the boat was an excellent place to shake out clothes and other items in the warm breeze that traveled down the open channel of the canal, unencumbered by trees. After an hour had passed, a horse-drawn carriage approached with Mrs. Hale and Aaron. As they stepped down from the two-seater, Mrs. Hale carried her embroidered cloth bag containing her various mixtures of herbal medicines.

She was quickly delivered to Margaret and after checking the patient, she agreed with the captain that Margaret had typhus. She opened her bag, which contained bottles and boxes of various herbs and medicines, and gave Margaret's mother two bulbs of garlic, to be administered over the next couple of days. She also mixed up some mint and chamomile teas and an herbal sachet to lie next to her pillow. She called for a meeting with the Connells and the captain.

"Margaret needs to see a doctor. When you get to Rochester, make sure you find a doctor right away."

"We will," replied the captain.

"Will she be all right?" asked Mr. Connell.

"I think she will make it. The garlic will help and give you time."

They thanked Mrs. Hale and paid her a modest fee for her service although, little known to Mrs. Hale, the Connells were almost penniless, as were most of the immigrants who traveled the canal. But the money did not matter as much as Margaret's health, so the humble payment was made without question. Mrs. Hale returned to her carriage and left for her home.

The horses had been changed so Aaron was out on the towpath and Billy was in the stalls cleaning, grooming, and feeding the pair he had just brought in. The boat started up again. The captain knew Margaret would be stable for a while but he did not want any delays before he reached Rochester.

Captain White had a broad knowledge of navigation as well as an extensive life experience. His years as the chief pilot on canal boats gave him a vast education in health, first aid, business savvy, and, most of all, skills in handling a wide range of people.

They hadn't traveled three miles out of Lyons when trouble was waiting for them. The towpath was a mix of trees and high shrubs with thick thorny underbrush along the pathway. The underbrush offered concealment for animals and men with evil thoughts. Conor came outside to talk with the captain, who was piloting the boat from the rear deck.

"Captain, how long is it to Rochester?"

"We will be there by daybreak tomorrow. How are you feeling?"

"Much better."

Unknown to Conor and the captain, three outlaws were listening to their conversation from the underbrush. These three bandits saw a distinct advantage, mistaking Conor as the third crew member of the boat. Their perception of Conor in his workman's clothes as a crew member were augmented by an afternoon of drinking whiskey in the sun waiting for a canal boat to come along. The would-be robbers were more unpolished thugs than trained criminals with honed skills. With all three crew exposed, the thugs thought, the boat was vulnerable.

The first bandit emerged just up the path from the horses as if he were taking a walk in the park. Aaron knew immediately that trouble was approaching; he looked back at the captain. The captain, sitting at the helm, also saw the man coming towards Aaron.

Even though this was their first trip this year, Captain White, Aaron, and Billy had worked together long enough to know what the other was thinking in times of crisis. Crews often consisted of new naive immigrants looking for jobs; rarely were there experienced crews who coordinated well with each other. Today was not going to be a lucky day for the thieves.

As the man met Aaron, the other two men emerged onto the towpath just even with the captain. Seven feet of water and earthen bank separated them. The closest robber pointed a pistol at the captain. "Don't move or we will shoot you both," he ordered.

Simultaneously, the first robber stopped the horses and threatened Aaron with a knife. Aaron was well aware that a knife was just as deadly as a gun in an experienced hand. Guns fired one round and then needed to be reloaded; knives could continue to stab and were a constant threat. All six individuals froze; it was time for a measured response.

"Throw the gangplank out," came the order from the gang's leader.

"Very well," replied the captain. He knew these crooks were amateurs if they did not bring their own boarding plank. They were probably highway thieves who had heard about lifetime treasures traveling in the packet boats and decided to give this crime a try. But this was a deadly game, not to be taken lightly.

Conor stood still. He thought how Mrs. Hurley would be frightened by these circumstances and he was glad she was not here to endure them. The passengers saw the events from the windows inside. Kathleen too thought how lucky they were that Mrs. Hurley was not here.

The captain slowly moved into the boat to retrieve the plank. The leader of the thugs, who did the talking, watched through the windows as the captain moved forward through the cabin. Captain White came to the door of the stall. The robbers did not know Billy was there. Billy had already removed the rifle from the rack, loaded and cocked it. The Captain did not look Billy's way but whispered, "You ready?"

"All set, Captain," came the hushed reply.

"Wait until both are on the plank," was the final advice from Captain White.

"Will do."

The captain opened the door and laid out the plank between the boat and the bank. He stepped aside. The two robbers, still with pistols drawn, moved to the plank. Billy had the rifle propped up and wedged into his shoulder. He waited for a signal to move. He looked out between the cracks in the stall and saw the two men approach the boat, each with a gun in his hand. The first man stepped on the boards and moved forward; the second followed.

Billy's eyes narrowed; his breathing deepened and slowed, all distractions dissipated. Tunnel vision set in. Billy was ready. He moved around the corner and had a direct line of fire down the plank. His focus was the pair of threats; all other activity escaped him. A person next to him could have yelled "Billy!" into his ear and he would not have heard. He saw the first man with the gun look directly his way. This was the point of no return.

His line of sight took in the doorway of the boat and only the objects within that frame. On the right side of that frame was Captain White. He needed to compensate for the captain's presence. He inched the gun left. He fired his one shot from the 45-caliber Leman rifle. The round struck the first man in the shoulder. The blow kicked the man back and made him unstable on his feet.

The crack of the rifle started a series of events. The captain immediately bent down and grabbed the plank before the first man had fallen, and with unusual strength and speed, he lifted the plank waist-high to send both men into the water. Upon hearing the shot fired, the robber guarding Aaron looked to the boat. The lapsing second was all Aaron needed to strike the man with his fist and send him backwards. Aaron quickly turned and dove into the canal out of harm's way.

On the boat, it was chaos: mothers grabbed their children and dove to the floor. Mrs. Connell clutched her ailing daughter on the makeshift bed. The captain threw the plank to the side and jumped in the water, followed by Billy, to disarm the men. The other male passengers scrambled to the door of the boat to assist with the apprehension.

The horses spooked and reared. The first robber, the thug with the knife, was underneath one of the rearing horses and was kicked as it came down. He scrambled into the underbrush to escape the oncoming assault by the horses. He fled the scene on his horse, trotting off into the distance. Conor jumped into the canal and swam to the bank. He ran up the towpath to assist Aaron out of the canal.

The two thieves were dragged onto the towpath by the captain, Billy, and two assisting passengers. Billy grabbed a rope and tied the hands and feet of their two captured bandits. The one with the shoulder injury started complaining: "My shoulder hurts."

"Too bad," stated Billy.

"The ropes are too tight."

"They should be around your neck," continued Billy.

"I didn't mean anything. You didn't have to shoot me."

It was clear that the packet crew and passengers were not sympathetic to the complaints of the thief. "Why don't you just keep quiet," the captain finally said sternly.

Kathleen offered to wrap the shoulder of the injured thief. She had knowledge of bandages from working at the hospital and felt basic aid was necessary. She applied an ointment to the entrance and exit wounds in the muscle tissue of the shoulder and found that no bones were struck and no blood vessels were ruptured. He would recover from the wound. Surely this thug would wear his injury and scars as a badge of honor, thought Kathleen. Maybe it was his lucky day. "What's your name?" Kathleen asked politely.

The thief took the question as a friendly gesture but also as a sign of weakness. "Ray. What's yours?" He smiled playfully as he replied.

Kathleen took a bottle of tonic and poured it on the open wound. Ray screamed with surprise at the sharpness of the pain as the tonic seeped into the wound, delivering a constant sting as the tonic flowed. Kathleen looked at Ray with contempt and finished the bandaging in silence. Ray had guessed Kathleen wrong. She had strength and courage.

The unwritten law in the early frontier was clear—you had a right to survive and defend yourself. These two bandits could have been dispatched to the afterlife right there on the towpath and little would have been said by anyone. But that was not the captain's moral view; he was known as an honorable, principled, and decent man and his livelihood depended on many more trips up and down the canal so his reputation needed to be solid. Under the circumstances his choice was between being known as a harsh man or a fair and decent gentleman not to be treated lightly. He chose the latter, not only in this situation but in most of his business and life dealings.

Now the two bandits raised another dilemma—what should he do with the two thugs? Releasing them was out of the question. Taking them to the next town, Newark, and delivering them to the authorities was the right solution but not an easy or safe task.

The captain decided not to place them on the boat, for many reasons, the strongest rationale being that the passengers would not approve and the two outlaws did not deserve an easy ride. So, he decided, the prisoners walked with the horses. Aaron was good with ropes and knots and he was assigned the task of securing them for the journey. He bound the two prisoners so they could walk with reasonable comfort except that their hands were tied behind them.

A rope was connected from the horses' harnesses back to the prisoners. This rope maintained slack but if the rope became taut, a loose-fitting noose around their neck would tighten. The device kept the prisoners moving and prevented thoughts about running. The driver walked with the horses, while the two prisoners walked behind them and Conor sat on the top of the boat, watching for any nefarious movements.

Aaron was young and immature in the ways of manhood. When setting the ropes, he tied a slip-knot with the rope between the boat and the horses' harness. If trouble occurred, he could pull the slip-knot, setting the horses free. Next, he would slap the horses' backs, causing both horses to gallop away, taking the two prisoners with them in a tightened noose. Aaron felt that was one less thing to worry about during any future crisis. He did not think through how he would explain the two dead thieves to the captain, who was ultimately responsible for the prisoners.

They were on their way again. Billy returned to the stall to finish caring for the horses and clean the rifle. Once the rifle was cleaned, the captain called for the rifle to be made ready again, in case the third bandit returned to liberate his companions. The captain did not say anything to Billy but he wanted control of the rifle because Billy had shot Ray at close range and only hit him in the shoulder. The captain realized that if Billy had to fire a longer distance onto the towpath, the path of the bullet would be unpredictable. A man or horse could end up being hit. A struck horse would probably have to be put down. Such trouble was needless, so the captain kept the rifle close for his own use.

The boat had an hour's ride to Newark at normal speed. The two additional pedestrians made the travel slower; however, at dusk the boat pulled in to the banks of Newark. Billy was dispatched to find a sheriff or an army garrison. He returned shortly with a platoon of cavalry soldiers. A lieutenant pulled up to Captain White, who was waiting on the bank.

"I am Lieutenant Poppa. I understand you had trouble on the canal."

"Yes, sir. Three men tried to rob the boat and passengers. We captured two of them but the third escaped."

The lieutenant looked at the two prisoners. "I take it these are the men?"

"Yes, sir. One was shot during the capture."

Captain White noticed the lieutenant mumbled while thinking and muttered his thoughts out loud. The first mumble: "Too bad he is still standing." Then he announced out loud in a commanding voice, "Sergeant, relieve the prisoners from the boat crew."

"Yes, sir."

Aaron and the sergeant made the trade of prisoners, who looked disheveled from the wound, the walk, the drinking, the fight in the water, and their own lack of hygiene.

"What punishment did you apply, captain?" asked Lt. Poppa.

"None, sir. I brought them directly here."

Another mumble. "Yeah, sure," as he examined the two prisoners.

"Are you going to take them to a court?" asked Captain White.

The authoritative voice returned. "I am in charge out here, Captain. We have martial law. You said that you administered no punishment. Well, I will." The mumbling started: "A whipping would be good, let's see." He spoke up. "Captain, how many miles from here to the scene of their unfortunate crime and capture?"

"About four miles."

Mumble: "Four, that's not enough." Again aloud: "How many people on board?"

"Sixty-five—no, wait, we lost two passengers, sixty-three."

"And four crew?"

"Yes, sir."

Mumbling: "Sixty-three and four, that's . . . sixty-six."

"No, sir, that's sixty-seven," interrupted the captain. The lieutenant was surprised the captain could hear him think.

"Sixty-seven, close enough. I am going to round it up," came the continued mumbling.

"Eighty," he announced.

Aaron and Billy were standing next to the captain. Both of them were trying hard not to laugh at the fluctuations of the lieutenant's voice, the high loud voice and the low mumbles.

"Forty lashes each," the lieutenant ordered. "And if they don't tell us the name of the third person, they will have to endure that man's forty lashes."

"Eighty." The lieutenant was uncomfortable and mumbled again: "Did I add it right? Eighty seems like a lot."

He said out loud as a final determination, "Yes, eighty, unless they reveal their co-conspirator. Then it's forty each. Tomorrow morning," he added.

Ray did not know what a co-conspirator was, but he knew what eighty instead of forty meant. The sergeant led the two men off to a place of detention for the overnight vigil and Ray complained again as he was led away that forty lashes were too many and that he wanted to go before a magistrate. Clearly, it was not Ray's lucky day.

"Captain," said the army lieutenant, "I will divide my men into two patrols. One will go eastbound towards Lyons to find this third person. The second patrol will go west, following you, so you do not have any further trouble."

"Thank you, lieutenant." Captain White realized that Lieutenant Poppa was not an educated man and had odd particularities about him but he was a strategist, and this would make him an effective lieutenant in the U.S. Army. All things considered, he respected the lieutenant.

"Captain," the lieutenant continued, "my men can only go so far in your shadow. Then they must return here."

"I understand."

"They can go as far as a place called Fairport and then turn around."

"I know where Fairport is."

The mumbling returned: "Of course he knows Fairport, he's a captain on the canal."

"Thank you again," said the captain as he turned to ready his boat. The captain was a man of details. He conducted periodic inspections of all aspects of his boat—tools, materials, and horses. He inspected the horses' harnesses before going aboard.

"What's this?' he asked, pointing to the slip-knot.

"I made that," Aaron said proudly. "If any trouble came along, I could pull the rope, release the horses and deal with the threat."

"The boat would come to a halt, unable to move. What if I called for the horses to pull us out of trouble or pick up speed? They would be gone and nowhere to be found. And if the horses took off, the prisoners would have dragged behind, right?"

"Yes, sir." Aaron could tell the captain was getting angry.

"Don't you ever do that again without my knowledge and approval. Do you understand?" came the stern reprimand.

"Yes, sir." Aaron was shaking but he knew the scolding was over. The captain would never bring it up again unless Aaron made another mistake. If that happened, Aaron would be left on the bank of the canal, jobless.

The army patrol followed a couple of hundred yards behind the packet, far enough not to be intrusive but close enough to see any threats. Aaron was brought in for his rest and at the same time Billy took his horse team out to the towpath and Conor joined him.

Conor started the conversation. "Today was an exciting day."

"The captain is mad at me."

"Why? You did great."

"I blundered the shot and only hit the thief in the shoulder. The captain thinks I should have hit him square in the chest."

"The captain is not a brutal man. He is probably happy that no one was killed. Did he tell you that you should have killed him?"

"No, not exactly. He took the gun away from me and he didn't want me to use it any more."

"Is that what he said?"

"No, but he made me give him the gun at the rear of the boat."

Conor understood Billy's trouble. His woe was not about the captain; it was about his own disappointment. "Have you ever shot anyone before?" asked Conor.

"No, but I have shot deer, squirrel, and rabbit many times."

"Shooting a person is a little different, don't you think?"

"It does make you nervous," admitted Billy.

"And sitting there, waiting for the right moment, makes you even more nervous?" asked Conor.

"Of course, and the captain was standing right there in between us. I did not want to hit the captain."

"You did fine, Billy. Everyone appreciates what you did."

"The next time, I'll blow his head off," Billy said, trying to sound valiant.

"Billy, there's no glory in taking a man's life. Look how this has affected you and you did everything right."

Billy thought a moment. "You're right. I was nervous about actually killing a man."

"I am glad you're sensitive enough to know when killing is the right decision. It's a tough judgment out here in the frontier where decisions are made in the quickest of moments."

"How do you know all this stuff?" asked Billy.

"You know, I grew up in the west of Ireland and even though we were poor, my parents insisted that my brothers and sisters learn right from wrong. We learned what was fair and decent and to be good Catholic Christians. Once, I saw my father catch a vagabond in our potato field stealing food, and food was scarce. My father could have killed him. He was mad enough to kill him, but he didn't. He grabbed him by the coat and told him if he ever returned that he would kill him. My father gave him two potatoes and told him to leave. He turned to me and said, 'That was the right thing to do. A man has to eat, just not out of our field,' and the man never came back." Conor finished with, "You don't have to be brutal to be effective." The two walked on.

Conor hopped aboard when the horses were changed. Kathleen was still keeping vigil with the Connells, who were closely monitoring Margaret's progress. Conor greeted them. "The night air is getting cool out there. How's Margaret?"

"Shh, she's sleeping," warned Kathleen.

"I am going to grab a sweater and go up above."

"I will join you for some air," said Kathleen. The top deck had a low bench in the front for passengers. Now Conor and Kathleen had time to talk alone with no one else close by. "How's Billy doing?" Kathleen asked.

"He's okay. What do you mean?"

"After today, I thought he would be a little shaken."

"Well, he was, but he is okay now. I think we were all a bit shaken."

"Not you, Mr. Tough Irishman," Kathleen said jokingly.

"I have to admit, when the rifle went off, I cringed. I thought another person was going to die and I was in the middle of another violent death. The sound of the gunfire jolted me. The noise was so loud; I felt like the gun was making a big announcement, that a big event was about to happen and so quick and so final at the same time."

Kathleen grabbed Conor's arm and held tight as he continued, "Billy did the right thing. He did the only thing possible to save all of the passengers and their belongings and I am glad no one died."

"So am I."

A chill wind blew down the canal bed.

Conor finally said, "Let's hope all this violence and death is over."

Occasionally, the passengers could hear the Army regulars talking, laughing, or arguing amongst themselves. Most of this trip from Newark to Fairport was after dark and into the midnight hours, so the soldiers on the first watch went to bed very late. Around midnight, the boat pulled into Fairport and the captain looked back; the soldiers were gone. The boat continued; they were now only a couple of hours from Rochester. All the passengers were bedded down for the night, but Aaron was still awake. He joined the captain at the rudder.

"Cool night," said Aaron.

"The air pressure has fallen. We could get rain," replied the captain.

"That lieutenant was funny today."

"The lieutenant helped us a lot, he is a good man. He took care of those two attackers to administer the proper justice."

"Too bad Billy didn't kill 'em."

The captain voiced a third perspective on the shooting. "It's a good thing Billy didn't kill him. He's too young. Just like you, too young to value the importance of human life, and I shouldn't have put him in that position. I could have tossed the plank aside without shooting first. I could have refused them boarding. I should have taken the gun myself."

"It all worked out fine, Captain," said Aaron.

"We learned; that's what worked out."

Close to four o'clock in the morning, the boat made the infamous turn on the east side of the Genesee River onto the aqueduct crossing the swift-moving, spring-swollen river. Once across the river, the captain found a place to tie up. He immediately went down to Mrs. Connell.

"How's Margaret?"

"Resting comfortably."

"Should we wake up a doctor or wait till sun-up?" asked the captain.

"I think we should let her rest as long as we can."

"Okay, I am going to get some rest. I am tired."

"You must be exhausted from today's events."

"I will see you soon." The captain left for his berth.

Shortly after sunrise everyone was awake except for the captain and Margaret. Billy, Aaron, and the passengers had agreed to let both of them get their needed sleep. Aaron went out to look for a doctor in the Corn Hill section of the city just south of the canal. With the extra time, Conor and Kathleen decided to walk around the main streets of Rochester in the early Sunday morning hours. Conor picked up Mrs. Hurley's bag, as the bag always remained close by, and they set out to stroll down Front Street, looking in the shop windows. A store with housewares caught their attention. They dreamed of their home with the dishes, silverware, and accent pieces.

Conor looked across the river and saw a steeple north of the downtown area. "Look, a church."

"Yes, and a Catholic one at that," replied Kathleen, noticing the cross.

"Let's walk over and see."

"Do you think we have time?"

"Sure, I don't think they will leave without us."

The Meighans crossed the river and headed up State Street. They turned at Platt Street; the church was one block down. Seven o'clock Mass was just starting.

"Do we have time for Mass?" Kathleen asked Conor.

"Of course we do. It will take a while to find a doctor and examine Margaret."

The early morning Mass filled a void in their spiritual core. They decided to meet the priest, Father O'Reilly, after the service. The priest was a pleasant and pious man, and both Conor and Kathleen took an immediate liking to him. They explained they had met on a ship and were married by the captain under some dire circumstances. Father O'Reilly laughed.

"That is not a marriage recognized by God," he exclaimed.

"We understand," said Conor, "and we are anxious to get married in a church soon."

"I hope so. You are living in sin until you are married in the eyes of God."

"Yes, Father."

"Where are you headed?"

"To Canada first, and then we must decide where to settle."

"No more fornication until you have a proper marriage."

Conor decided not to give the details of their marriage on the steps of the church. "Yes, Father," was his reply.

After Mass, the Meighans walked to the south side of the canal in the Corn Hill district, home to many prominent Rochester citizens. The stately mansions and manicured lawns and gardens were a surprise this far into the frontier. As they walked, they discussed their future. They liked Rochester and Father O'Reilly, but they had only seen the wealthy section and the market district. They were unsure about the availability of jobs for unskilled laborers like Conor. They needed to wait before making any definite plans. Eventually they circled around and returned to the canal dock. The doctor was examining Margaret.

It was close to 10:00 a.m. before Captain White woke up; he could hear street noises and movement on the boat. He immediately knew it was late in the morning. He quickly got dressed and entered the dining area. The doctor was finishing his examination of Margaret.

"Hello, I am Captain White."

"I am Dr. Henry Briggs. Margaret is a very sick girl. I have asked her parents to leave the boat, so that I may care for her."

"I guessed it was typhus. Was I right?"

"Yes, I believe so. And the actions you took with the herbal medicine kept the illness at bay and probably saved her life."

"I have kept her quarantined from the others as best I could and no one else seems to be bothered by it."

"You are lucky. When it strikes, it spreads quickly,"

"Yes, I have seen it hit before," acknowledged the captain. The captain summoned Mr. and Mrs. Connell: "The doctor agrees that Margaret has a case of typhus. What are you going to do?"

"We have no choice but to get off and care for Margaret."

"Okay, I think that is best. I wish you luck. Margaret is a great girl, and I hope everything works out for you."

"Thank you for everything, Captain."

"You are welcome. You are in good hands. Rochester was hit with an epidemic of cholera a few years back and good care stopped the disease."

The captain's reference to the cholera epidemic and the good care was based on a religious revival that had taken place in Rochester and across the Western New York area, where certain lifestyles were believed to be the cause of cholera. The disease struck early and quickly to "drinkers, overeaters, and those who recklessly excited their stomachs at cards, horse racing, and other diversions."

The message delivered by the popular orator Obediah Dogberry was that good religious people who did not live a risky lifestyle were spared or recovered quickly, and that the reckless were the heathens and the disease was an act of God as a Divine intervention. The medical community had not yet caught up to the causes but was on the verge of identifying the microscopic organism responsible for cholera, even though it was not yet an accepted medical certainty, and therefore the religious reaction gathered momentum. Physicians recommended a good diet without fruits and vegetables, which were known to be hard on the stomach—additionally fresh air and rest were required; in other words, the lack of the excitement of night life.

Aaron and Billy helped Margaret off the boat into a waiting carriage. The Connells and their two younger children said goodbye and left the boat as well. It was a sad departure for the passengers. They were bonding as a group and leaving was difficult, but under the circumstances of possible death, the grief would be even more intense. For everyone's safety, the captain ordered another scrubbing of the boat, disregarding the belief of Divine intervention especially in the case of the virtuous child Margaret. The *Tuscarora* left Rochester just past noon, heading west.

Even though Captain White was upset about losing time, he understood the necessity for the delays. He maintained his cheerful disposition despite the disappointment of lost time. He felt this next leg of the journey between Rochester and Lockport should go fairly smoothly.

There were no locks to contend with for seventy miles and the scenery was pleasant, as they traveled along the lower ridge of the Niagara Escarpment overlooking the long fertile slope leading to Lake Ontario, known for its production of fruit. Several small towns had started along the canal for trade, goods, and services for the canalers, as well as budding industries; accordingly, every few miles contained one of these communities.

The first small settlement was Spencerport. The captain liked this section of the canal because of a series of low-lying bridges through the area. Any passengers riding on top of the boat had to be warned of the upcoming bridge. The first bridge was approaching.

"Low bridge. Everyone get down below," the captain bellowed. Even the captain had to duck from his perch on the boat or his head would have struck the low bridge.

Adams Basin was the same circumstance. "Low bridge, everybody get down."

Four such bridges kept the passengers running for cover on this afternoon. The captain reported that a few non-believers about the low bridges ended up in the water with a good-sized headache. The passengers laughed at the comical order and everyone scurrying to get below.

The packet made up lost time as they moved west with little interruption. The boat approached Lockport just after sunrise on Monday morning. The early morning rays of the sun created a spectacular scene as the boat came around the bend and the village came into view on the high cliffs above the canal. They were welcomed to the small western village of Lockport by the small black-capped chickadee whistling a song.

Nature promised a good day on this sunny morning as a warm breeze blew from the west into the faces of the canal travelers. The temperature and humidity were in perfect harmony, reminding the passengers of the brightest, cleanest, greenest day in Ireland. It felt like home.

Captain White announced that they were pulling up to Lockport and the boat would take a while to go through the five locks.

He suggested passengers exit the boat and visit the village while he moved the boat through the five tiers of locks. The passengers could see the cut layers of rock forming large steps, with gates to control the water.

The captain said to the small group watching on the topside of the packet, "This rock formed a ridge between Lockport and Tonawanda that was blasted out to form the canal. Many lives, arms, legs, and eyes were lost during construction due to the black powder blasts. The fragmented rock was then wheelbarrowed out—a tedious and laborious job."

"Truly amazing piece of engineering," said a passenger.

"Yes, Nathan Roberts is credited with the design construction of these locks," replied the captain, and then added, "A man named Orange Dibble invented a horse-drawn crane that lifted the blasted rock out of the canal bed. We will see the deep cut, after we pull out of Lockport, where the cranes were erected seventy feet apart for three miles to lift the rock out."

Lockport was a vibrant village that was exploding with commerce. The canal and the locks offered a natural stopping point for business dealings and a distribution point for needed supplies as well as a place to pick up locally made goods. The village was growing, and became an attraction point for the skilled and unskilled labor forces. All the elements existed for successful economic and industrial growth.

The canal rose seventy feet at Lockport through a limestone ridge that was blasted to make way for the canal. A westbound canal boat had to pass through these five locks on the right to make this rise. There were another five locks on the left to lower eastbound boats heading towards Albany. When the boat pulled up to the lower lock, the passengers exited the packet and walked up a steep incline to the main streets of Lockport. The early morning merchants were hustling about to start their week. Conor and Kathleen walked to the first intersection where Church Street crossed a bridge and met Main Street.

"I like this town," said Kathleen.

"Yes, it has a good feel to it," agreed Conor.

"Let's get some breakfast over there," Kathleen said, pointing to a small restaurant next to a hotel on Main Street.

"Okay," said Conor.

They entered the restaurant and sat close to the front window to watch the activity of the street. A waitress, who was also the cook, came by and asked if they wanted "The Breakfast."

"What's 'The Breakfast'?" asked Kathleen.

"It's the good Irish breakfast that you have been waiting for," said the waitress.

Conor had been waiting for years to get a substantial breakfast, or any meal for that matter. They ordered the restaurant's specialty, "The Breakfast." A few townspeople people had already arrived at the restaurant for their "Breakfast" and shortly the cook came around the counter and became the waitress again. She brought the breakfast of eggs, sausage, toast, and small bowl of oatmeal. She returned with a small pot of tea.

"You are new here. You're traveling the canal?" the waitress asked in an Irish brogue.

"Yes we are," answered Conor.

"Where you headed, if you don't mind me asking?"

"Canada."

"Canada? You don't want to go to Canada. It's too cold." The waitress was half serious and half playing with her two guests.

"It's just across the lake. How much colder can it be?"

"You don't want to go to Canada. Right here is where you want to be. Ain't that right, Mr. Hogan?" she said, and turned to address the gentleman at the table across the room.

"There are a lot of opportunities right here, if you are looking for one," agreed Mr. Hogan.

"We are looking for a job opportunity but we must go into Upper Canada first."

"What for?" asked the waitress.

Kathleen looked up at the waitress. She could not help but like the forward-talking lady. "We need to meet with some people in Canada."

"Ah yes, family obligations. Some special message from Ireland, I suppose. I could imagine what message me Ma would send to me: 'Come back and clean the kitchen, Bridget.'" She laughed at her own family discord. "Yeah, I'd go back in a fancy dress and say, 'See, I ain't the tramp you thought I was.'" Bridget turned and went back towards her kitchen filled with dirty dishes and pots and pans in heaped-up stacks. She stopped and turned to Conor and Kathleen. "You have a good trip."

Kathleen replied, "Thank you, Bridget."

Mr. Hogan got up from his seat and walked over to the Meighans' table. "Do you have a skill?"

"I can do a lot of things. I was a farmer in Ireland so any general maintenance I can do," replied Conor.

"A farmer? That means a strong back."

"Yes, it does."

"If you decide to come back to Lockport, come and see me. My name is Bill Hogan."

"I am Conor Meighan and this is my wife, Kathleen."

"What is it that you do, Mr. Hogan?" asked Kathleen.

"I am a foreman for a construction company. The state is widening and deepening the canal just west of here. It's all rock. We have been hired to blast the rock and move it out. I am going to need some strong backs." He hesitated. "Do you like the whiskey?"

"I drink very little and then it's only a pint."

"Good to hear. The Irish boys here like their whiskey. Some days are a slow go."

Conor thanked him for the opportunity and Mr. Hogan left the restaurant.

Bridget returned. "Anything else you like?"

"No, we're fine," said Conor.

"Mr. Hogan is a good man. He works hard and raises a good

family. It's sad though; his wife got the cough and passed away. He has to raise his little ones. He'd be a good catch."

"Yes, he seems like a nice man," said Kathleen.

"I'll be looking for you to return this way," announced Bridget as the Meighans left the restaurant. Once outside and a couple of doors away from the restaurant, Conor reacted by letting out a squeal, "Yeah," he yelled. "I have a job if we want to come back here."

"'Tis true," said Kathleen with equal excitement.

The couple strolled back to the packet, which had been raised to the upper level for its final journey to Tonawanda and Buffalo. The two hopped aboard as the boat pulled away and headed into the heavy rock walls that lined the canal. Conor saw the job of blasting the rock that Mr. Hogan and the Captain had described. There was plenty of work for a long time.

As they passed the "cut," Conor stated to Captain White, "Mrs. Hurley mentioned how this was 'the longest canal made in the least time, with the least experience, for the least money and the greatest public good,' and now I see how significant those words were."

"I agree, this canal has been a magnificent enterprise for the state and for the development of the country," said the captain. "It used to take a month of hard journey by boat, with portages and carries and going out to Lake Ontario before the canal was built. Now the journey can be made under much safer conditions in about a week."

"Safer, is it? Highwaymen attacked us and Mrs. Hurley lost her life. Certainly faster and more efficient, but I don't know about safer."

"Yes, we have had our troubles, but before the canal was built, the boats would travel into Lake Ontario. That lake can be very treacherous at any time, not just during a storm, so many boats were sunk trying to get from Oswego to Niagara and going back the other way. Besides, there was constant harassment from our neighbors to the north—Canada. Assaults were made on the shipping boats and the guilty were on both sides of the lake, but the attacks were about economic advantage, and gaining access to the resources of the interior of North America. Lake Ontario, and the St. Lawrence River for that matter, were not safe routes."

"Are passenger boats harassed?" asked Conor.

"No, just the cargo ships. You see, the inland waterway is a much better and more efficient operation."

"I see," said Conor, relieved at the good news about passenger boats.

Within a few hours, the boat arrived at Tonawanda. The docks along the canal were busy with the activity of loading and unloading cargo for the canal voyages. Tonawanda was the gateway to the upper Niagara River, where the boats turned south to go upriver towards Buffalo. Likewise, the opposite way, Tonawanda was the gateway for the canal going east towards Albany. This was Conor and Kathleen's departure point, and they thanked the captain for his skillful voyage up the canal.

They took a moment to remember Mrs. Hurley. "I am sad that Mrs. Hurley will not have her reunion with her daughter," said Kathleen.

"Yes. It is very disappointing that she did not complete her journey," said Conor.

The captain confessed, "I regret placing Mrs. Hurley on the deck the night she died."

Kathleen tried to comfort him. "It could have happened to anyone leaning over the edge to watch for logs."

"I still feel responsible," said the captain. "I will never forget her. Good luck to both of you on your journey and may God be with you."

"Good travels to you, too," said Conor and, turning to Billy and Aaron, "I wish you well for the future."

"Thank you." Billy pointed across the canal and said, "Anguish's Tavern is a good place to have a meal and a beer, but be careful, it gets a little crazy later in the evening."

"Good to know," said Conor.

Conor and Kathleen waved goodbye as the packet boat pulled away and they started their last leg of the trip to Buffalo. Captain White was perched in his skipper's seat in the rear of the boat. He made one last turn and waved as the boat headed around the bend to the Niagara River.

"I feel like I am leaving my family again," said Kathleen.

"I guess so, even though I didn't really have the chance to say goodbye," said Conor. "Do you know what arrangements Mrs. Hurley made for her arrival in Tonawanda to continue her passage to Peterborough?"

"No, I don't think she mentioned it," said Kathleen. "Let's walk down to the travel office and check for reservations."

Along the southern edge of the canal, they found the travel office and entered.

"Good morning," said the elderly gentlemen, who was dressed in a well-worn suit and sat behind a grated window.

"Good morning," said Kathleen. "Do you have a reservation for a Mrs. Ellen Hurley?"

"Why yes, I do. Are you Mrs. Hurley?" asked the agent.

"No, I am not. Unfortunately Mrs. Hurley was killed in a terrible accident on the canal. We have her belongings and are taking them to her daughter in Canada."

"Oh, how dreadful," said the agent. "I shall cancel the reservation."

Conor spoke up. "We would like to use the reservation and continue her route. How was she getting to Canada?"

"Mrs. Hurley had a reservation for a coach to Lewiston. I don't know her plan after Lewiston. Maybe she was taking a boat to York, I mean Toronto. They changed the name a few years back and I can never remember Toronto."

"Mrs. Hurley was eventually going to Peterborough in Canada," said Kathleen.

"Peterborough, where's that?" asked the agent.

"It is in Canada, that's all I know, but she was going in this direction to get there. Can we get to Canada from Lewistown?"

"That's Lewiston, madam," said the agent. "Yes, you can. You can go across the lake or go across the river. Both ways will get into Canada."

"Can we use the reservation to go to Lewiston?" Conor asked again.

"Sure, you may," answered the agent. "The next coach leaves tomorrow morning at seven o'clock."

"We will be here," said Conor.

Tonawanda was a bustling village that had developed trade industries like the other border towns along the canal. The village was becoming a large lumber supply area. Stacks of hardwoods were arranged along the docks for shipment, including hickory, oak, black cherry, and maple, which would become home furniture, desks, wall coverings, pianos, and ships. There were stacks of softwood for construction of homes, factories, and barns. A railroad terminus was being built for this boom in the lumber and commodities trading as well as for moving people.

Conor and Kathleen checked into a hotel for the night and took a short rest before going to dinner.

"I feel like my body is still in motion from the travel on the packet," said Conor.

"I know how you feel; I still sense the sway of the water too."

Conor checked Mrs. Hurley's bag to account for her money. Kathleen had been tracking expenses and writing down expenditures. "All the money balances, we're accurate," said Kathleen.

"I still am angry over that thief taking your money in New York."

"He gained a small fortune as a reward for his immoral and criminal deeds," answered Kathleen.

"It's not right," said Conor, closing the bag and hiding it under the bed.

At dinnertime, Conor and Kathleen went to Anguish's Tavern which Billy had pointed out. When they walked into the dark tavern they stopped for a moment so their eyes could adjust. Their hesitation caused all the patrons to turn and look to size them up. Once they determined the newcomers were no threat, they returned to their conversations, ignoring the new arrivals.

"Let's take the table over there," said Conor, pointing to a table near the rear. They walked in silence to the empty table.

Many Irish laborers were at the bar drinking and celebrating the end of the workday, even though it was Monday. Conor and Kathleen felt like celebrating too; they had traveled a long way and overcome many obstacles and hardships along the way.

"What'll you have?" came a voice from somewhere near the bar.

"Something to eat," Conor said towards the bar.

"I meant to drink; my wife will serve the food."

Conor could now see the man behind the bar. "I'll have a beer."

"Anything for the lady?"

Conor looked at Kathleen and she shook her head. "No, she's fine."

Within a minute, the barman brought a jar of brew. "This is a local pale ale brewed by some German immigrants in the area." It was clear that the barman was Irish and, when setting the glass on the table, he leaned down closer to Conor. "'Tis a shame there is no Guinness here."

"Ah, such a shame," answered Conor, feeling the warmth of an Irish welcome.

"My name is Paddy O'Toole," said the barman, holding out his hand.

"I am Conor Meighan and this is my wife Kathleen," Conor said, taking the hand and solidifying the greeting.

"Nice to meet you, Mr. Conor."

"No, my first name is Conor."

"Your first name? I thought Conor was a last name. Are you related to the Conors who live up the canal road about a mile?"

"No, I don't know anyone in the area, and I was named after my great-grandfather on my mother's side.'

"Oh, I see." While he was speaking, a short, portly woman appeared at the table "I'll leave you with Ma," said Paddy.

"I heard you wanted something to eat?"

"Yes, what's for dinner?" asked Conor.

"Ham and potatoes," said the woman.

Conor looked at Kathleen and she nodded. "We will have some," he said.

The beer was light and smooth compared to the dark, heavy porter he was used to in Ireland and it went down easily. The wait for dinner was not long and "Ma" returned with two plates. "If you need anything else just call me, I'm Caitlín."

"Thank you, Caitlín," said Kathleen..

After the meal, Caitlín returned and offered a homemade apple pie made with apples from the New York fruit belt area along Lake Ontario.

"Apple pie?" said Kathleen.."I would love some apple pie."

"I don't think I ever had apple pie," said Conor.

"Oh, you are in for a treat," said Caitlín.

"I'll have another beer to go with the pie," stated Conor.

As they were enjoying their dessert, the rowdy bar erupted into song and patriotic Irish ballads were the songs of choice. Each new singer tried to outdo the previous balladeer by singing louder or hitting higher and lower notes. Laughter and gaiety filled the bar. Conor sang along with some of the songs as the beer eased his inhibition.

Kathleen said, "I should have brought my violin." Conor had ordered his third beer.

"Are you sure you want another beer?"

"Yes, this is too much fun," answered Conor.

Kathleen became concerned and felt nervous at the bar patrons' exuberance for drinking. The songs quickly turned into songs of rebellion and the heroes of Irish resistance to English rule. Kathleen's anxiety was growing. "I think it's time we should go."

"Oh no, not yet. You sure you don't want a nip of something?" Conor was starting to slur his words.

"No, nothing for me," she said nervously. Conor was having a good time with the festive atmosphere along with a few drinks and the company of the woman he loved. He was not ready to leave the celebration. Kathleen gave in and tolerated the party atmosphere for a few more songs. By now they were starting to sing the same songs a second time and Conor was on his fifth beer.

The high-alcohol German beer was affecting Conor, who rarely drank and never experienced this level of intoxication. He was happy, but Kathleen's anxiety was turning to a mixture of fear and anger. She was truly uncomfortable and the relaxed level of propriety among the patrons became easily noticeable. They spoke with ease about things that were kept at bay in a sober state: such topics as the overthrow of England and the persecution of Anglicans, and the ease of using curse words, troubled Kathleen.

"We need to go now!" she said with authority. It was going to be hard enough walking past the partyers to the door but entering the street with Conor in his drunken state scared her further.

Conor saw the change in her mood although he did not understand why, but as drunk as he was, he realized it was time to leave. He stood up and weaved from side to side. Kathleen grabbed him around the waist and started for the door. Conor cheered Ireland as he walked past his fellow countrymen. A big hoopla erupted in agreement. With Kathleen holding him up, he waved as they exited the bar.

Kathleen walked her husband down the darkened street towards their hotel. She listened carefully for footsteps behind them, a response she would never shake. She heard nothing.

They passed a house and a barking dog ran up to the fence in the front yard. The dog surprised and scared Kathleen. Conor tried to pet the dog, but neither Kathleen nor the dog wanted his erratic movements. Kathleen caught her breath and, within a short distance, they reached the hotel. The clerk watched Kathleen maneuver Conor through the lobby; he was amused. When she entered the room, the clerk showed up with a bucket. "Just in case," he said.

Conor sat on the edge of the bed to take his shoes off. "Kathleen, you are wonderful. I love you, my dear wife."

"Yes dear, I love you too," she said matter-of-factly.

As soon as Conor lay on the bed, the room started to rotate. Soon Conor needed the bucket. The celebration of the fine dinner, drink, and song was over.

Chapter 12

Lewiston

A t 6:00 a.m. there was a pounding on the door. "Mr. and Mrs.
Meighan, time to get up," announced the overnight clerk.
Kathleen heard the knock but Conor was sound asleep.
"We're awake," she answered back.

"Very good," came the reply as she heard footsteps trail off down the hall.

"Conor, time to wake up," she said and shook the near lifeless body next to her.

"Oh, what do you want?" growled Conor.

"It's time to get up and catch the coach."

"Can't we take a later one?"

"No, now get up," she insisted as she pulled on his arm.

"Not so fast. My head hurts."

Conor slowly sat up, squinting at the early morning sunlight. He groaned again and again as he moved, but finally, he rose to his feet and worked his way to the water basin to splash cold water on his face. "That doesn't feel any better," he said.

They got dressed for the day's travel and prepared to go downstairs for a cup of tea before leaving. Kathleen made the bed.

"I don't think you have to do that," said Conor.

"I don't want the hotel to think I don't make my bed in the morning."

"Humph." Conor was not in the mood to make needless decisions or arguments.

They went downstairs and had tea and toast in a room off the lobby. Just before 7:00 a.m. they left the hotel to catch the coach. Conor moved slowly as he carried Kathleen's bag.

At the travel office the coach was waiting along with another young couple. The driver took their bag and said, "I'm Tim Clancy and we are being joined by Bob and Ethel Ostrander."

"Nice to meet all of you," said both Kathleen and Conor.

"We're heading for Youngstown and making stops in Niagara Falls and Lewiston," announced Tim, who could not have been more than twenty-four years old.

"Niagara Falls? We're stopping in Niagara Falls?" asked Kathleen.

"We are," replied Tim. "Would you like to see the waterfalls?"

"Oh, that would be grand." Kathleen was excited at the thought of seeing the world-famous falls.

"Well, step into the coach and we'll get started."

The passengers climbed aboard and Tim pulled the coach and four-horse team away from the office. The carriage headed down a road known as Portage Road which had been used as a land trail around the falls for centuries. The native Indians, traders, military troops, and now immigrants looking for a new home had traveled the Portage Road route. Tim would take a detour off the road to make the stop at the falls.

Conor was feeling better but the rough road made his head hurt. He slouched in his seat and placed his head on Kathleen's shoulder. Kathleen thought to herself, "You got what you deserved." No more needed to be said until Bob Ostrander asked, "Are you feeling all right?"

Conor just mumbled, "Yes, I'm fine."

Kathleen was not going to let the moment pass. "He had a little too much drink last night."

"Oh, one of those nights," said Ethel.

Kathleen had found a comrade. "Yes, too much beer and song."

Conor found enough energy to say, "It was a great night, I loved it, right dear?"

"Yes, that's right, dear," she said with a note of playful sarcasm. "You loved it and now you are paying for it."

"I won't be doing that again any time soon," said Conor.

"No, you won't," was Kathleen's reply.

Conor snuck in the last word. "But it was fun."

Kathleen shook her head in that knowing gesture of "I'll make sure you don't do that again." At the same time she felt a wave of concern, she shivered at the thought of the bar and the loss of control under the influence of alcohol. She leaned back and took a deep breath.

As the carriage approached the Falls at Niagara, the passengers could see the mist of water floating up into the air through the windows of the carriage. Gradually the roar of the water could be heard and, as they got closer, the sound grew louder. The excitement of seeing the falls up close permeated the coach. Conor and Kathleen switched seats so that Kathleen could see better out the windows as they approached the misty air, a by-product of the thundering water.

The swift-moving waters above quickly developed into the rapids. They passed an island in the river, where people could cross a small bridge over the rapids. The carriage pulled up to a stopping place, at which point they knew they were close. The door of the coach opened and even though it was a clear sunny day, they could feel the moisture in the air against their faces.

"Here is Niagara Falls," said Tim.

"This is exciting," said Kathleen as she stepped away from the coach. "Look there." She pointed across the smaller American Falls to the larger horseshoe-shaped falls on the other side of the island.

"The water, the roar, the mist—this is truly a Wonder of the World," continued Kathleen.

"That's Canada over there," added Tim.

"So close," said Conor. The bright sunlight hurt Conor's eyes but the moist air felt good on his head as the mist drifted through the air from the water cascading over the river's edge. It reminded him of the frequent mist in Ireland.

They walked to the edge of the river and looked down the mighty 175-foot drop to the bottom. A constant rainbow glistened in the gorge of the river.

Tim explained, "The top side of this ridge is known as the Niagara Escarpment, a rocky rim of limestone going along New York State into Canada and up as far as Lake Huron, one of the Great Lakes. This ridge also forms Niagara Falls. The rock is so dense and hard that the constant flow of the Niagara River did not erode the upper riverbed, but underneath the hard limestone becomes a softer level of shale.

"Hard on top and soft underneath, this erosion occurs slowly but steadily over the centuries. The ridge keeps moving backwards or upstream as the lower level supporting shale washes away and the upper-level rock collapses under its own weight. You can see the collection of rocks at the bottom; that is limestone fallen from the last cycle of erosion."

Kathleen looked across a section of the river to an island. "So that island will someday fall into the lower river?"

"Yes, but we will be long gone when that happens. By the way, that is Goat Island."

"Where does the water originate?" asked Bob Ostrander.

"The Niagara River is fed from the four upper Great Lakes: Erie, Huron, Michigan, and Superior," said Tim.

"That's a lot of water," said Ethel.

"Yes it is, and it flows out into Lake Ontario to the St. Lawrence River and into the Atlantic Ocean," added Tim.

A pensive Bob thought out loud: "No wonder they built the Erie Canal. You can't sail a ship up this river."

"No, you can't get a boat up the river, but they didn't want to either, because of the troubles between Upper Canada and the United States."

"Yes, we heard that on the packet," said Conor.

"We don't have time to walk over to Goat Island. We must get moving," Tim announced to the group. He waited a few more minutes and then called the passengers to the coach. They boarded and headed back to Portage Road to resume their journey down to Lewiston.

"Such a sight," said Kathleen. "Did you hear the power of that water crashing to the rocks below?"

"Oh, I was so amazed," said Ethel. "Do you think many boats get caught in the rapid flow and get swept over? No one could survive such a treacherous ordeal."

"I'm sure accidents occur," said Conor. "God bless those who fall over."

The gloom of the thought settled the discussion of the falls as the carriage headed north towards Lake Ontario.

Bob and Ethel Ostrander were traveling to Youngstown to catch a ferry to Toronto. The small village of Youngstown sat at the intersection of the Niagara River and Lake Ontario. They were worried about the crossing. "I hope there's no problem leaving New York or entering British North America," Bob stated.

"Why, what do you mean?" asked Conor.

"There's a lot of trouble at the border. There have been clashes over the land boundaries."

"Yes, we heard that on the packet."

"There's tension, and British soldiers are posted at all the border stations looking for troublemakers trying to enter Canada."

"Where's the trouble? Where are these border stations?" Conor asked, hoping to pinpoint the location of the soldiers.

"From what I'm told, they're everywhere along the river and the lake."

The news made Conor nervous about being questioned by British troops. "There's no place to enter without going through all that scrutiny?" he asked.

"Not that I know of. And besides bounty hunters, the marshals are watching for runaway slaves on the American side. So you get the inquiries and inspections on both sides of the border."

Conor looked at Kathleen, who was also listening intently. They both took a deep breath. There was no discussion on the coach, but they needed a plan.

Tim brought the carriage into the small village of Lewiston on the Niagara River, where it flowed north away from Niagara Falls but before reaching Youngstown and Lake Ontario. The Falls originated at Lewiston 12,000 years earlier and the thundering water had eroded the base layer of shale causing the Falls to slowly retreat seven miles upstream.

Conor was looking out the window of the coach where he could see the swift-moving water confined to the rock canyons of the riverbed. It was full of treacherous whirlpools, eddies, and currents. Conor saw that a person could not swim across the river and expect to survive the swirling waters. Also, the river between the

Falls and Lewiston had sheer rock canyons, which made climbing the walls nearly impossible. Sneaking across the river from New York to Canada in either direction was an unlikely feat.

Conor and Kathleen exited the carriage. While Tim took care of his business of delivering mail and other goods, the two Meighans walked over to a small park across the way. Conor asked, "Should we just try to sail across and see what happens?"

"What if they detain you and figure out who you are?" asked Kathleen.

"How are they going to know me? I'm half-way around the world from Ireland."

"If they search us, they're going to find the money. What do we tell them?"

"Tell them the truth: we're delivering the money to Mrs. Hurley's family."

"An English soldier assigned to the American-Canadian border will seize the money and that'll be the last we see of it. He'll put us in jail for smuggling a quarter of it and he'll keep the rest. What are we going to say: 'No, there is more, he didn't report all of it and we would like it back?'"

"You're right, we can't chance it. You saw the river; it is impossible to cross undetected." Just then Tim walked across and announced the coach was leaving. Conor decided to take a chance. "Tim, you're from Ireland, right?"

"Yes, I came here when I was twelve years old with my family."

"You can't trust the British any more here in America than you could in Ireland, can you?"

"No, they're the same here as they are there. My advice is don't trust them at all."

"We need to get into Canada without any British hassle. Do you know an easy way to do that?"

Tim looked at Conor. He thought to himself, "Another Irishman with a secret; on the run from something."

Conor did not allow the silence to force him into disclosing his reason for asking.

Tim answered, "Your best bet is to cross here at Lewiston."

"But the river is treacherous."

"Yes, it is," replied Tim, who talked more slowly and started to measure Conor.

"Where are you from again?" asked Tim.

"County Clare." Conor knew something was disturbing Tim.

"Cad is ainm duit?" Tim said suddenly in the Irish native tongue, asking for Conor's name.

"Connacher Ó Miadhachain atá orm," Conor answered with his name. He knew he was being tested for something and continued, "Is leor nod don eolach," which was an Irish saying reminding him that a hint is sufficient for the wise.

Tim reverted to English after realizing Conor was fluent in Irish and most likely a true Irish national. "There may be a way to get you across, undetected."

"You're being cautious about something."

Tim eased his reluctance. "Go to the tailor shop," said Tim as he pointed down the street, "and see Josiah. Tell him your troubles. He can help you and you can trust him."

"Go raibh maith agat," said Conor.

"Beannacht Dé ort! (God bless you!)" added Kathleen.

The Meighans waved farewell to Tim and the Ostranders as the stagecoach headed down the street and disappeared from sight. The two travelers walked towards the tailor's shop with Kathleen carrying her bag and Conor carrying Mrs. Hurley's bag.

When they entered the tailor's shop, a middle-aged man approached them.

"Can I help you?"

"We would like to see Josiah."

"I'm Josiah, can I help you with something?"

"I was sent to see you. I was told that you could help us."

"In what way; do you need a new suit or something?"

"No, we need to get into Canada without the knowledge of the British troops."

"Really, why did you come to see me?"

"Tim Clancy sent us here to see you."

"Tim did, did he?" Josiah was just as cautious as Tim. "And why are you afraid of the British?"

"The British would like to catch me for some things that happened back in Ireland."

"Canada is controlled by the British. So why do you want to go there?"

"To meet a family there."

"I don't support rebels and I don't support clandestine meetings between rebels."

"I'm not a rebel. I got caught up in a bad situation, that's all."

"I'm sorry but I can't help you."

Kathleen spoke up. "Please help us. We are not troublemakers. We are just trying to start a fresh life."

"I'm sorry, but I think Tim sent you to the wrong tailor shop."

Conor and Kathleen left the shop dejected. "Where do we go now?" asked Kathleen.

"I don't know. Let's go across the street to the tavern."

"No beer," said Kathleen with a serious tone and a testy look.

"No beer. My head still hurts. I didn't drink that much but it was potent beer."

Kathleen grunted as they headed across the street and entered Hustler's Tavern on Centre Street. The bar had a few mid-afternoon regulars. They took a table in the corner as the barman approached. "You getting a new set of clothes?" the barman asked.

"No, why?" replied Conor.

"I saw you coming over from the tailor shop," he answered, pointing to the shop through the front window. "I thought the tailor was going to make you a new coat. He does that to welcome new folks to the village."

"No, we just talked to him."

"Oh," said the barman in a baffled voice. "What'll you have?"

"Tea," said Kathleen.

The barman turned to Conor. "Would you like a cocktail?"

"A cocktail?"

"We are known for our cocktail. The drink contains a mixture of gin, sugar, and bitters with the tail feather of a stuffed cockerel. It is smooth and fine for the lady too. Even Fenimore Cooper wrote about us in his book."

"No, we'll just have tea," Kathleen said firmly.

"Two teas. Where are you from?"

"Ireland," answered Conor.

"As if I couldn't tell. And why are you in Lewiston?"

"We're just passing through, if you must know," answered Kathleen. "You ask a lot of questions."

"Just being friendly. We're a small town here."

When the barman left the table, Kathleen leaned over and whispered, "This is a strange place here. Don't you have a funny feeling about this town?"

"It is strange, but I'm not sure what to think about it. I don't know what to do from here. I'd rather not go to Youngstown and chance crossing under the eyes of the British. I wonder if there is a way to cross here on our own?"

"You saw the river. It is too dangerous to cross without knowing where to go or having knowledge of the river."

Conor sat back in his chair and thought of the different possibilities. He considered buying a boat with Mrs. Hurley's money or renting a boat and dressing like fishermen for a trip onto the lake, but such thoughts were not realistic. Conor sat there watching out the window sipping his tea. He saw a man nervously walk down Centre Street, stop and check up and down the street, and then enter the tailor shop. Shortly after, the man left the shop and hustled back in the same direction.

A few minutes passed and another man entered the shop but he was not nervous. He was confident and self-assured, a man who could be rough with people or pleasant, however he chose. About twenty minutes passed and the man left the shop. He looked across the street at the tavern and walked over.

When he entered the bar, he was greeted the same way as

the Meighans were, with a series of questions. Only this man acknowledged that Josiah had offered to make him a new coat. The barman's approach changed; he was friendlier but the questions continued. The barman introduced himself as "Hank" and the new visitor said, "Just call me Gunner."

Kathleen was the first to pick up on the scenario. There was a relationship between the tailor shop and whether or not you received a new coat. The coat had significance. The next level was the barman. She watched with interest for the next step with the man and what the barman would do. He informed the barman that it would be about an hour and a half for his coat, which he thought was fast to tailor a new coat. He could use a new coat, and a free coat was even better.

The barman returned to the Meighan table. "Anything else?"

"Could we just sit for a while?" asked Kathleen.

"Sure, what are you waiting for?"

"We're just passing time," answered Kathleen.

"Yea, take as much time as you need."

"You have a slight British accent, don't you?"

"Yes, but don't say it too loudly. The British are not popular around here. I'm trying to lose the accent and the connection."

"Why do you want to lose your connection?"

"This town was burnt to the ground by the British during the war. All buildings and homes were lost except the Hustler Tavern. That was twenty-five years ago; most of the people here were young and impressionable. The impression has lasted and it was not good for the British."

"So why don't you settle where the British are more acceptable, like Canada?"

"This is home now. I have a job. I like the pub life and living on the border is like living on the edge—you never know what's going to happen."

Kathleen had not developed enough rapport with Hank to ask further questions so she let the conversation lapse and Hank returned to the bar.

The conversation in the bar turned to personal stories of living on the frontier and politics, neither of which Conor or Kathleen wanted to discuss. They kept to themselves at their table, but Hank and Gunner could be heard bantering throughout the establishment. Gunner had traveled a long way to Lewiston and the beer loosened his tongue. At one point Gunner stated that he was a bounty hunter looking for runaway slaves and two men in particular. Conor and Kathleen could not hear names, but Gunner had traveled from Virginia to find these men.

"Good luck," said Hank as Gunner left to get his coat at the tailor shop. As soon as Gunner had left the bar, Hank and a couple of regulars had a laugh but no words were exchanged. Kathleen was puzzled.

Shortly, Gunner left the tailor shop wearing his new brightly colored coat. Hank said, "There he goes." They laughed again.

Kathleen asked, "What's so funny?"

Hank looked down the bar at the regulars and said, "Aw, never mind, it's nothing."

The next time Hank came to the table, Kathleen said, "You asked us when we came in if the tailor was making us a coat. What's the deal with the coat?"

"I told you, they're gifts for new folks to town."

"But he's not staying, he's just a bounty hunter passing through. It is a nice gift for someone just passing through."

Hank grabbed a chair at the next table and slid it between Conor and Kathleen. "You said that I asked a lot of questions; now it is you who are asking too many questions. Just mind your own business."

Kathleen said, "We asked Josiah for help and he wouldn't. It seems that he helps some but not others."

Hank looked at them for a moment and then turned and looked back at the bar. Although no one was looking directly at him, he knew most were listening. "That's true, he helps some but not others." Hank rose from the chair and returned to the bar.

Kathleen leaned in to speak to Conor "They don't trust us. It's not about money, they're not looking for money, it's something else."

"If we could figure out what these people are up to, then we would know what to do."

The afternoon sun was lowering in the western sky and cast a yellowish hue over the small village. It was a beautiful ending to a beautiful day but Conor and Kathleen were distraught at getting stuck so close to the border.

"Maybe we should forget the crossing," said Kathleen.

"No, we need to continue our journey into Canada even at the risk of detention, arrest, or other trouble; there is no other option. We have a responsibility to Mrs. Hurley and her family. Anything less is an affront to our values and that would haunt us forever."

Conor was looking out the window of the tavern when a coach came down Centre Street and stopped in front of the tailor shop. Tim Clancy stepped down from the driver's seat. "Look, there's Tim," exclaimed Conor.

Tim walked around the back of the carriage and disappeared from sight. "Where did he go?" asked Kathleen.

"I don't know. I think he went into the tailor shop."

"What should we do?" asked Kathleen.

"I'll wait for him to come out and then I'll tell him that Josiah didn't help us," answered Conor.

Five minutes went by and Tim was out on the street.

"Look, there he is," said Kathleen. But Tim was already on his way across the street towards the tavern. Conor rose and was preparing to leave in case Tim was heading somewhere other than the tavern. However, Tim walked in Hustler's door and greeted Hank at the bar. He looked to his right as Conor was walking up to him.

"Tim, can we talk to you for a minute?" asked Conor.

"I was just coming to see you."

"How did you know we were here?"

"Nothing happens in this town without people knowing about it. I knew where to find you."

Tim and Conor went over and sat down with Kathleen. "Beer," yelled Tim in no particular direction.

"Coming up," was the reply from across the room.

"Josiah won't help us," Conor started.

"Yeah, I know, he told me."

"What can we do?" was Conor's rapid and desperate reply.

"Slow down," started Tim. "I talked with him and he will help you. You just have to be patient while we set up your crossing."

"You must know Josiah pretty well for him to change his mind." asked Kathleen.

"He trusts me."

"Thank you for helping us," added Kathleen.

"We'll see how it goes. Wait here until five o'clock and go down the street to the Presbyterian church. Go inside and see Christopher."

"Go inside a Presbyterian church?" asked Kathleen.

"Yes, do it, and don't worry about being inside a Presbyterian church." After Tim gave this instruction, he got up and left the tavern and went to his carriage. As fast as he had come, he was gone.

At five o'clock, Conor and Kathleen went down Centre Street to the First Presbyterian Church as Tim had instructed them to do. They entered the church and were greeted by Christopher, who did not ask questions or want to make small talk. He thrust them to a back room. The room was dark. Christopher rolled back a small rug and then picked boards out of the floor.

"Down here, and quickly." He shone a candle above the hole to illuminate a ladder.

Conor went first. It was dark and damp and he waited for Kathleen to make her way down the worn ladder. Christopher whispered, "Don't make any noise. I'll be back in about five hours." The remaining floorboards were replaced and they found themselves in total darkness.

Kathleen was disgusted. "We walked down here in bright daylight and sat all day in the town pub and now we have to sit in a dingy basement."

"Shh," Conor whispered softly.

"And we're in a Presbyterian church, not a Catholic church."

To Kathleen, it seemed like an eternity sitting in the dark for the five long hours. Then they heard a faint noise followed by footsteps getting closer. The floorboards were being removed. Kathleen had had enough of the church cellar. She followed Conor up the ladder, not knowing if her weight would break a rung and send her crashing to the floor. She thought, "Then I'd be stuck here for another five hours."

Christopher helped her off the ladder into the church room but he did not replace the floorboards. Shortly a figure appeared on the ladder following her to the top. The figure came into view. It was a black woman. "Where did she come from?" wondered Kathleen. Another image came into view—a child, followed by another child, and then a black man appeared at the top of the ladder.

"Where were you?" asked Kathleen.

"We were down the passageway from you," answered the black woman.

"You were there the entire time?"

"Yes, ma'am."

"Why didn't you say something?"

"We didn't know who you were or why you were there."

"For five hours?"

"We waited for many hours, for as long as it would take."

Kathleen looked at Conor, distressed but amazed at their discipline.

"Come," ordered Christopher as he led them forward to the front of the church and over to a side door. Christopher had his hand on the handle of the door when he stopped, looking back. "Stay close to me and don't say anything." He opened the door and exited into the darkness of the night. The six of them followed.

The route went three blocks towards the river and down a pathway towards a house on the edge of the cliff. It was a moonless night and vision was limited. They were led into a house, through darkened rooms, and down a set of stairs, followed by a second set of stairs, then a third. Eventually the group went down six sets of stairs before going through a door that led back outside. One by one, they descended the long, steep stairways to the riverbed.

A long, deep rowboat was waiting. Each evader stepped into the boat and was ordered to go to the back of the boat and lie on the floor. Four or five assistants were organizing the boat but Conor could not make out the people.

A familiar voice whispered, "Just stay down and be quiet and you'll be fine." Conor looked up and saw Tim Clancy.

"Okay," he answered.

The boat shifted as it moved away from shore. The effects of the current could be immediately felt as the front moved left and the back swung around to the right. Strong strokes from the rower straightened the boat and subsequent strokes took the boat to the middle of the river.

The silhouette of the rower showed a large muscular man, who let up his hard pulls and allowed the boat to float down-stream. Then a couple more strokes and the boat headed towards the Canadian side of the river. Kathleen shivered in the damp, cool April evening. The lingering mist from the falls chilled her entire body. She snuggled into Conor. He placed his arm around her to comfort her; she was looking for warmth.

A thud indicated they had arrived in Canada. The six passengers were hustled out of the boat and up the bank. A horse and buggy were waiting for the Negro family. They were loaded into the buggy and pulled away into the night. Tim led the Meighans down a narrow road to a house. Instead of entering the house, Tim took them around to a barn.

"Wait here." Tim disappeared into the barn. They could hear horses stirring. A wagon emerged from the dark barn. There were two people in the wagon: one was Tim and the other was the rower from the boat. "Get in the back under the sacks," Tim commanded.

Conor helped Kathleen into the back of the wagon and onto the floor. He continued to move the sacks around, placing them on top of Kathleen.

"Stop doing that," yelled Kathleen.

"Shh," said Conor and Tim. Conor finally realized that these sacks were forty to fifty pounds each and that excessive weight was resting on top of Kathleen. That was one thing when the wagon was stationary, but a bumpy road could cause grave injury to her over a long journey. He pulled the sacks away and moved Kathleen to the front and placed the sacks around her.

He leaned forward and asked Tim, "Do you have a canvas cloth?"

"Wait." Tim climbed down off the bench and went into the barn. He returned with an old burlap blanket and threw it on top of Conor and Kathleen, who had crouched down between the sacks. "Here, and by the way, this is Carl. He will be traveling with us."

Each gave a muffled "hello." The wagon started up, jerking and shifting the sacks into place. Conor had to readjust the sacks and their seating to fit. The trip took about two hours to go fifteen miles to the port of St. Catharines, traveling the back roads and using caution at each intersection. Conor and Kathleen were being jostled in the wagon.

"How much farther?" she asked Conor.

"I don't know," he whispered back. "I don't know where we are going."

Tim pulled up hard on the reins of the horses. Distant voices. Tim proceeded slowly. The voices increased, then passed and tapered off. Tim picked up speed again, making frequent turns. Conor could tell the wagon was traveling through a populated area because of the frequent turns. The wagon stopped.

Tim whispered, "Don't move." After a few seconds, he said, "We have to change our route, we're going a different way," and abruptly pulled away.

"Something is wrong," thought Conor.

The wagon made a few more turns and Tim announced softly, "The wagon isn't going to stop, but when I give you the word, jump out. Carl will take you." The wagon slowed and Tim said, "Now!"

Conor threw the cover back and got up. His muscles were stiff from lying in the awkward position for the last two hours and Kathleen was slow to get up too.

"Move," said Tim again anxiously.

"We're trying," Conor answered. They jumped down. As soon as their feet hit the muddy street, Tim slapped the reins on the back of the horses and they sped off.

"This way," said Carl, as they headed down an alley. Kathleen gripped Conor's arm. A few steps into the alley, Carl stopped. "We can't go to the church; soldiers were around. We are going to a different place." Carl started a half-run, crouched over, head up, looking and listening as he went. Conor and Kathleen followed.

They crossed over two streets and through a back yard, up to the back of a house. Carl stopped at the door; he listened and rapped lightly. Without waiting for an answer he opened the door and entered. "Father?" he called.

"Here, son," was the reply.

Conor and Kathleen followed Carl into the kitchen area of the house. An older man and woman entered from a front room carrying a lantern. This contact was the first opportunity for Conor and Kathleen to see Carl in the light. He had a dark complexion and weathered skin. Carl was native to North America; his people had lived in this area long before Europeans explored and settled there. He introduced his father, Maska, and his mother, Kibbe, and said, "These people need a place to stay for the night."

"They can sleep in our front room," said Maska without asking why.

"Thank you," said Kathleen.

Kibbe could see that Kathleen was still shivering and she directed her guests into the front room. The house was a small one-floor cottage. The front room contained various brightly colored pillows positioned on the floor in a semi-circle. The three men, Kibbe, and Kathleen entered and sat down. Kibbe handed Kathleen a heavy woolen blanket, hand-made with various stitched symbols interwoven throughout. Kibbe went back into the kitchen area and returned with three bowls of a vegetable stew, as if she knew these guests had not eaten. Kibbe took her place next to Maska on a well-worn pillow, as she had for the past thirty-four years.

Carl explained to his parents, "These people needed to enter Canada like the black people—avoiding the watchful eyes of the British soldiers or American authorities. They are going to travel east of the Mississauga nation." Carl turned to Kathleen and Conor and said, "East of Toronto." Maska nodded to his son in acknowl-edgment.

Conor asked, "What's the story about the tailor shop in Lewiston?"

Carl smiled. "You entered what is known as the Under-ground Railroad. Josiah is a conductor on the railroad who moves people through the network. He is an extremely important con-ductor because it is a crossing point into Canada and freedom for the slaves. He's a very cautious man because there are many bounty hunters and marshals along the Niagara River looking for runaway slaves. It's a dangerous area. The bounty hunters will shoot if they encounter resistance and the slaves will fight because they're so close to freedom."

"What's the significance of the coats?"

Carl laughed out loud. Maska and Kibbe joined in the humor. "Josiah has a warning system concerning the bounty hunters. He gives them brightly colored coats, so people know who they are."

"Are the slaves safe in Canada?"

"They're free people in Canada."

"That's why Hank, the barman, asked if Josiah was making us a coat. He wanted to know if we were bounty hunters."

"Yes, men and women have come looking for slaves."

Conor looked at Kathleen, as they both understood the odd behavior of the townspeople. "This blanket is beautiful. Did you make it?" Kathleen asked Kibbe.

"Of course," Kibbe stated softly and matter-of-factly. "It tells our story." Kibbe would not tell the story unless someone expressed interest. Her humble personality would not assume anyone was interested.

Kathleen had just met this woman and she did not want to appear to be forward. "I'd be interested in your story, if you cared to share it."

"We are native to this area. Our ancestors lived on this land for many centuries, as you can see by the seasons of sun and snow." Kibbe leaned over and gently touched the blanket on the image of the sun. "We hunted in winter; here is the symbol of deer and rabbit. We cultivated and preserved corn, beans, and squash in the growing season." She touched the blanket which had muted rows of corn throughout the patterned blanket. Her touch was tender, as if she was connecting with centuries of relatives.

"We were a peace-loving nation called the Attiwondaronk, but the Seneca from the Iroquois nation came and conquered our people." She pointed to symbols of falling arrows. "We were friends with Hurons but the Seneca defeated the Huron and the Seneca took us too." There was sadness in Kibbe's voice as she told the story of the warring nations and the loss of their independence as a sovereign Indian nation. "The French called us the 'Neutrals' because we would not side with either."

Kathleen said, "I feel honored to be warmed by your history."

Conor decided to share his reason for entering Canada. He explained, "I was present when a British soldier was killed in a pub."

"Many troubles have come out of pubs and men drinking too much," said Maska. "Our people do not approve of drunken behavior but our youth fall prey to the enticements of jovial merrymaking under the effects of this poison. They do not see they are making themselves fools. Our leaders see this as disrespect to our soul."

"Many Irish see the bad effects from too much alcohol and it hurts our people too," said Conor.

"This is sadly true," said Kathleen. "We have scholars, writers, talented musicians, and even saints, along with the very good, hard-working people of Ireland, but the few who drink too much and, like you said, make fools of themselves, hurt all our people."

"I am on the run from Ireland," continued Conor. His hosts nodded in response. "I jumped on board a ship heading for America without knowing where I was going to end up." Again, Maska and Kibbe nodded in acknowledgment. "I met Kathleen on the ship and we were married."

Maska spoke first. "You did not know Kathleen before getting on the boat?"

"No, we met on the ship," Conor said with a slight smile to his wife.

"No one, including yourselves, had a chance to see whether you were a right match or not?" asked Kibbe.

"Oh, we are a right match," Conor said quickly, missing the point that Kibbe and Maska were trying to make.

"You have many moons to live under and no elders to guide you. I am afraid you might get lost in the woods."

"Lost in the woods?"

Kathleen interrupted, "What they are saying is that we did not have enough preparation time and now we have no elders to help us if we have difficulties in our marriage."

Conor opened his mouth to affirm the solidity of their relationship but he stopped before saying anything once he realized the depth and wisdom of the question. Finally he said, "I see."

Kathleen answered for him. "We are both tough people with a strong faith in our Creator, and moral beliefs. Together, we can work through our difficulties. Since we have been traveling through New York, we have lived through having our money stolen, the death of a dear friend, being threatened by highwaymen on the canal, and crossing the border into Canada. This proves our union has strength and commitment. If we could not endure together, the last ten hours would have destroyed us. We will weather our hardships."

"I see how strong you are," said Maska. "You have tested your resolve."

"Are you are going to live in Canada?" asked Kibbe.

"No," said Kathleen. "We must find the family of our friend who died and give her family the property belonging to them."

"We must travel to Peterborough," said Conor.

"I think we need our rest," announced Maska. "You still have a long journey ahead." Kibbe arranged the front room for Conor and Kathleen. Within a short time, they fell into a deep sleep and rested comfortably under the protection of their Canadian hosts.

Chapter 13

Peterborough, Upper Canada

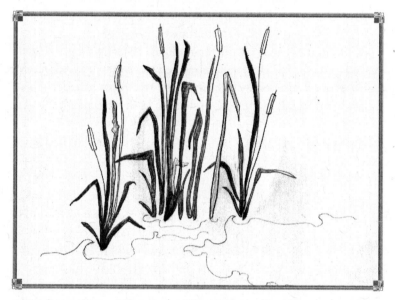

The early sun illuminated the room and Kathleen could hear noises from the kitchen. She rolled over and sleep took her away again. The next sounds were voices and the room was filled with light, which meant it was time to rise. As soon as Kathleen got up, Conor stirred. Carl, Maska, and Kibbe were in the kitchen and ready for the day. Kibbe served a potent hot tea in the front room and Conor quickly came to life. Breakfast consisted of cornbread dipped in the boiled sap from a maple tree.

"This bread is delicious," announced Conor.

"Glad you enjoy," said Maska.

As soon as breakfast was over, Carl declared that it was time to go. "Quickly, we have to leave."

Conor and Kathleen gathered their bags along with her violin. "You have been most kind; thank you for your hospitality and sharing your home with us," Kathleen said to Kibbe and Maska.

"You have safe travels," said Maska.

It was a Wednesday and the warm streets were alive with market activities. Carts full of breads, cheeses, dairy goods, and spring flowers were passing through the streets of St. Catharines' normal business flow. Carl and the two Meighans headed down Niagara Street towards Lake Ontario, without hiding or concern for interruption now that they were clearly in Canada.

The lake was a considerable distance from the downtown area, so Carl turned down a side street to recruit a friend with a wagon. The friend's house was just off Niagara Street and the man Carl was looking for was in a small barn behind the house. He spoke away from Kathleen and Conor and they could not hear the conversation. No introductions were made, they were just told, "Climb in."

The friend drove the wagon as the four people headed to the edge of the lake. Towards the end of the trip, they made a number of turns through various side streets and traveled over a bridge before arriving at a desolate U-shaped cove at the edge of the lake. Carl thanked his friend for saving time with the ride. The five-mile walk was not considered a long walk for Carl, but he wanted to save time for travel on the lake.

They walked another thousand feet along the shore before going to a small dock area containing three boats moored in waiting. The short pier swayed under the motion of the three people trying to walk in unison and maintain their footing. They jumped aboard a small twenty-one-foot fishing boat with a single mast. Conor looked skyward and saw dark but sparse cloud cover, which gave an ambiguous forecast as to whether rain was imminent or not.

"This boat is small enough to be navigated by one person," said Carl as he made the boat ready to sail. Conor assisted as best he could with the lines and sail. Soon the boat was ready and Carl pushed off from the dock.

"You are taking us all the way to Peterborough?" asked Kathleen.

"No, I will sail you across the lake to Oshawa. Someone else will get you to Peterborough."

· "How long will it take?" asked Conor.

"It depends on the wind. Once we get out on the lake we can tell how strong the wind is and which direction. There is a steady breeze along the shoreline but it is likely to increase on the open lake."

Just as Carl predicted, the boat started slowly, catching a mild breeze coming out of the west off the port side of the boat. Once they had traveled a couple of hundred feet from shore, the wind increased slightly and the boat picked up speed. Soon Carl turned the boat from a northerly direction to head eastward. The sail caught the full energy of the westerly wind, causing a boost in the push on the boat.

As the boat moved farther east and entered the centre of the lake, the waves were more pronounced and the boat rose and then slapped down as it traveled past each wave. The forward motion gave soothing rises and slapping falls, which made for an amusing up-and-down ride as the boat cut through the water for many hours. Conor was glad his hangover was gone.

The wind blew Kathleen's long black hair around her head in a tangled mess. She lowered herself onto the floor of the boat, out of the influence of the wind. Conor slid down next to her. "We are getting close, I can feel it. I'm tired of traveling," said Conor.

"Me too," agreed Kathleen. They cuddled in and took a nap, swaying to the constant rocking of the boat. When they awoke, the sun was descending in the western sky.

Carl kept the boat away from the Canadian shoreline out of the eyesight of any British patrols. He pushed the rudder, and the boat edged towards the port side. The wind shifted and the sail swung around and caught the crosswind. Land came into view again to the north. "Stay down," stated Carl.

Conor and Kathleen's anxiety started to rise again as they anticipated landing. From their low position they could not see the horizon or any activity beyond the boat's gunwales. An occasional seagull would hover over the boat but would then fly off. Carl wished he had a couple of fish in the boat to keep the attention of the gulls, which would indicate he had been fishing. However, the gulls studied Conor and Kathleen and flew off squawking, realizing there was no chance for a free meal here.

Carl manipulated the rudder as he was heading in. His eyes grew narrow with a look of concern. He was dodging some hazard but Conor could not see what it was. Suddenly Carl raised his hand and waved with a smile. Nothing was said but Conor could see the tip of a tall mast go by. The mast was flying the Union Jack—a British ship. Carl kept his course steady.

A few minutes later, Carl spoke while keeping a stoic look ahead: "I maneuvered to their starboard side so the sun would be in their eyes as we passed."

"That was risky," replied Conor.

"They don't expect Indians to follow the rules of civilized navigation. I just gave them what they expected."

Conor liked Carl even though he was hard to get to know. Carl, like his father, did not speak except when necessary. His manner was soft and quiet, but his values were clearly strong and unyielding. Conor respected his modest style.

The gulls were circling more frequently, indicating land was approaching, and Carl tightened the sail to slow the boat. They entered a small cove and a channel leading to the town of Oshawa, which was an immediate left turn. Carl went past the turn, which led into tall reeds that lined the back of the cove. Another channel appeared which snaked through the natural camouflage. Carl lowered the sail and used a pole to propel the boat deeper into the channel.

As they moved across the channel, Conor remarked to Kathleen in a low hushed voice, "Aren't you amazed at the help these people have given?"

"Yes, they have risked so much for us."

Conor thought for a moment and said, "And you would think the Native people would resent the Europeans encroaching on their lands."

Carl, standing at the back of the boat and looking straight ahead, said, "We share our bounty. As long as we can live in peace, we will share the riches of the land. Now keep quiet."

The channel soon left the open area of the cove and entered a wooded creek. Carl pushed the boat to the bank. "Okay, out," ordered Carl.

"Are you coming?" asked Conor.

"No, I have to leave right away."

"Carl, thank you for your help. We need to repay you."

"Go now," was Carl's only reply.

"Where?" asked Kathleen as she stepped out.

"There's a house just up the path. Go there."

As soon as Conor stepped onto solid ground, Carl pushed the boat back into the channel. Conor knew enough not to yell any further words. He just stood on the bank looking at Carl, holding his hand in a farewell gesture. He felt he was losing a friend even though he had only known Carl for less than twenty-four hours.

Conor's gratitude for the risks that Carl had taken to get them here was overwhelming. He stood immobilized. He marveled at the enormous difficulties involved in crossing the river and lake as well as the huge danger posed by the soldiers along the borders. He silently asked these questions to himself: Why did he work so hard for us? Why did he risk his life, his freedom for no recompense? He took us to his parents' home. He trusted us without really knowing us. Conor realized the generosity of the people associated with this Underground Railroad would stay with him forever.

Kathleen grabbed his arm and they started up the path. The wood gave way to an open meadow. At the edge of the path sat a small cottage. Cautiously they approached the cottage, hoping it was the one that Carl meant for them to find. Conor knocked on the door. It opened a crack. A woman's face was seen in the darkened slit of the door's gap.

"We were told to see you. We are trying to get to Peterborough."

"Peterborough," the woman chuckled. She continued to look at Conor and Kathleen without further comment.

"Carl sent us," Conor added.

"Carl?"

"Yes, Carl from Lewiston."

"Lewiston?"

"Carl from St. Catharines," Kathleen added.

"Carl the Neutral?" the woman said.

"Yes," replied Kathleen.

"Come in," the woman said as she opened the door. "Did anyone follow you?"

"No, I don't think so," answered Conor as he and Kathleen stepped in.

The woman closed the door. The room was the same as Kibbe and Maska's front room, lined with pillows instead of chairs. A gesture was given to sit down. "You want to go to Peterborough?" asked the woman.

"Yes, we are Conor and Kathleen Meighan. Carl helped us get into Canada and we are going to Peterborough," explained Kathleen.

"You needed help getting into Canada?"

"We didn't want the British to know."

"I understand. Now that you are in Canada, do you still need to travel secretly?"

"No, I don't think so," said Kathleen looking at Conor.

"No," Conor hesitated. "As long as we are not stopped on the road."

"If we travel in a coach, will we be safe?" asked Kathleen.

The woman chuckled again. "A coach" was the only answer given by the woman.

"Yes, a coach," said Kathleen after a few moments of silence.

"You can travel by coach." The woman, who never introduced herself, said, "I will get you to the coach. But tonight you will stay with me. I will fix you an area to sleep. Are you hungry?"

"Yes," said Kathleen.

The woman was as Native-looking as Kibbe and Maska, with a dark weathered complexion, but this woman was not as friendly or engaging as Carl's parents. She took care of their needs and was hospitable to her traveling guests but her demeanor had a disapproving tone, as if Conor and Kathleen did not qualify as destitute or endangered. She provided comfort as expected for this link in the system, as well as shelter and food to her travelers in need. She knew that only those in need were sent to her door and she would not judge, pry, or demand a satisfactory explanation, but her attitude was clearly condescending.

Kathleen tried to connect more personally with the woman and asked, "Carl was from the Neutral tribe. What tribe are you from?"

"A tribe, as you call it, is different than a nation. Carl is from the Attiwondaronk nation, which was shortened to the Neutral nation by the Europeans. My ancestors and I are Mississauga. We have lived on this land for many centuries."

Kathleen understood that she was being corrected and schooled regarding who owned the land and the fact that Europeans were the invaders, the conquerors, and the squatters on Native American land. Kathleen was puzzled by the woman's forward, curt answers. She tried another approach. "What name would you like us to call you?"

The woman stopped working with the food and stared at Kathleen. Although Kathleen was trying, she realized she had made another annoying statement. "You may call me by my name, Hurit."

"Thank you for helping us enter Canada, Hurit."

Silence hung in the air as Hurit prepared a meal for three. Kathleen did not try to make further conversation.

But Hurit had not said her fill, even though she did not like to question her visitors' motives. These two travelers were different; they struck a different nerve in Hurit. The typical visitors were slaves on the run from oppressive slave owners, not European couples. "You've committed crimes in the United States?" Her question was more of an accusation.

"No, we landed in New York City and traveled through the state."

"Oh?" answered Hurit. She waited and let the silence linger. After a while she continued, "We don't help criminals."

"Why do you think we are criminals?" Kathleen asked.

"You are not slaves; why else would Carl help you?" The question went deeper than Carl's assistance. Hurit knew that many people were involved in the Underground Railroad and, for some reason, these visitors had passed the test of needing imminent and covert assistance.

"Like we said, we need to avoid the British authorities," said Kathleen.

"What she means," said Conor, "is that we will be sent back to Ireland if the British find us. It's more political than criminal."

"Oh," murmured Hurit. "Political, meaning they are trying to assassinate you?'

"No, I don't think assassinate is right. Maybe prejudice is a better word."

"Political or prejudice, do you think I do not know these words?"

"What do you mean?"

"My family has lived on these lands for many moons. I know political troubles, the prejudices of people, and assassinations. We openly welcomed newcomers and made trade agreements to help each other but slowly we lost our lands. 'Ownership' they called it, as if they could take the land away and now say they owned it. Yes, I know prejudice. We walk through the streets and people call us names, laugh at us, and throw dirt, manure, rotted fruit, or whatever they have. And why? Because we have a different heritage, perform different customs, or wear clothes unusual to their eyes. The white man cannot be trusted."

At this moment, the couple in Hurit's house represented ridicule, prejudice, and land stolen from Hurit and her people. They also represented all the stories she had heard from the people on the "Railroad" of the oppression and cruelty to slaves in the United States. She did not realize the couple had experienced their own version of oppression.

"And you feel that we cannot be trusted?" Conor said, pointing to Kathleen and himself.

"No, you must be all right," said Hurit. "You must be good people if Carl brought you over."

"We try to be," said Kathleen.

Regardless of her historical instincts, Hurit decided to help these people on the "Railroad" to find safety.

After dinner, Hurit went to a box next to the fireplace and opened the cover. She removed a handful of tree leaves. She dipped them into a bucket of water and tossed the leaves into the small fire. The leaves sent a thick smoke up the chimney.

Shortly a young teenage boy opened the front door and entered. When he saw the two Europeans he announced to Hurit, "I'm here." Hurit spoke to the boy in her native language. Even though Conor did not know the language, he knew they were the topic of conversation due to the frequent looks and hand gestures. The conversation was short and the boy left.

Hurit turned to Conor. "Bobby will be back tomorrow morning to take you to the coach."

The evening was quiet, with little conversation, while Hurit worked on a beaded scarf. Kathleen read from the Bible she kept in her luggage and Conor offered to cut and split wood, but his offer was refused. After dark, the three inhabitants retired for the night, each of them yearning for morning light to place the travelers back on the road.

Bobby returned early the next morning. They were happy to leave Hurit's company, although they were grateful for her assistance in the network to enter Canada.

Conor said, "Thank you," and offered her some money for her troubles. Hurit considered it for a moment but then refused the payment. Bobby took them out onto the path, which led the Meighans into the woods towards the coach to Peterborough.

"The path is demanding but we need to keep moving to make the coach."

The walk through the wood was difficult. The path was uneven and wet. In late April, the ground along the southern Canadian border was saturated from the melting snow and spring rainstorms. The three hikers had to carefully dodge mud holes along the slick trail. The creek that flowed into Lake Ontario ran along their left and thick vegetation lined the pathway. Many times they could not see the creek from the dense underbrush but they knew it was there. They could hear voices from the other side but no one was visible.

Bobby signaled to be quiet. An uprooted tree, blown over during the winter, lay across the path. The tree was about six feet in diameter and created a considerable obstacle. Bobby quickly scrambled up onto the horizontal trunk and rolled over the top. Conor thought about doing the same but he was wearing traveling clothes that made agile leg movement hard, and he did not want to throw Mrs. Hurley's bag over to Bobby. Likewise, he knew Kathleen would not have the upper body strength to pull herself up and over.

Exposed and torn roots supported the base of the trunk off the ground, so a small gap was available to crawl under the trunk. Conor did not like the idea of crawling in the mud to go under; consequently, the only option was to go off the path into the thick underbrush and around the tree.

A crater in the ground had been formed when the tree toppled, taking the soil along with the root system and leaving a pool of water and mud in the depression. They needed to go the long way around the tree. Conor managed his way through the web of branches and thicket until he found an opening near the top end of the tree.

Branches pulled and tugged at their clothing as they made their way through the uncomfortable detour. Occasionally, Kathleen would let out an "ouch" or a heavy breath when an unco-operative branch slapped back. Conor carried Kathleen's bag through the underbrush while she managed to carry the violin. They caught up with Bobby waiting patiently on the other side of the trunk. He chuckled and Conor scowled.

Bobby moved along the path with skill and ease. The path was alive with bird activity and Kathleen watched little chickadees darting among the branches. The chickadees seemed very trusting and friendly birds, and they flew close to the walkers apparently without fear. Their colorful appearance and pleasant song made for nice hiking friends.

Although Bobby warned his companions to remain quiet, he walked upright as if he did not care who was watching their move-ment. Suddenly Bobby stopped. About fifteen feet behind, Conor and Kathleen quickly stopped too and started to crouch down, anticipating imminent danger. Bobby slowly thrust his hand into his coat pocket. He removed his hand, tightened into a fist. Conor tried to see what he had but the fist was tight.

Bobby slowly extended his hand and opened the fist. A small black but obscure object could be seen in his palm. Soon a small chickadee landed on Bobby's hand and took a black sunflower seed and flew off. A second chickadee did the same. Bobby closed his hand again and placed the remaining seeds back into his pocket.

Conor hustled up to Bobby. "That was a little dramatic, wasn't it?"

"No, not at all. The birds are my scouts. When they are around, I know no one is following me, otherwise they would be scared off. I feed them to keep their vigilance for my walks."

"But we were following you."

"Yes, they have been watching us since we left the cottage. They saw me wait for you at the fallen tree. Now that I have fed them in your presence, they will trust you."

"The birds are smart," remarked Kathleen.

"Don't give them too much credit. They want food," advised Bobby.

They continued on the path towards the road to meet the coach. The path wound uphill as they moved farther from the lake. The path now had more dry spots as they walked, with a meadow of grass to their right. Within ten minutes they reached the end of the path at a well-worn road.

"The coach will be here shortly," said Bobby.

"Are you leaving?" asked Conor.

"Yes, you will be fine from here to Peterborough. Good luck." Bobby returned to the path and disappeared into the stand of spruces that lined the roadway.

Kathleen found a small stump to sit down on. "I'll be happy when we get to Peterborough. I'm tired of this traveling and sneaking from place to place."

"I will too, but Peterborough is not necessarily the last stop. We might be there just a short time, maybe one day," answered Conor.

As Bobby had predicted, the stagecoach pulled up and stopped. An older man with long thin graying hair was driving. He rose slowly off the driver's bench and found his footing on the rungs of the steps to climb down.

Before he reached the bottom the door of the coach swung open and a young man stepped out. The man was about thirty years old, with fiery red hair and pale white skin. He was dressed in a simple traveling suit with a tie—a man of modest means but one who knew the proper etiquette for coach travel. The young man extended his hand for a young lady to grasp as she brushed aside her long traveling dress to find her footing. She too had the light complexion common to the people of Irish descent. The combination of her blue eyes, dark hair, light skin, and engaging smile gave her a charming appearance.

"Hello," said the young man to Conor and Kathleen.

"Hello," they answered back.

"Here, Jake, let me help you," said the young man to the driver as he grabbed the driver's arm to steady his step onto the ground.

The passengers and the driver seemed to have a good relationship and congenial personalities, which reassured Conor. They bantered about the driver being old and fragile and the passenger being outspoken. "So where you going?" the driver asked.

"Peterborough," replied Conor.

"Good, because that's where we're going," said the equally outspoken driver.

Conor recognized the man's Irish accent but Kathleen was concerned about the light-hearted tempo; she realized the serious nature of traveling on the well-traveled Erie Canal but this had been true wilderness travel. She knew the conditions could change at any moment. Their individual experiences had taught harsh lessons in vulnerability and survival.

The driver loaded the bags into the back of the coach and turned to his passengers. "Let's go before the horses leave without us."

The young man extended his hand again for the lady. "Thank you," she said, clearly impressed with the attention she was receiving from the man.

However, the man did not follow her in. He waited and offered his hand to Kathleen. She took it as she climbed the steps into the carriage. Conor stepped forward. The young man withdrew his hand and said, "You are on your own." Conor grinned at the man's sense of humor.

The man's attention moved to the driver. "Jake, can you get up on your own or am I going to have to get a rope and pulley?"

"Young man, this old body can manage just fine. And get yourself inside or you'll be running behind for the next fifty miles."

The man stepped in and yelled out the door, "Jake, I'm in but we're still missing the comfortable chairs you promised."

"He ya," Jake shouted and, with a snap of the reins, the horses pulled the coach into a jerking start.

The passengers settled in their seats. The young man looked at Conor. "You're going to Peterborough?"

"Yes," Conor said cautiously.

"Good town, we lived there for a while. Do you have family there?"

"No, not exactly. We are looking for someone there."

"Oh, who's that? Maybe I can help. I know just about every-one."

There was a comfortable feeling with this friendly man that put Conor and Kathleen at ease. Conor did not feel guarded in explaining their reason for traveling to Peterborough.

"The daughter of a woman we were traveling with. The woman's name was Ellen Hurley. We don't know the name of the daughter."

"Well, there are some Hurleys in Peterborough."

"I am afraid that she does not go by the name of Hurley any more because she is married."

"That could be tough. What do you know about her?"

"I know she moved to Peterborough about seven years ago and she grew up in Ireland in a small town called Crookhaven."

"Maherly O'Keefe is who you are looking for. Her husband is Michael O'Keefe. She lives in Peterborough, not one of the set-tlement towns adjacent to the village."

"How do you know this?"

"I lived in Peterborough for eleven years. I was a farrier with the town blacksmith. That's how I know the people." He started to turn towards the younger lady but stopped and said, "I'm sorry. I've not introduced us. I'm Dennis McCarthy and this is my wife Johanna. We were married last year in Lockport in New York."

Conor replied, "This is Kathleen and I am Conor Meighan. We were married a month ago in the middle of the Atlantic Ocean."

"How romantic," said Johanna.

"Yes, it was romantic in one sense but we have been on the move ever since. We can't wait to settle down," added Kathleen. "We stopped in Lockport while traveling the canal; it's a nice town."

Dennis explained, "Yes, we like it. We've decided to make it our home because of the work there. We're going back to

Peterborough to visit our families. We haven't seen them since our wedding."

"You were born in Canada?"

"No, both of us were born in Ireland, County Cork, and brought to Canada by the English to start a new life."

"The English? That's unusual."

"Yes, it was. A Canadian official by the name of Peter Robinson led the settlement project by bringing over two thousand starving Irish into Canada—well, let's see, that was twelve years ago. And we appreciated the opportunity to start a new life and Mr. Robinson was a wonderful man. He was kind, generous, and most of all, honest about the assistance he would provide. I'm afraid neither of our families would have survived the conditions in Ireland had we stayed."

Johanna said, "My father died on the ship coming over and my mother had a difficult time starting a new life with seven children. My mother never recuperated from her grief. She always introduced herself as 'the widow Sullivan.' Dennis lost his father too but his mother's nature was stronger and her grief turned into determination."

Dennis broke in before Johanna's emotion overcame her. "The English helped many families go from starvation to self-sufficiency. The settlement program was a wonderful opportunity for many people. However, many lost mothers, fathers, or children in the process of moving from Ireland, so upon arrival in Upper Canada there were no familiar family members to assist with clearing land, planting, harvesting, and raising children."

"We miss our families, too," said Conor. "I left without saying goodbye. One bad night in a pub and I was banished from ever going home. I've been hiding and running ever since."

"They call this the New World, and we all have new lives, whether we like it or not," added Kathleen.

The carriage moved along the lake on the main road and the two young couples conversed easily. However, when the coach turned off the major east–west route and headed north in the less traveled direction towards Peterborough, the road was uneven, narrow, and less maintained.

Muddy conditions from recent rains turned the path leading to Peterborough into a sloppy mess of ruts and puddles of water that the coach bounced through and around. These conditions slowed the horses to a careful walk and time seemed to slow as well, because the passengers knew the destination was close. The passengers felt the exaggerated bouncing, which at first was funny but rapidly became a nuisance. The terrain was rough in this remote area of the interior away from the lake. Clouds rolled in and the sky darkened as the threat of more rain loomed. Jake pulled the team to a halt.

"Bad weather ahead," he announced. The passengers heard Jake climbing around on the top of the carriage.

"Anything I can do to help?" yelled Dennis out the window.

"No, I'm just getting my rain gear and securing the luggage from any dampness. Do you know how to close the flaps on the windows?" asked Jake.

"Yes. We'll take care of it," Dennis answered back.

The rumbling of thunder could be heard in the distance as the coach inched forward. The storm hit quickly. Lightning, thunder, heavy rain all appeared instantly. The horses kicked and reared in the tumultuous weather. Jake was working hard to control and calm the horses. At the peak of nature's tempest, Jake pulled the carriage to a stop and disembarked from his bench on the top of the coach.

The passengers expected him to open the door and climb in. Johanna started to squeeze in closer to Dennis to make room and Kathleen and Conor did so as well, but the door did not open. They could hear Jake's voice calming the horses. The carriage would make slight jerks forward as the agitated horses reacted to the nearby flashes of light and the pounding thunder.

Kathleen whispered to Conor, "I am afraid.'

"We will be fine; this will pass soon."

"We have been through too much already; I do not want any more excitement."

Conor patted her leg. "We are in the company of good people."

"Actually we have been in the company of some very good people all along the way; we have been lucky," said Kathleen.

"Yes, and I have a good feeling about the McCarthys here, too." Johanna heard the conversation and looked over at the mention of their name and smiled.

Conor pulled the curtain back to see the storm but rain found a way to fly in across the interior and saturate the passengers. Now the wheels were sunk into the waterlogged dirt roadway as the horses pulled and tugged. Jake yelled again for the horses to move and they pulled again. The carriage began to rock. It released with a sucking sound from the muck, and the carriage moved forward.

Jake was in between the horses with his hand on the bridles to pull and coax them. He was soaked through his coat and a draining flow of dirt, mud, and water ran down his pants and into and out of his boots. Between the resistance of the mud and the skittishness of the horses, the coach moved slowly.

The front of the storm passed by and the lightning and thunder drifted into the distance. The rain, however, continued. The horses settled down but Jake still had his hands full, making calming strokes on the horses' necks and keeping them on the move. A half-hour passed and the carriage had advanced only a short distance. Jake was afraid to stop for fear of the carriage sinking farther into the mud while stationary. He knew of a small opening in the trail ahead and headed into a wider, grassy area to stop. The horses followed Jake's lead into the open part of the road that had firm ground among the thickly rooted, clumpy grass.

Kathleen leaned towards Conor again. "This would have been a hard ride for the baby: bumps, thunder, my own anxiety with the lightning, and scared horses."

"You seem to be worried about something?" asked Conor.

"No, not that I can tell, but I have this uneasiness. Look out the window, what do you see—nothing but forest. We are in the middle of nowhere. If we get stranded here, what are we going to do?"

Conor was slow to reply. "I'm not sure, but you are right, I have no idea where we are."

Johanna and Dennis heard these concerns but were hesitant about interfering. Finally Dennis spoke up. "We are about twenty miles from Peterborough—straight up this road. If anything were to happen just walk straight to town." He pointed to the east.

"What kind of town is it?" asked Kathleen. "Does it have a place for us to stay and eat?"

"Oh, yes. It is a very modern town for being so far off the beaten path, with thriving businesses, a bank, and a hotel."

"I feel a little better," said Kathleen.

"I don't mean to pry, but did I hear you say you had a baby?"

Maybe it was the isolation of the wilderness or the dismal rain or just a melancholy mood, but Kathleen collapsed with emotion and started to weep. It started with a little whimper, followed by an immediate full uncontrollable cry with flowing tears. Conor reached around Kathleen as she tried to gain control of her sobbing.

"I am so sorry," said Johanna.

Dennis comforted his wife, who felt responsible for the outburst. "That's okay, you didn't know." Although he did not know what he was apologizing for, as nothing indicated a baby.

After a moment of silence and fighting the sudden outcry, Conor said to Kathleen, "Would you like to tell them or shall I?"

"Go ahead and tell them if you like," said Kathleen.

"No, please," said Dennis. "You do not have to tell your business."

"That's right," said Johanna. "We can step out of the carriage for a moment, if you need."

Conor looked at Kathleen to read her disposition.

"No need to go out into the rain," said Kathleen. "We lost a baby during our voyage on the high seas. It was during a storm." Her voice filled again with emotion.

"I am so sorry to hear that," said Johanna. "We have lost two babies since we were married less than a year ago. Neither was the result of a storm or a traumatic event. Both passed in the night."

Kathleen looked up at Johanna, as a bond had just been established between the two. Kathleen at nearly eighteen years old and Johanna, who had just turned nineteen years old, connected. "Do you ever think about them?"

"Yes, I do, and I worry that we may never be able to have children," answered Johanna.

"Oh, such a terrible thought," said Kathleen and turned to Conor. "I think I am all right now."

"I'll get you some water." Conor exited the coach.

"Need water," he yelled to Jake.

"Look up," said Jake, "you can have all you want." Conor walked up to Jake. "What I really need is a cup to hold the water."

"Climb up top, son, and in that front box are cups. Help yourself."

"Thank you." Conor climbed up to the cargo hold on top and found a tin cup in the box. After descending, he went to the back of the carriage and saw that a pool of rainwater had gathered on the canvas cover. He stretched the cover and the rainwater flowed off into the cup.

The rain remained steady through the day as Jake waited for clear weather. The passengers passed the time playing cards in the coach. The cards, dampened by the humidity, stuck together, but they made the best of their circumstances. By late afternoon the rain had stopped. Jake pulled out an extra set of dry clothes and changed. He had one pair of boots and his feet remained soaked.

He approached his passengers. "If we leave now, the road is wet and muddy and we will not likely go far. So we will wait until the road can dry up and drain. We will set up camp here for the night." The carriage had provisions for emergency stops such as this and Jake prepared a small dinner of bean soup. The rear of the carriage had a foldout bed with a canopy for two passengers, and the interior of the carriage allowed one person on each of the cushioned bench seats. Jake slept on top with a tarp.

No additional rain occurred through the night and in the morning the road was passable enough to set out. The journey continued and the road dried as the sun became more intense. The McCarthys and the Meighans rekindled their conversation once the coach was under way and again the talk came easily between the two couples. Dennis spoke of his job in Lockport working on the canal.

"The work is hard but steady."

"Are there opportunities for people like myself?" Conor asked. "We met Bill Hogan, who said that he would hire me because of my strong back."

"Yes, I know Mr. Hogan; he is always looking for good, strong, honest workers. Especially those who don't let the drink get the better of them," Dennis said.

"You should consider coming to Lockport to work," said Johanna.

Conor looked at Johanna. "We will consider it. We talked about the possibility of heading back to Lockport."

Without their realizing they had stopped, the door suddenly flew open and Jake was standing there.

"Are you going to get out or am I taking you back with me?"

Dennis looked out the window and saw the familiar town where his family had settled. "Jake, you are a fine driver to get us here with hardly a bump in the road." Dennis remained playful after a difficult journey.

"Yeah, yeah, come on and get out so I can keep my schedule."

Dennis jumped out first so he could turn and assist the women from the coach to the street. Conor was the last to exit, as Dennis turned to the stationhouse. He was surprised to see Jeremiah standing there.

"Jeremiah, good to see you."

"Hi Jeremiah, how have you been?" Johanna asked.

"Dennis, I'm fine, and how are you two?" answered Jeremiah.

"Good. I would like to introduce you to Conor and Kathleen Meighan, who just arrived in America from Ireland."

"Nice to meet you." Jeremiah turned back to Dennis. "What took so long? I have been checking the station every day for a week. I have been waiting for you." Conor observed that Jeremiah looked up to his brother and most likely missed his presence in Peterborough.

"Late start. I had to get some work done before we left. How's Ma?"

"Very good. I have been checking on Mrs. Sullivan like you asked me to. They're all good too," replied Jeremiah.

"Thanks for doing that, Jeremiah." Dennis turned to Conor. "By the way, Maherly O'Keefe lives down Water Street in a yellow house. Is it still yellow, Jeremiah?"

"The O'Keefes' house, yes, but why would anyone want to go there?"

"It's their business, Jeremiah, never mind."

Dennis pointed towards the hotel. "You can find a room over there."

"Thanks," said Conor.

Dennis added, "I would like to introduce you to the rest of the McCarthy family. Would you have dinner with us tomorrow?"

"Sure, thanks for the invitation," replied Conor.

The two couples separated, with Dennis extending his hand in farewell to Conor. "Welcome to the Americas. Good to meet a fellow Irishman."

"Indeed," replied Conor. "We are looking forward to meeting your family tomorrow."

Dennis, Johanna, and Jeremiah walked down the street carrying their luggage to head home. Conor observed there was no carriage; they were still a poor family struggling to fulfill a dream.

Conor turned to face Kathleen but she was already smiling and about to break into a laugh. "What's the matter?" asked Conor.

"I think we are in for an interesting trip to the O'Keefe house."

"This trip has been one adventure after another."

"Let's check into the hotel."

After settling into their room and enjoying a hot meal, Conor and Kathleen left the hotel on George Street in the early evening carrying Mrs. Hurley's bag. They felt a mixture of apprehension and a sense of accomplishment regarding their pending conversation with Maherly O'Keefe. The bag symbolized the rigor of their journey, Mrs. Hurley's accidental death, great wealth, and a history of greed, theft, and personal destruction. Now, with the bag, they had to inform a stranger that her mother had died en route to see her. The gravity of the impending conversation produced an increasingly melancholy mood as they advanced down Water Street looking for the yellow house.

Folks were out in their yards and sitting on porches, watching the faces of new arrivals and old friends walk through the neighborhood.

The houses were large and probably owned by the business people of the community. After walking down a full block and crossing over to the next, they found the yellow house, which was guarded by a picket fence to keep out the forces that would disrupt their safety and security and hold in the tranquility of a home. It was a large house indicating a well-to-do family, with three floors and many windows giving it an airy and comfortable presence. Each window had lace curtains and half-pulled shades to control the light and exposure.

Conor held the gate open and Kathleen stepped through. The house had a large wrap-around porch accessed by four short steps and Conor looked at Kathleen as he walked up and knocked on the door. Nothing was said but their eyes locked and shared the sadness of the looming news.

A woman in her thirties opened the door. She held an infant in her arms and she asked, "Yes?"

"Maherly O'Keefe?"

"Yes."

"We are Conor and Kathleen Meighan. We just arrived from Ireland. Can we step in to speak to you?"

Maherly looked down at Conor's hand and observed the embroidered bag he was holding. She quietly gasped for air, which was not meant to be heard by the visitors, but was. Maherly was caught off guard and her face changed from surprise to anger. "What do you want?" she started.

"To speak to you about your mother."

"I want nothing to do with that bag. You can send it back to her."

"Mrs. O'Keefe, that's what we want to talk to you about."

"I can see that, but you can leave now and don't bother me any further."

Kathleen spoke up. "Maherly, your mother has died. She died on her way to see you."

"Yes, I knew she was coming."

"May we at least speak to you?" Kathleen asked again.

"No, that bag is bewitched." Mrs. O'Keefe was now showing her anger. "Get it out of here. This is my home; you can leave now." The door slammed shut. Conor and Kathleen stood on the porch, stunned; they had not planned on this reaction.

"Oh," said a surprised Kathleen. Both stood motionless while thinking of their next option and whether to re-approach Maherly. Through the door, they could hear the baby start to cry. Kathleen was heartbroken. "I'm sorry that we disrupted a home with tragic news and past horrors."

Conor sat down on the top step. "What should we do?"

Kathleen sat next to him. "I don't know. We can't leave the bag on the porch at the door; she thinks the bag is bewitched or possesses some strange power."

"Well, I'm anxious to get rid of it myself—not that we have bad luck. I'm just tired of carrying it and worrying about protecting it."

The front door of the house opened again and a man stepped out. He was a tall man and appeared more so because Conor and Kathleen sat on the step below him. They stood up. "You're still here. I thought my wife told you to leave."

"Yes, but we were trying to decide what to do," answered Conor. "We were not sure if Mrs. O'Keefe wanted to hear what happened to her mother."

"What happened?"

"She drowned in a boat accident on the Erie Canal on her way here to see her daughter."

"That's too bad," Mr. O'Keefe said genuinely. "Now you can leave."

"What should we do with the bag?"

"My wife wants nothing to do with the bag. Do with it what you please."

"It contains a great deal of money."

"You don't understand. My wife does not want the bag or its contents."

"We feel that it is not our money and we don't know what to do about that."

The man hesitated. "What's your name?"

"Conor Meighan."

"Conor, I am an accountant. I know money. I know its value and its problems. You want to relieve your conscience, take half for your troubles and donate the rest to the church. Now you must leave."

"Thank you for your help, Mr. O'Keefe," said Conor, and he descended the steps. Kathleen followed.

As they retraced their route back to the hotel, Kathleen broke the silence. "I have a better idea. We divide it into thirds: we give a third to the church, we donate a third to the Underground Railroad because they helped us, and we keep a third, as Mr. O'Keefe suggested."

Conor gave a firm and formal reply. "We are not keeping a third." They walked in silence. Then Conor said, "I like the idea about the Underground Railroad and donating a portion to the church. This is what I think we should do: take our original fifty pounds sterling we lost and split the remainder between the church and the Underground Railroad."

"We should take a portion that Mrs. Hurley was going to pay us for our time and troubles."

Finally Conor found a reason to laugh. "For the troubles we had I don't think there is enough money."

"See, I think we've earned a portion."

"We can pay ourselves a reasonable sum and donate the rest."

"I agree," said Kathleen with resolve. "But how do we give it to the Railroad? They're secret."

"We'll go back to the tailor shop or we'll give it to Kibbe and Maska."

"Here we go again," said Kathleen.

Chapter 14

Cobourg

he next day Dennis walked into town to pick up Conor and Kathleen. He found them at the hotel. "Do you mind a six-mile walk in the mud?"

Kathleen replied, "We have been riding in ships, boats, and coaches for seemingly months. I am ready for a long walk."

Conor carried Mrs. Hurley's bag instead of leaving it in the hotel. He had lightened the load considerably by paying expenses in coins. Merchants appreciated the gold and silver coins more than paper money, especially now that there was an international monetary crisis in the Western world. Dennis thought it unusual that Conor had the bag with him but said nothing. They started their journey north to Smith Township.

"Did you meet Maherly O'Keefe?" asked Dennis.

"Yes, we found her. Thank you for your help."

"A pleasure. Did you get your business done?"

"For the most part, we did."

The shortness of answers and lack of information struck Dennis as odd, but the topic of Maherly O'Keefe and the bag remained a mystery.

After a long pause, when each person became uncomfortable in the silence, Conor felt he had come to know the McCarthys through the long carriage ride and overnight stay on the road and now he was welcoming them into his home. He decided to speak. "Mr. McCarthy, you know your way around Upper Canada and New York and I need your help, but I need to know whether I can trust you or not."

"Yes, you can trust me to do the right thing. I am well known around Peterborough, if you want to inquire. However, if you are going to ask me to do something wrong, you're asking the wrong person."

"We are in a quandary about what is right," informed Conor.

"I will give you the right answer, the best I know. You will be free to decide on your own after that."

Conor started the story by describing O'Malley's Pub. "And the evening ended with a fight with the British soldiers. One was killed." He stopped the story long enough to judge Dennis's reaction and gauge whether to go on or not.

Dennis replied, "I have no love for the British soldiers in Ireland. However, I am grateful for the British generosity and benevolence in bringing our families to Canada. It was hard, what with losing the land, sickness and death, but they gave us an opportunity we would not have had otherwise."

"I understand," said Conor, and he continued the story of the ship. "Kathleen and I met on the ship, fell in love, and we got married. When we arrived in New York, we met Mrs. Hurley and agreed to assist her to Peterborough, but she died coming up the canal and that is why we are traveling into Canada—to deliver her possessions to her daughter. I have to be careful crossing the border because of the British troops and what happened at home. We sneaked across Lake Ontario and now we have to sneak back."

"Is that your dilemma?" asked Dennis.

"It is one of them."

"Well, I know a smooth way to cross between here and Rochester in New York," Dennis said.

"I remember Rochester. It's a nice town."

"Yes, it is, and we can sail easily into the harbor with no British soldiers to worry about. The British soldiers on this side of the lake are not worried about Irishmen leaving Canada, just those coming in." Dennis chuckled.

Conor felt more at ease and continued. "This bag," he said, raising the bag slightly, "belonged to Maherly O'Keefe's mother, Mrs. Hurley. We went to Mrs. O'Keefe's house but she doesn't want the bag."

"Well, don't bring it to our house; we don't want it either," replied Dennis.

"The bag is very valuable. That's why we didn't leave it at the hotel."

"Oh." Dennis was clearly not impressed with the bag.

"It contains a lot of money: all of Mrs. Hurley's savings and family . . ."—he hesitated on the next word—"treasures."

Dennis was surprised. "And Mrs. O'Keefe did not want the money?"

"Right, she doesn't want the money because she feels it is stolen or haunted or both. Mrs. Hurley said the money came from pirates off the coast of Ireland and that her family has had it for generations. Mrs. O'Keefe does not want stolen money."

"I can understand her feeling, and I know the history of looting and pilfering of ships along the southern coast of Ireland."

"But the money is not ours—what do we do with it?"

"That's quite a question," agreed Dennis.

"Kathleen and I thought that we would reimburse the money stolen from us at the dock when we helped Mrs. Hurley."

"I can see the connection," agreed Dennis.

"We thought we would take the remainder and split a donation between the church and the Underground Railroad which helped get us into Canada."

"How much are we talking about?"

"Hundreds of dollars."

"In that bag there?"

"Yes."

Dennis stopped on the road and thought for a moment. In his mind he was reviewing all the pertinent dilemmas he had studied or read about, including scripture and literature. These folks did not want to steal and made a valiant attempt to return the money to its rightful heir, so the obligation to the rightful owner had been fulfilled. Charity was a logical next step. The church and the Railroad were noble sources to donate to.

"I think that is a good plan."

"We don't know what else to do."

"Incidentally, a new St. Peter in Chains Church is being build in Peterborough. You could donate to that church and the money will stay in Peterborough, where it was destined to go originally."

"That's true," confirmed Conor.

"I like that idea," said Kathleen. "The money stays close to Mrs. O'Keefe."

"True, and it helps poor Irish, many of whom were the victims of pirate activity, especially in County Cork," added Dennis. "I believe your plan is solid."

"That's a relief," said Conor. "I was worried about crossing the border again with the money. At least I will have only half of it."

Dennis stated, "I appreciate your concern about being searched at the border, as there are still hostilities between the British and the Americans. Large amounts of money traveling across the border would be suspect—and investigated."

"And then I would have to tell the whole story, a story I do not want to tell."

By the time they arrived at the 11th line, the road on which the McCarthys had settled, the dilemma had been resolved and they had a plan in place. But Conor had one further point to discuss. "Dennis, please do not chat about this conversation or reveal the amount of money we have in our possession."

"I am glad you confided in me, and I have offered you safe transport to New York and Lockport. So your safety is my safety, particularly if we are traveling as a group. Your secret is safe with me. I will let Johanna know some detail as to our concerns for safe travel."

"We understand," agreed Kathleen.

The dinner and evening was filled with pleasant talk of Ireland, the voyage over the ocean, and life in the New World with the two couples, along with Dennis' mother also named Johanna, and Jeremiah. As a result, Conor and Kathleen Meighan looked forward to settling in Lockport.

The next morning, Dennis and Johanna walked part of the way back to Peterborough with Conor and Kathleen until they reached the turn-off for Emily Township, where the McCarthys were headed up to see the Sullivan family and Johanna's home. Before departing, they made arrangements to meet again in town for the return trip to Lockport.

"We will meet you at the hotel tomorrow," said Dennis.

Once in Peterborough, Conor and Kathleen went to St. Peter in Chains Church where they made an anonymous donation to aid the start of the new parish. After that business, they returned to the hotel and waited another day for Dennis and Johanna to return. During this waiting, Conor's anxiety began to mount;

crossing a border guarded by British troops renewed his fear of detention, arrest, and deportation to one of Britain's notorious prisons. His other fear was that his apprehension would show at the wrong moment, thereby drawing attention to himself.

The next day, Dennis and Johanna came to the hotel as promised and the two couples walked over to Andrew Dennehy's livery. "Andy, you here?" yelled Dennis as they walked in.

"Back here," came the reply. Soon a man about the same age as Dennis walked from a back stall.

"Dennis, you old farrier," said the man and they clasped hands.

"Andy, these are friends, Conor and Kathleen."

"Good to meet you," said Andy. "What brings you to Peterborough?"

"Just visiting," said Dennis. "We have a home in Lockport now and we came to see our mothers and family."

"Want a job?"

Dennis turned to the Meighans. "I used to work for him before leaving Peterborough." They nodded in understanding.

"No, we just need a carriage to Cobourg."

"Of course," said Andy, who stepped out into the street. He looked across the way and yelled, "Kevin, go get Niall and tell him to come down right away."

"Okay, Andy," said Kevin.

Within a few minutes, Niall walked in. "What do you need, Andy?"

"Do you remember Mr. McCarthy, who used to work here?"

"Sure do. How are you, Mr. McCarthy?"

"Very well," said Dennis. "You have grown since I last saw you."

"Ahh, probably."

"Can you take us to Cobourg?"

"Sure, it will be just a minute to hitch the horses," said Niall. Shortly, a carriage came around from behind, ready for travel. "Hop in," said Niall.

Dennis turned to his old friend. "Thanks, Andy; here is the fare."

"You keep it for your travels; I'll cover Niall."

"I hope to see you soon," said Johanna as they climbed into the carriage.

The team started towards Cobourg some twenty miles from Peterborough, following the Otonabee River to Wallace Point, where the river bent left and they took the road to Cobourg to the right. After a few miles they passed the township of South Monaghan and headed down towards the western tip of Rice Lake.

Suddenly, Dennis said in a low voice. "This area has many Protestant Irish and they follow the Orange Order. You should know in case we stop."

Within a few miles Dennis's prediction came true. They were interrupted by a crash of wagons in the roadway. A woman had been hurt when her horses ran uncontrollably into another wagon. Now she lay on the dirt road and people from the area had gathered to assist. The carriage stopped as the road was littered with debris from the loaded wagons. A crowd had gathered around the injured woman and Kathleen went over to offer help.

"Can I help? I used to work in a hospital." Even though she had limited training, on the frontier any medical knowledge was helpful. The woman was in pain but had no visible injuries, and Kathleen immediately said, "Be careful handling her. Is there a doctor close by?" she asked.

"Yes, a few miles away," said someone in the crowd.

"Can we have some of the men lift her? Get along each side of her and lift carefully."

Dennis and Conor moved into place with the other men and, at Kathleen's direction, they slid their hands under the woman and lifted her gently. They cautiously placed the woman in the back of the wagon and she was taken to the doctor.

A man, who also stopped to help, said, "Thank you, madam."

"I am glad I could help," said Kathleen.

"You sound Irish?" he asked.

"Yes, we just came over from Ireland, County Clare."

"Ah, I am from the north, Strabane near Londonderry," the man said. Both parties had stated their origins and understood the differences of location, politics, loyalty, and religion. No need to speak such matters aloud. He continued, "You're from County Clare, are you? There is hatred at home but here we all help each other. Welcome to Upper Canada, and thanks again for your help. As soon as we clean up the roadway, you can stop at our house for some lunch. We are just up the way."

"Thank you, but we have to catch the ferry at Cobourg," replied Kathleen.

As they walked back to their carriage, Kathleen said to Dennis, "He was a nice chap."

"Yes, he was. You never know what you're going to get. Some people are welcoming and see Canada as a mixture of many people all trying to survive together and others just can't give up the old ways."

"Everyone here, everyone who stopped, were good caring people," Conor said.

"'Tis nice to see," added Johanna.

They started their journey again to Cobourg and when they arrived at the lake, the dock had a small hut, with a British soldier in the doorway, and Conor could see another soldier on the inside. He braced for an inquiry but Dennis, who was in the lead, just walked past and said "Hello." The soldier grumbled a "Hello" back but took no notice. However, the soldier in the doorway watched Conor closely as he passed and Conor stared back wondering what was going to be said. The soldier had a good look at his features but gave no indication of a problem. Conor kept moving to the boat moored at the edge of the dock. When he got to the gangplank, he turned to look. The soldier had followed him down.

"Where are you going?" asked the soldier.

"To New York," said Conor.

"Are you returning to Canada?"

"No plans to come back," answered Conor. The soldier

nodded and walked away. Once out of hearing, Conor whispered to Kathleen, "That was close."

"I think we are fine, now," she said.

"I hope so and I truly have no plans to return."

Kathleen looked at Conor. "Let's go find a home."

"I can't wait to get there," said Conor.

The trip across Lake Ontario from Cobourg to Rochester was uneventful. Government agents on either side of the border took little notice and asked few questions of the two couples traveling together.

The lake had its usual two-foot-high waves hitting the boat on the starboard side, pushed by the western wind, but the large ferry hardly felt the push as it headed south to Charlotte, in New York State, the landing port for Rochester.

Dennis and Johanna stood at the back of the boat, apparently lost in their reminiscence of family and friends in Peterborough. Johanna was describing some point on the horizon along Cobourg's harbor area with her arms stretched out but Conor could not hear her words. The scene moved Dennis, because he placed his arms around Johanna and pulled her in to his chest. She looked up at him and he kissed her gently but with a strong embrace.

Kathleen could see it was a magical moment for the newly-wed couple and she turned away to let them have their privacy. Conor came up beside his wife and likewise placed his arm around her shoulder in an unusual public display of affection. The damp air must have had sentimental droplets as it blew across the deck, bringing each couple a romantic moment.

Inside the main cabin, the boat had benches lined up for the passengers and Kathleen found two vacant seats; she motioned Conor to the seats. "I think I am going to like Lockport and its people," she said.

"I think we will feel the closest to home with its Irish Catholic settlement," said Conor, "and I will be happy to stop running. I don't like constantly looking over my shoulder."

She took his hand and squeezed; both felt the stress of their journey easing. The relief from running and hiding with clandestine movements was inviting, but most of all they had the vision of being settled. Their connection with Dennis and Johanna had brought relief through friendship, their strong faith, and avoidance of alcohol.

Chapter 15

Michigan Street

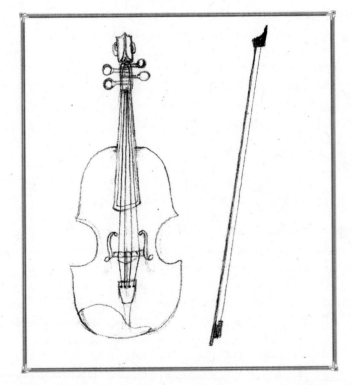

Once they had a footing in Rochester, Conor breathed easier. "I hope that is the last border crossing for a long time. I'm not used to being sneaky or watching over my shoulder."

"You should be fine from here on," replied Dennis as they boarded a coach for the eight-mile ride alongside the muddy waters of the fast-flowing Genesee River to the centre of the town. As they approached the main trading district of Rochester and the intersection of the Erie Canal, the steeple of St. Patrick's Church towered over the shops. At the corner of Platt Street both couples looked down one block and said nearly simultaneously, "There's St. Patrick's Church."

They laughed together, and Dennis asked, "Have you been there?"

"Yes, we attended Mass there during our trip up the canal," said Conor.

"We were married there," interjected Johanna.

"Oh, the priest there, I forgot his name . . ." started Kathleen.

"Father O'Reilly," added Johanna.

"Yes, Father O'Reilly, wanted us to get married right away. We promised that we would but," she leaned forward and whispered, "we haven't been married in the Church yet."

Dennis further added, "There's a church and priest in Lockport that can marry you."

The carriage stopped at Main Street, within a short walk up Exchange Street to the canal. The group waited for the next westbound packet as the canal boats had a continual flow of traffic in both directions for goods and people. Late in the afternoon, after less than a two-hour wait, they were boarded on a passenger packet and headed west towards Lockport.

"You can stay with us in our home," offered Johanna as they started to make plans for their arrival in Lockport.

"Thank you, but we can stay at the hotel until we get situated."

"You are welcome at any time," was the final offer.

They arrived in Lockport in the middle of the night. The boat tied up on the lower side of the locks and would traverse the locks after daybreak. As soon as the sun rose, so did the passengers, and the four travelers disembarked before the hour-long passage through the locks. They headed through the village.

Conor went to see Bill Hogan for a job and found him at the construction hut.

"Mr. Hogan, I met you last week in the restaurant on Main Street," said Conor.

"Yes, I remember. You have a strong back," said Mr. Hogan.

"I can work hard," answered Conor. "And I don't drink the whiskey." Conor remembered the question from their original meeting and Mr. Hogan's concern about the whiskey-drinking Irish.

"Good to hear. When can you start? Tomorrow, I hope."

"I have some business to tend to first in Lewiston, but in two days' time I will be ready."

"Good, settled."

The next day, Conor and Kathleen hired a carriage to take them to the tailor shop in Lewiston. The driver was inquisitive. "Why are you traveling all the way to Lewiston to see a tailor? There are good tailors right here in Lockport."

Conor diverted the question. "Just business."

The driver grinned as if he knew something, but Conor never let on the nature of his business. "All right, hop in. it's a good day to travel."

The carriage pulled out and headed west towards Lewiston, going along the "Upper Mountain" route. Although there was no mountain in the area, the trail followed an upper ridge of a low-lying plateau that paralleled Lake Ontario—the Niagara Escarpment.

Lewiston sat on the edge of the Niagara River below the escarpment, which Kathleen and Conor had experienced after leaving Niagara Falls, and when the carriage arrived in Lewiston, it stopped in front of the tailor shop.

"We will be right back," Conor informed the driver as he and Kathleen headed into the building.

"Josiah," Conor said as the shop owner came from the back room.

"Yes?" asked Josiah, who recognized his visitors.

"We have come to repay you for your kind help."

"There is no charge for the service I provided."

"Indeed, you helped us, and we would like to make a donation so your important work may continue," Conor said, the conversation carefully crafted not to mention the service.

"No need," said Josiah as the front door opened and a stranger walked in.

After looking at the stranger, Conor turned back to Josiah and laid Mrs. Hurley's embroidered bag on the table, "This is for you." Both Conor and Kathleen turned and left the shop, leaving the bag, which contained several thousand dollars.

Conor opened the carriage door for his wife. "That's a relief, and our work is done."

"Now we can start our new life," Kathleen responded.

Conor looked up to the driver. "Please take us back to Lockport."

"Okay, back up the hill we go."

During their ride, Conor considered the task they had just completed. "I think we helped many people today. The imprisoned, the wretched, like us when we left Ireland."

"We gave new hope to many people," said Kathleen.

"Do you think Negroes are second-class people?" asked Conor.

"Do you think the Irish are second-class people?" replied Kathleen.

"The English think so."

"So, are you?"

"We all deserve a chance at a good life," said Conor. "We have been kicked around on the bottom level of the social structure. We came to America and still we are being kicked around, but I see it changing, like the Protestant man when we helped with the broken carriage. He saw that we are in this life together. The effort to change attitudes sometimes needs to be drastic, like leaving Ireland and coming here to see the difference and make change happen."

"I agree," said Kathleen. "That man who offered us lunch was a kind and nice man, which made him easy to like, but he didn't have to be nice. We have our differences but we don't have to kill him for it, or hang him or ruin his crops—just let him be."

"I think that is what I am hoping for. I like this idea of democracy and electing the people's government, but even if ruled by a king, I want to be left alone, to grow my own crops and feed my family without the soldiers coming into my life trying to pick a fight just to see who will win. And if I win, more soldiers will come. Those odds are against me. Leave me alone and if I break the law, well, I will answer for it. That is only right, but if it's someone else's fight, leave me out it."

"Can you rest here comfortably? Are you always going to be looking over your shoulder?" asked Kathleen.

"Of course, I will always wonder what will happen; each day I will live under a cloud of suspicion. Just like the Negroes, who will wonder whether their master—hah, their 'master,'" he said with emphasis, "will come after them. And like any Catholic, like all the Irish, we need to be treated with respect."

"What about our children? Will they have to watch over their shoulders too?"

Conor replied, "Our hope is they will become industrious and contributing people. If so, they will be fine as long as they are accepted as good people, otherwise nothing will have changed from Ireland to here."

"I hope so," said Kathleen.

After returning to Lockport, they asked the driver to stop at Michigan Street at the edge of town. Dennis and Johanna had established their homestead among the other Irish in a shanty settlement in this western end of Lockport. They decided to visit their friends and inform them that they had completed their business in Lewiston. The McCarthys had spent the past two years, 1836 and 1837, becoming adjusted to their new life, and now Conor and Kathleen were looking forward to settling down as well.

As Conor and Kathleen walked along the street, they saw home to many hard-working immigrants trying to establish a better life in America. The canal construction had brought hundreds of Irish laborers to Lockport and in the early 1820s they were mostly Protestant Irish. Exact numbers of Irish immigrants are not known because canal construction was built by a series of contractors, who did not keep records of immigrants versus settled laborers. Many Irish stayed, and now the canal was expanding wider and deeper to allow larger boats and increased traffic, and the Irish were again recruited as laborers.

This time, a decade later, it was the Irish Catholics who swarmed the area for the jobs. This recruitment caused tension with many settled Americans, and accentuated the conflict between Protestants and Catholics. The new Irish, labeled the "Wild Irish," were willing to work for less pay. But they were a difficult lot to handle—they drank, fought, and caused general mayhem. The large influx of these Irish Catholics came from Ireland under the duress of near-starving conditions and religious persecution.

Adding to the issue, the Protestants were convinced that Irish Catholics adhered to hierarchical and superstitious practices. Such accusations were a direct insult to the Pope and the Catholic reverence for statues of saints, rosary beads, and other artifacts of their faith. Fights were frequent, in part because of the whiskey-fueled arguments and the century-old feuds but also because the Irish Catholics, even though often badly displayed, were looking to establish their respectability in the New World. The Irish newspapers wrote that "America was the best poor man's country, a place where affordable farmland and work opportunities abound." The west end of Lockport was one of those places in transition.

The ethnic groups interacted reasonably well within the confines of the daily business of the community, which allowed general harmony except for one spot—the bars. Heritage and background took on a new importance when liquor and social contact came into play. Arguments were plentiful and divided along ethnic lines when under the influence of a good stout beer or a couple of shots of whiskey.

Even though most drinkers were familiar with each other prior to the night's discussions, when strong insults or provoking opinions were spewed, especially around religion or politics, a fist-fight was the likely outcome. This appeared to be the town sport. Sunday morning Mass, after a hard Saturday night, was attended with bruises, black eyes, sore ribs, and tarnished honor. Respectability came at a price and, for many, it took generations.

But calm prevailed, especially when industry flourished, and Lockport would soon grow out of its adolescence into a thriving community. It would become a successful boomtown that survived its initial turmoil. Even though the drinking became a notable point in Lockport's history, the Irish laborers were a hard-working lot that reflected their own history of industry and bravery on this new frontier. Most Irish were pious and sober members of the community. They were an inspiration for other immigrants, showing that hard work was rewarded with respectability and prosperity.

After the two days promised to Mr. Hogan, Conor went to work on the canal. He was assigned to carry wheelbarrow loads of rock that had been blasted out of the escarpment to rock piles at the edge of the canal. Indeed, he needed his strong back but he was happy with his employment and income.

They lived in the Niagara Hotel for a few days, but the noise from the bar downstairs was more then they could handle. The rowdiness started in late afternoon and lasted well into the night. Kathleen felt compelled to stay in the room after 3:00 o'clock in the afternoon for fear of going downstairs and walking through the lobby with the adjoining bar, which scared her.

Conor and Kathleen looked for a home in the Michigan Street area near the northwest end of Lockport and found a place to move into. It was sparse but the young couple was happy. Kathleen made friends quickly with the established residents and time was spent sitting together, knitting and reminiscing about the old country. Many of the stories were sad, with sickness and trouble, but they found their joy in family connections, funny events, and their new home in America. Added to their joy was the gratitude to have food, which was, at least, available to them, although meager from the low pay. They would never forget the dire circumstances from which they came.

Kathleen found solitude away from the hotel and the frequent fears of being close to the nightlife. Now after completing their travels, she felt whole again having a house and a husband. The fortitude and confidence that she had developed in her youth returned.

Soon after moving in they were able to get a bed, a table with two chairs, and a few kitchen utensils, mostly donated by the various immigrants who had settled previously in the neighborhood. Now, they felt the relief of completing their treacherous journey. "We have been through a lot to make it this far; the blessings of the Lord have been with us," Conor said.

"Oh yes, every day I say a prayer of thanks for our good fortune and being together," said Kathleen. "Just as was said in the Prophecy of Isaias, chapter sixty, verse one: 'thy light is come, and the glory of the Lord is risen upon thee.'"

"Oh, a quote from the Bible, very good. That is what Isaias was saying, out of darkness comes light—our faith in Jesus and our goodness, especially with handling Mrs. Hurley's money, has brought us earthly rewards." Conor continued, "I feel good today, let's go for a walk to the market."

They left the house as clouds rolled in and now a typical western New York drizzle fell, driven by a cool breeze against the faces of the two weary travelers. Conor stopped to let the rain hit against his exposed cheeks and forehead and dampen his long, straggly red hair. This rain felt familiar, of times gone by in the fields of Ireland. He spread his arms as if to welcome the soaking, and tilted his head upward to catch the full effect of the shower. He smiled and closed his eyes. He was at peace.

In a moment, he opened his eyes and Kathleen was standing there, smiling too in her Irish moment. Her bonnet sagged from the rainwater and circled her youthful face which beamed with the same satisfaction as her husband; together, they had found love. She gave Conor her disarming smile and there in the middle of Niagara Street, they embraced and kissed.

"Ah," said Conor, breaking the connection as he started to walk along the dirty rutted street, "we have found our refuge."

"I think we have," Kathleen said.

"But here in Lockport, I see many displaced Irish, people who have escaped a personal bondage from the old country, like myself who was on the run from a situation beyond my control. Everyone here has their story of forced immigration, landlords looking for past payments, or trouble with some aspect of the English law. Even the Underground Railroad is designed to bring people out of bondage."

Kathleen added, "As you were saying, I think it is more than just the Irish. I think many nationalities are here escaping their personal demons that they would not have been able to shake if they stayed in the old country. We are just one example."

Conor pondered the thought of the reality for a moment. "We cannot go home, for there is no returning. We are now Americans—forever."

"Flight of the wretched," said Kathleen.

"Oh! What do you mean?" asked Conor.

"Two hundred years ago, two of our beloved Irish chieftains were forced into exile, which we know as the 'Flight of the Earls.' Now, I see Ireland's poor and wretched people being forced out in the same way. We have become the exiled, just like the earls, driven by circumstances beyond our ability to control."

They continued their walk with a sense of relief and belonging to their new community. Conor turned to look at Kathleen and said, "You know, we started this trip penniless, then we had some money from your father, then we were penniless again. A while later, we had a whole purse full of money, and now, we are nearly penniless again."

"That may be true, but we are not poor. We have a lot together and that is everything," said Kathleen.

"You're right."

"Are you worried about being penniless?" asked Kathleen.

Conor stopped and looked skyward, took in a deep breath, and thought over the question. "Not at all," he finally said. "With a job, we will eat, and that's easy enough here in Lockport, but with you, I have everything. This trip has been a fairy tale of excitement, with frightening and inconceivable mystery; the things we saw were almost unreal but, most of all, it brought me you. And I would do it all again for you. I am not worried in the least."

They started walking again and Kathleen said, "You know, we have to get married again. This time in a church."

"That is tomorrow's task; today we rest."

The two walked down Niagara Street hand in hand. Conor was carrying their most cherished possession, the violin. They had found home.

"Give me your tired, your poor,
Your huddled masses yearning to breathe free,
The wretched refuse of your teeming shore.
Send these, the homeless, tempest-tost to me,
I lift my lamp beside the golden door!"
Emma Lazarus (1883), "The New Colossus"

Appendix I

Once Conor and Kathleen settled in the Lockport area, they communicated back to their homes in Ireland. They needed to be careful sending correspondence going to and from the Meighan household lest the letters regarding Conor's whereabouts should be intercepted. The Irish were attuned to cautious and secret messages in order to keep loved ones safe. Kathleen took the lead:

November 27, 1840

Dear Mr. and Mrs. Meighan,

My name is Kathleen O'Grady from nearby Ennis. Three years ago I emigrated from Ireland to America. During my trip over, I met your son Conor on the ship and I am very sorry to inform you that some highwaymen killed Conor during a robbery as we were coming up the Erie Canal. He was a brave man trying to save our possessions and us. I wanted to let you know that Conor spoke very well of you and loved you very much.
My thoughts and prayers are with you.

Most sincerely,
Kathleen O'Grady

Appendix II

After learning the "truth" created for the benefit of the letter's hostile British readers, Conor's mother responded:

February 25, 1842

My dearest Kathleen,

Thank you for your letter of last year informing us of the sad news about Conor's death. I hope the news of his death will close the final chapter of that terrible incident in O'Malley's Pub.

After Conor left, we endured more than a year of constant persecution from the soldiers and in particular one sergeant who was behind it all. At one point they burned down our barn but that did not matter; we have nothing and lost nothing. One night, someone killed the sergeant while he was sleeping. They believe Seamus Burke's younger brother Michael was responsible. But I don't believe it, why would Michael want to avenge that sergeant. Anyway, the harassment stopped.

Our poor Claire died two years ago this month of the sickness, may her soul rest in God's peace.

Your parents rode out from Ennis to visit us and told us of your trip to America, and we were happy to hear that you found a wonderful husband. All our love to you and your husband and congratulations on your new baby; we are sure that she is beautiful.

The Meighan family

Irish family members on both sides of the Atlantic could now rest easy knowing that Conor and Kathleen had embarked on a new life safely and without fear of British reprisal.